D1602921

Rare as Earth

Gregory Zeigler

OWL EYE PRESS · JACKSON, WYOMING

OWL EYE PRESS
JACKSON, WYOMING

ISBN: 978-0-578-65138-5
eISBN: 978-0-578-65139-2
LCCN: 2020909414

Cover art by Jane Lavino
Graphic design by Lindsay J. Nyquist, elle jay design

Printed in the United States of America
1 3 5 7 9 10 8 6 4 2

Contact the author: gzeigler@wyom.net
Visit the author's website: gzeiglerbooks.com

Dedication

For my three children, Jamie, Alex, and Wil.
Thank you for loving me unconditionally.
You have made my world a better place.

Also by
Gregory Zeigler

Travels With Max:
In Search of Steinbeck's America Fifty Years Later
2010

The Straw That Broke:
A Jake Goddard and Susan Brand Thriller
2013

Some Say Fire:
A Jake Goddard and Susan Brand Thriller
2015

View Zeigler's award-winning short film about
John Steinbeck at https://vimeo.com/131129928

*It's sometimes annoying when people say, "Oh, you children are the hope, you will save the world."
It would be nice if you could help a little.*

The fact that you are staring at a panel of young people testifying before you today pleading for a livable earth should not fill you with pride; it should fill you with shame.

Greta Thunberg

November 6
Sunday Evening

"Who am I? Amanda Fry. Fight for Right and Never Say Die!" Mandy's voice carried through the darkening woods. She stumbled over a rock in the trail, then walked a little faster and chanted a little louder, her battered Nikes scattering ankle-deep leaves.

Sure, the cheer was silly; some of the older kids even called it weird. Well, they could throw all the shade they wanted. Whitey, Mr. White, the school counselor, had suggested it when she appeared at his office just after getting cut from the cheerleading squad. She felt a little silly now, remembering how she had blurted out through tears that the coach had said she lacked physical confidence.

Mandy brushed a cobweb out of her auburn bangs and adjusted the blue bandanna on her head. She pushed past several spruce boughs stretching across the trail and ducked under oak branches curving down like hairless claws.

After climbing a short rise to a large opening in the forest, she paused, breathed in the autumn air, and sighed. A large gibbous moon hung dead center above the tree line in the lavender sky to the east. Behind her, the western sky glowed pink.

It was getting late and it was getting cold. Earlier while hiking, Mandy had realized she had totally spaced the time change. Dusk arriving an hour early was not in her plans, such as they were.

Of course, if she hadn't killed the battery on her phone, she might have been better able to keep track of the time. Ms. Hatcher, her dorm parent, was going to be majorly pissed.

She zipped her school fleece up to her neck and marched down the slope through the trees on the far side of the clearing. "Who am I? Amanda—" A sound deep in the woods stopped her dead. She listened. Nothing. Had she actually heard something? See, that's the problem, Mandy, she thought. You get caught up in what you're doing and forget the time, and now these Goddamn Pennsylvania woods are getting scary and you're imagining things, girl. She charged down the hill, singing even louder.

Mr. White had said the mantra, as he called it, might help her two ways. It could give her courage, which could also boost her confidence. She'd be her own little cheer squad, rooting herself on to victory. Mandy also hoped it would help her work on her rhythm and timing because, although the coach had not mentioned it, she had always been a spaz and sensed it was obvious in the tryouts.

Mr. White said he got the idea for the chant from the Cowardly Lion in *The Wizard of Oz*. He said it had helped a lot of kids like her. Huh? There were actually other kids like her? Who knew? One thing Mandy knew for sure—the silly chant helped. It helped a lot. Whitey was the GOAT.

Night was rapidly descending on the woods. Apart from her voice, the only sound was the ripping of dead leaves grasping at her ankles like withered hands. But then there was that sound off in the woods again, stopping her in her tracks. Only this time it was closer.

Off she went, almost running now. She rounded a bend in the trail and thought she could discern the lights of the campus. That was a relief. Now she could focus on the next pressing problem. Hiking alone off campus at any time was against the rules; arriving back at the dorm on Sunday evening after dark—strictly forbidden.

At least she had a shot at talking herself out of this one. Ms. Hatcher was also the student newspaper advisor, and Mandy had scored big-time earlier that afternoon with pictures and evidence she felt were strong enough to capture front-page coverage in the *Saint Mike's School Times*. That'd be pretty amazing for a girl who had only been on the newspaper staff for the first two months of her freshman year. I mean, look what the Parkland kids had done, reporting on their school shooting. Who needs lame cheerleading anyhow?

Mandy rushed past a large vine-covered tree chanting, "Who am—" The words caught in her throat as two hands reached out of the darkness, crushing her airway and stifling her scream.

October 30
Sunday Afternoon
(One Week Earlier)

"How's things at Super Foods?" Jake asked from his reading chair as Susan kneed open the cabin door laden with cloth bags full of groceries. Cool fall air rushed in around her. The sun slanted through the living room window. A swaybacked black horse belonging to their neighbor grazed the brown grass along the fence bordering their side yard.

"*Stupid* Foods? Still can't believe we have to drive sixty miles round trip, Boulder to Escalante, for mediocre produce that's seen better days. 'Course, driving through Grand Staircase-Escalante National Monument—incredible. Never gets old."

"Yep. Small price for living in a Utah paradise, angel."

Susan shot him her eye roll/headshake combination and placed her bags on the kitchen counter.

Jake stood to help with the carrying. "Well played, babe. Amy couldn't have expressed that body language smackdown better."

Susan paused with her hand in a grocery bag. "Aww, I miss Amers." She bobbed her head and smiled. "Even her evil eye and that sweet little blow-off conversation-ender, 'What*ever*, Mom.'" She pulled out a bunch of carrots, opened the fridge, and placed them in the bottom drawer.

Jake headed for the door. "Speaking of the little devil, got a call from Saint Michael's this morning."

"Whoa, whoa, whoa," Susan said, turning. "The groceries can wait. Is Amy in trouble?"

Jake stopped and smiled. "No. For once I heard from the school for reasons other than your daughter's habitual tardiness or my tardy alumni gift to the annual fund."

"What did they want?"

"She. It was Joan, the school head."

"You heard from Mrs. Bailey? What about?" Susan asked.

"Joan wants the services—or at least the advice—of the two principal private investigators of Goddard Consulting Group."

"Principal and only."

"She's offered to fly us both out to Pennsylvania and put us up. No money in it, but I just guessed you wouldn't mind paying an unscheduled visit to your daughter, considering we've got nothing else going on, professionally speaking. I'll tell you all about it after we put the groceries away." He turned back to the door. "I just put some beer and wine in the fridge. We have something to celebrate. Three years to the day since I placed a bet on anything."

Susan turned. "That's right. Pittsburgh Steelers, right?"

"Correct. Dropped two hundred. Last time."

"Proud of your discipline, Jake."

Jake banged the screen door and thumped across the deck past two decorative pumpkins, toward Susan's Toyota Tacoma.

Susan crossed to the door and called out. "And hey, I want to get a run in while that wine chills."

Jake flashed a thumbs-up. "As long as you are extra careful. There're ghosts and goblins out there tonight. Not to mention the odd vampire." He opened the truck's passenger door.

November 7
Monday Morning

"There are few places more beautiful than Saint Mike's in the fall," Jake said. He and Susan were crossing the school quad. Stately redbrick buildings surrounded them—several adorned with ivy. "Pride of sleepy Coalville, Pennsylvania. The small town that never changes."

"This is pretty for sure, but a few weeks ago, with the Appalachian Mountains in color, it must have been gorgeous around here." Susan scooped up a blood-red maple leaf from beside the sidewalk, held the stem between her fingers, and twirled the lobes. "Is it always this sunny and warm in November?"

"No. Not from what I recall from my student days. I remember running late to early-season wrestling practice, all bundled up against the cold."

"Different century. Different world," Susan said.

"Different climate," Jake added.

"I keep telling you, longer summers is the upside to climate change." She winked at him and shoved him off the sidewalk, one of many that crisscrossed the flat, grassy quad under the watchful presence of mature oaks, elms, and maples.

"Tell that to Zullie Jen. Longer summers means jumping into more late-season forest fires." Jake recovered and rejoined her on the sidewalk.

"Haven't thought about my BFF for a while. Need to get in touch now that her fire season has ended."

A tall, attractive African American boy, wearing the school colors of green and gold—in his case, a gold school polo under a green school sports jacket and khakis—smiled as he passed them, heading toward Dormitory Row. Four beige brick-and-stucco buildings capped by dormers. The student was carefully avoiding stepping on the cracks of the sidewalk.

Susan tickled Jake's neck by placing the leaf on the collar of his flannel shirt. He brushed it off. "Now you behave, or I'll report you to the dean. Cliff's office is right down the hall from Joan's in the admin building."

"You can kiss up to the head and rat me out to the dean in the same visit."

"Worked for me when I was a prefect—oh, excuse me, for the *public*-school educated, a 'prefect' is a student mentor. I carried the heavy burden of leadership when I walked these hallowed halls. Of course, some of the kids wrote me off as a narc."

"It's what you do best, Jake."

He pulled up.

"I wasn't referring to narcing," she reassured.

He relaxed and resumed walking.

"Jake Goddard takes care of others and occasionally guides the misguided back to the path of righteousness." A campus dog, a blue-gray Australian shepherd, furiously wagging the distant memory of a tail, sidled up to Susan for a brief greeting and a head scratch. "I hope Amy, if she goes the distance here, will follow in your footsteps."

"When we surprised her last night in the student center, I'll never forget the look on her face," Jake said. "She still expresses that spontaneous childlike affection. Even to me, now."

"That's really important, considering how rarely her father visits. His lame excuses about how guiding in Alaska has picked up, and how he can't afford to pass up the work, have gotten really old. I hope she never loses that sweet quality."

"Now that's the upside to climate change," Jake said. "A warmer Alaska means we don't have to deal with your flaky ex as often."

"Isn't that the cryin' truth." She adjusted the gold chain at the V-neck of her maroon tunic sweater. "I was a hard sell, I admit, sending her so far away to school. But I feel this experience has done wonders for my relationship with my one and only baby girl."

"Like I predicted, she gets a sense of independence, and you get to appreciate her more when you aren't waging daily battles over turf littered with shoes and dirty underwear."

"Amen to that."

A bell rang. Students heading to their next class gushed out of the buildings and surrounded them with chatter and laughter. Jake and Susan walked up the front steps and onto the gray wraparound porch of the two-story white clapboard admin building.

Joan Bailey's office was formal and a little staid, yet comfortably appointed. Clustered around her neatly organized desk were several wooden chairs adorned with the Saint Michael's crest. On the wall above her desk hung two framed diplomas. Lining the walls around the windows were built-in bookshelves jammed with large volumes and multicolored binder notebooks. Some of her hanging, framed photos displayed her engaging with students; others depicted her in a hard hat flanked by important-looking men and women in suits and similar headgear, ceremoniously breaking ground with shovels.

Joan gestured for Jake and Susan to sit on a leather couch flanked by two matching armchairs facing a gas fireplace. She took the armchair to their right. A coffee table covered with school publications sat in front of the couch. "How does it feel to be back at your school, Jake?" Joan asked. She wore a tailored black pantsuit with a cream-colored blouse.

"Always a wonderful trip down memory lane." He glanced around the office. "But I have to admit, still feels a little weird to be called into the head's office."

"You're not alone. It's the school head's secret weapon. Don't think for a minute my colleagues and I don't leverage that superpower when asking an alum for a donation or trying to get a parent to toe the line. Everybody was a school kid once upon a time. And these days, we sometimes need every advantage when Mom and Dad *bulldoze* up to campus with an agenda regarding their precious child." She shifted her gaze to Susan. "Present parent company excepted, of course." Joan leaned over and squared up two magazines on the table. "Are you finding our guest accommodations comfortable? I just got those funded and remodeled a year ago. There is nothing else suitable anywhere close to the school."

"Everything we need is right there," Susan said.

Jake added, "That's a beautiful location, tucked back in the woods off the golf course. I even figured out the remote last night and caught the end of the pro football game."

"Go Philly Eagles," Joan said. "I couldn't stay awake, but I saw the highlights this morning. They're on a roll. Penn State too." She looked at her cell and placed it on the coffee table. "I have to run to a meeting in a few minutes. Just wanted you to know the casual investigation that you and I discussed on the phone, Jake, has taken an interesting and possibly frightening turn."

"Fill us in," he said.

"I have a student who claims she captured pictures of illegal dumping into the Susquehanna River yesterday afternoon and then was assaulted on her way back to school.

"Let me first say we don't know the girl in question well enough yet to be able to gauge her truthfulness. And I have to state the obvious: until we have concrete evidence that what she claims did indeed happen—and if so, it is the first time anything like it has occurred in this safe rural school's one-hundred-plus-year history—I can't risk panicking my parents."

She paused, then leaned forward. "This must stay between us while we sort it out. This is a small town. For now, I don't even want my security folks to know. For the record, Bill Warski, the local police chief, was contacted last night. That was against my better judgment, given the historic tension between Coalville and the school—town and gown, always interesting—but Cliff Hall, the Dean of Students, insisted. Warski chatted with our student this morning, investigated the site of the alleged incident, and found nothing. He said we should take it from there. The student promised me for the time being this will go no further. Until I inform her otherwise, her dorm parent is to be the only one to know. I think the child is just relieved she is unharmed and not in serious trouble with the school. At least, not yet."

"You can count on us to be discreet," Jake said.

"And objective," Susan added.

"Wonderful." Joan turned toward her. "If I remember, you were a policewoman before joining Jake as a private investigator?"

"Yes. First in Phoenix and then on the Jackson, Wyoming PD."

"I'm pleased to have a woman of your experience on board."

"Susan's background in law enforcement has added tremendously to the professional credentials of Goddard Consulting Group," Jake said. "Especially since I started out as a humble researcher of historical documents."

Susan shook her head. "My husband's being modest, Joan. Early on, Jake's research and investigative skills helped catch a nutcase who made his living forging historical Mormon documents in Salt Lake City. The guy murdered several people with pipe bombs. It made the national news.

"Jake also saved my life—and the life of a young friend of ours who we were trying to rescue from kidnappers—by, believe it or not, lying down in the road in front of the moving truck in which the two of us were being held at gunpoint." She smiled at Jake. "I knew at that insane moment I was going to marry him."

"Just so she could tease me about it for the rest of my life," Jake said.

"That all had to do with corruption regarding Colorado River allotments and retaliation by radical environmentalists, but that's another story," Susan told Joan.

"Wait. You two were somehow involved in that catastrophic conflict over the Colorado River?" Joan asked.

"'Somehow' is the correct word," Jake said.

Joan laughed. "I had no idea about any of that. Very impressive. Both of you. And promise me you won't worry about your daughter's security. This is a safe campus."

"I'm not at all worried. I'm really pleased with Saint Michael's, just as Jake said I would be," Susan assured her. "And very grateful for the financial aid you offered Amy. Just hope we can be of some assistance in return."

"Great." Joan opened a file folder she had carried over from her desk. "Here's what I know. Amanda Fry, entering freshman like your daughter, returned late yesterday from an unsanctioned off-campus hike with a wild story of being accosted. I've heard my share of whoppers when students know they are in hot water, but this one is a doozy."

"Is she all right?" Susan asked.

"Yes. School nurse says not a scratch on her, just a little sore and shaken up. We're trying to reach her parents, but they're on a cruise in Asia so it's proving challenging." Joan tucked her thick, collar-length gray hair over her right ear with a perfectly manicured nail. "Mandy claims—of her own volition, mind you—that she was taking pictures she hoped the school newspaper would print. She was snooping around the hydraulic fractured well operating just off school property. Our kids aren't dumb. They know we are concerned about our water supply being contaminated as well as other deleterious effects from the well. It's the very same well I was hoping you two could, let's say, 'research' for us." Joan's cell rang on the table. She glanced at it, then picked it up and silenced it. "Mandy was in violation of several rules, starting with being off campus alone after dark, but I'm afraid her desire to be an investigative journalist with a scoop trumped her better judgement. She claims when she was nearing campus on the River Trail . . . you remember it, don't you, Jake?"

He glanced down at his hands. "Remember it very well." Then raised his eyes to Joan. "We must have hiked to the river a hundred times."

They heard a shout. Students teased and taunted playfully outside the office window. Joan smiled. "There is nothing quieter than a boarding school when classes are in session, and nothing more boisterous than when they are out. I spend a lot of time fighting battles, penned up here in my office. The sound of that youthful vigor, full of possibility, is what keeps me going."

"It's a wonderful sound," Jake said. "Transports me right back to my years here."

Joan returned to the subject at hand. "Mandy reports that she was almost back to campus when she was forcefully grabbed from behind. While the perpetrator held one hand over her mouth, he reached around and searched her right jacket pocket with the other. Then she was shoved face down in the leaves, and he released her and ran away."

"Wow! Scary for a kid. Glad it wasn't worse. Did she get a description?" Susan asked.

"No. It all happened so fast, and it was almost dark. She did say that—and this is the part it's hard to imagine a kid making up—she said she felt something small but hard, metallic or plastic, when she was pulled backward and pinned against his chest. I say 'his' because she's pretty sure her assailant was a large, strong man and that he was wearing what she called 'rubber gloves.'"

"Latex, maybe," Jake said.

"Perhaps. Hard to say. That's all she could remember of the attack."

"Did he say anything? Take anything?" Susan asked.

"He said nothing. But yes, Mandy claims he took her phone."

"Sounds like we better visit that well first thing," Jake said.

Joan closed her file. "We have less than two weeks before we send the kids home for Thanksgiving. I hope you two can shed some light on this situation by then."

"How would you like us to report to you?" Susan asked.

"Let's see . . . I really want to keep this quiet, and too much time here in my office is bound to get people talking. I walk on the track most mornings, just after sunrise. We live in a fishbowl, but you two walking with me shouldn't arouse much suspicion."

"Good way for us to get our laps in," Susan said.

Jake nodded. "See you at the track."

November 7
Monday Afternoon

Jake and Susan exited the woods on the River Trail and crossed a narrow open area to a large oak on the bank. A knotted nylon rope hung over the water from a high, straight limb. The river flowed past, stolid and steady, at a width of fifty or sixty yards. Swirls formed on the surface of the dark water and hurried downstream.

After a few minutes at the tree, they walked a quarter mile upstream, skirting around a family of Canada geese foraging in the grass on the bank. The oil well that had attracted Mandy Fry's attention faced the river no more than thirty yards from the water.

The well was surrounded by a chain-link fence covered in No Smoking signs. Several green pipes rose up through a concrete pad and then bent at bright yellow joints, creating ninety-degree angles. Three tanks—the height of a two-story building and painted green but rusted in places to brown—stood side by side. The most prominent feature was the pumpjack poised like the head of a praying mantis, and at the moment dormant. The only object that broke with the color code was a silver box the size of a large refrigerator on long metal legs. Attached to the box was a white sign that listed as operator Beauford Oil and Gas of Nanticoke, PA. It also provided an address and additional information about the well. There was no one around and no sign that the well was not operating properly, but Jake wondered whether the site was under some sort of hidden camera surveillance. Perhaps that's how they'd discovered Mandy's snooping and decided they wanted her phone badly enough to jump her in the woods.

He turned to face the water, adjusted his ball cap, and murmured, "Wonder if we're being watched?"

He walked across the grassy, leaf-covered field toward the river and stopped a few yards from the bank. Susan flanked him.

"Nanticoke is about sixty miles from here as the crow flies on the east branch of the Susquehanna. This is the west branch." Jake gestured to the wide expanse of deep, dark water moving silently past. Although the river was lined with tall trees casting long shadows, the trees blocked little sun, for their leaves had fallen weeks ago. Susan had stripped off her windbreaker and tied it around her waist, and was enjoying the sun on her arms, bare below the sleeves of her blue L.L.Bean T-shirt.

"What we got?" Jake asked.

"Not a whole heck of a lot." Susan pushed her short blonde hair behind her ears. "I'm sure we examined the correct tree based on Joan's description of the location of the assault. The vines growing up it, some as she had mentioned cut at the bottom by students playing Tarzan and Jane, were unmistakable. There was no evidence of foul play, but you could lose a car in those leaves—a CSI nightmare."

Jake nodded back toward the well. "And that monstrosity? Might be a tad too close to the water for this environmentalist's comfort, but it at least looks legitimate."

"I can't see what Mandy got so excited about." Susan said. "We're going to need to interview her as soon as Joan gives us the green light."

"Unless . . ." Jake thought for a moment. "Unless they do something on weekends that they don't do on weekdays. Maybe to avoid surprise visits from inspectors. Which I'll bet happen—"

"Only on weekdays," Susan interjected. "Interesting theory. And just about all we've got to go on for the moment."

"Let's head back up the trail toward the school. Tarzan want to see Jane swing on vine in tight jeans one more time," Jake said, grinning.

Brown-stained fingers like sausages flipped the phone and inspected the back.

The thick digits were connected to a burly man dressed in a blue workman's jacket soiled with dirt and oil. The name tag pinned on his jacket indicated his name was Lester.

Lester leaned against the chain-link fence under a No Smoking sign, squinted into the setting sun, and puffed on a short roll-your-own stuck to his lower lip.

The man decided against trying to check the pictures on the device. What did it matter? No one was going to see them. He stubbed out the cigarette against the bottom of his mud-caked right boot and walked to the river's edge, flicking the butt into the current.

Just as he was about to toss the phone in, he hesitated. The water was clear, and the phone had a silver back. If it wasn't carried downstream by the current, it could reflect light. Someone might see it and fish it out, he thought. It was a long shot but definitely possible. Lester tapped the device against the palm of his right hand and poked two fingers into his scraggly blond beard.

The big man walked away from the river, past the enclosed well, and pushed through dense shrubs under denuded trees filtering late-afternoon light. He stood at the edge of a partially hidden trench. A crow cawed in the distance.

The sump was filled with brown drilling sludge covered with dead leaves. It was long and narrow and had a mud-stained concrete rim. Despite the rapidly cooling evening air, a fetid stench rose off the surface.

Lester chucked the phone. It slapped flat onto the fluid, the viscosity and floating leaves dampening the ripples. The device rocked on the surface until brown ooze crept around the edges, covered the face, and sucked it under. Lester sighed and scratched at his crotch. Time to face the boss.

"So?"

"So like I said, I took care of it. It won't happen again."

"Did you hurt her?" Raymond Beauford, a stout, balding man, paced back and forth behind his gunmetal-gray desk. He wore a dingy white shirt and a loose brown tie. He held a 7-iron by the grip.

"Nah. Mighta scared her a little." Lester shifted his weight from foot to foot. His eyes darted about and then settled on the dead flies littering the sill of the window behind the desk. The dirty glass emitted yellow light from an exterior pole, illuminating the sour expression on the boss's face.

"First the previous president takes our coal jobs—four big producers gone and Moray Energy recently filing chapter 11. Now that bunch of elites at the school you moonlight for is sniffing around our oil and gas." Beauford rapped the 7-iron on his battered desk. "That Goddamn school is a pain in my ass." He muttered to himself, "I can't believe my brother thinks my nephew is better off with those rich brats than at a decent American public school." Beauford drilled a look at his security guard. "Next time you fall asleep when you're being paid to protect my well, you're fired." He swung the club at his empty trash can, and it shot across the room. "Got it?"

Lester jerked. "I got it, Mr. Beauford."

"Good. Because if we're exposed, I won't have to fire you. Your job will be the first to go. She never should have been able to get that close on a weekend, let alone take freakin' pictures."

"I know. I know. And like I said, it won't happen again."

"Yeah, you did. Some security. A little school bitch, for Chrissake."

"I'm really sorry."

Beauford held the grip in both hands and pointed the club at Lester's head. "You should be." He pointed to the door. "Now get the hell out of here."

The big man backed toward the door, turned, and said, "I'll watch her every move, boss." He went out.

Beauford tossed the golf club against the wall, sat hard on the edge of his desk, blew out air, and shook his head.

November 8
Tuesday Morning

Susan eased the little Toyota rental up to the curb outside Joan's office. Jake sent the school head a text from the back seat.

Joan pulled back the drapes of her window and pointed toward them. A few moments later, Mandy, in green school polo and khakis, barreled through the glass double doors leading out of the administration building, then bounded through the pillars and down the four steps to the car. She opened the door, swung her black backpack onto the floor, and slid into the front passenger seat.

"You're Amy's mom," Mandy said.

"That is my greatest claim to fame." She held out her hand. "Susan."

"And I'm Jake."

Mandy swung around and beamed a smile at him.

"Hi, Jake." She turned back to Susan. "Mrs. Bailey said you had some questions for me."

"Buckle up and we'll steal you away from school for a while," Susan said, adjusting the rearview mirror.

Mandy looked perplexed. She studied the digital clock on the dash. "Hmm. 10:14." She grinned at Susan and then at Jake. "Means I miss algebra. That'll be a real tragedy." She bounced around in her seat and buckled her seatbelt. "I'll only agree to this abduction if it also causes me to miss French class after algebra."

"Let me guess, not your favorite subjects?" Jake said.

She frowned and shook her bangs. "Back-to-back. Two hours of daily torture."

"*Mon Dieu, mon amie.* Takes me back to my years here," Jake said, patting Mandy's shoulder. Susan pulled the car away from the curb. "Four years of French never breaking the B ceiling—lovely language for which I apparently have no natural ability. Struggled with algebra too. Had to take it over during the worst summer of my teen years. Girl after my own heart."

"Jake would much rather be writing lyrics for country songs, Mandy. Numbers and foreign languages are not his thing." They had passed the yellow-brick-and-glass school athletic center and were flanked by athletic fields.

Mandy said, "I love country music."

"Ah-ha, I sense a soulmate in this kid," Jake said.

"And I'm kind of a science nerd. And I like to write too. Mrs. Bailey said you two were private investigators. We have that in common too."

"Yes . . . we do." Susan said. "And, um, we hope you'll bring us up to speed, then hand over your covert operation so you can concentrate on important things, like—"

"Like algebra and French, right?" Mandy frowned.

"Yeah, for starters. But I'll make you a deal. If you trust us to finish your work, someday I'll brief you on the training that led me to be a police officer and then a private investigator."

"A top investigator. One of the very best, Mandy," Jake said. "There is nobody better you could learn from if investigative journalism is what you want to do someday. And as soon as we have permission from Joan, uh, Mrs. Bailey, you get first crack at our intel for the school paper," Jake said.

"Deal?" Susan asked.

Mandy smiled. "Deal."

Susan drove around the security kiosk, past gates adorned with Saint Michael's crest, and headed toward the small town of Coalville perched on the bank of the west fork of the Susquehanna river.

Mandy stirred her mocha coffee to cool it. They sat in a café at a square table in front of a defunct fireplace on the first floor of a converted house that had seen better days as a brownstone residence.

"When Miss Bee—that's what we call her, and it's bee, buzz, like the insect—called me in this morning, I thought for sure it was to say pack my bags." She looked up with a mock-serious face. "Boy, would that put a crimp in Ben and Melissa's grand tour of Asia. Get pulled out of the cruise ship buffet line and told their darling little girl just got the boot from Saint Mike's.

"I just about fell on the floor when she said you two wanted to interview me." She grinned and swiped two fingers across her forehead. "Whew. Dodged a bullet."

A waiter dressed in a plain black T-shirt and black jeans came around the corner from the kitchen and placed a mug of brewed tea in front of Susan. She nodded her thanks and added milk from a pitcher.

"How're you doing, Mandy? This had to be a frightening experience for you," Susan said.

"Scared out of my mind at first. But I realized two things right away. First, the guy was huge, so if he had wanted to hurt me, he could have; and second, I was onto something important, or else why bother with me and take my phone?"

"Yup. She's going to make a great investigator someday," Jake said.

"*Someday*, Mandy, as in after high school and college," Susan added.

Mandy struck a hand-on-hip pose, dragged on an imaginary cigarette, and exhaled up through her bangs. Jake and Susan both laughed.

"That better be an investigator who doesn't smoke," Jake said.

"Thanks, Dad." Mandy winked at Jake and sipped her drink.

Jake pulled out a small red spiral notebook from his breast pocket. "Just a couple of quick investigator-type questions. Mrs. Bailey said you were grabbed from behind."

"Yes." She placed her hands on her throat. "By the neck."

"And it sounds like your attacker knew where to look for your phone," Susan said.

"Yup." She patted her right side. "Went right for it."

"And you're pretty sure he was a large man wearing gloves, like surgical gloves," Susan said.

"Yes."

"Tell us about the hard object you felt," Jake said.

Mandy touched the back of her head with her right hand. "I've given that a lot of thought. Could have been a large button or metal snap."

"How about a badge or name tag, even?" Jake asked. He took a sip of his water.

"Could have totally been a name tag."

"Is there anything else you remember? Did you see or feel rings under the gloves, for instance?" Susan asked.

"Or see his shoes—what he was wearing?" Jake added.

"No, and no rings that I was aware of. It all happened so quick, and it was getting dark."

"Anything else we should know?" Susan asked.

After a pause, she shook her head.

"Please let us know if you remember anything else. Mrs. Bailey knows how to get in touch with us," Jake said.

"I will, I promise."

"Okay, great job, sweetie," Susan said, sitting back in her chair.

They heard glass shatter in the kitchen. Jake looked pensive and then perked up. "I just thought of a line I might be able to use in a lyric."

"Uh-oh. What is it?" Susan asked.

He grinned. "People who live in stone houses shouldn't throw glasses." He jotted it in his notebook.

"That's great, Jake," Mandy cried. "I love that."

Susan pulled a mock sour face. "Don't encourage him, Mandy." In a hurry to change the subject, she said, "Joan has been too busy to brief us on the drilling around here. We know a little about fracking from a controversy in Wyoming over allegedly contaminated groundwater, but what can you tell us about hydraulic fracturing in Pennsylvania and how you got interested?"

"Blame Mr. Marlowe. Two months ago, when I arrived here as an innocent freshman, I was clueless. But the first thing Mr. M does in his STEAM class—"

"STEAM?" Jake asked.

"Science, technology, engineering, art, and math." Jake looked impressed. "Yeah, I know, right? Only thing missing is sex ed. Amy will get STEAM next semester—required for freshmen. Anyhow, the first thing he does is teach us kids how the school works. What's sustainable and what's not. Where the water comes from. How to test it for contamination. Where the waste goes, etcetera. Then Marlowe gets us researching fracking, which he says is fine and even, uh . . . good? Oh, what's the word I want?"

"Advantageous?" Jake asked.

"Yeah, advantageous, especially natural gas as a lesser evil to water- and air-polluting coal burning, but only in regions where alternative energy is not available and when drilling companies play by the rules. Next thing I know, we're discussing impacts from a driller who is operating right at the school's back door—Beauford—who I think Marlowe thinks is shady."

"How so?" Jake asked.

"He didn't exactly say it, but he suggested we Google Beauford Oil and Gas. When I did, I found the company has been busted several times, resulting in thousands of dollars in fines, including a very steep one in a nearby county for cleaning up a five-thousand-gallon hydrochloric acid spill that wiped out fish—"

"Acid? What would they be doing with hydrochloric acid?" Susan asked.

"Something like 90, 95, 99 percent. I don't know, like I said, I suck at numbers. But after the hole is bored, most of the drilling liquid is water and sand injected under high pressure. The remainder is a secret formula added for lubrication. I think it's called 'priority.'"

"'Proprietary.' Industries call their secrets 'proprietary,'" Jake said.

"Gotcha. Anyhow, hydrochloric acid is used after the hole is bored but before the sand and secret slickening fluid is added. The acid cleans out crap from drilling and helps open up the shale fractures."

"That spill sounds pretty serious," Jake said.

Mandy stopped her cup mid-sip. "That's nothing. I learned online that in Lincoln County where Beauford spilled the acid, they also had methane gas in well water, and a gas well blowout—Beauford's into gas too—all in, like, fifteen months. Great for the climate, don't you think? This is like a gold rush in Pennsylvania. Mr. M says neighbor states New York and Maryland don't even allow fracking. What does that tell you?"

"Sounds like a lot on the line," Susan said. "But we visited the well by the river, and it looked legitimate. At least on the surface."

Mandy sat back in her chair. "Oh, it is, totally—on weekdays. But on weekends they are dumping something—probably drilling fluid—straight into the river through an underwater pipe."

"We didn't see any fluid storage," Jake said.

"It's in the woods up behind the well. Get close enough, you'll know. 'Cause it stinks." She wrinkled up her nose.

"And that's what you photographed with your phone?" Jake asked.

"Yup—both the sumps and the outflow in the river. Check it out. Unless they're taking a break after I caught them, you'll see a nasty brown stream gushing out of the bank and polluting our beautiful river. Look for dead birds too. A million birds a year die in open wastewater sumps."

"How'd you learn about the pollution?" Susan asked.

Mandy looked out the café's window to the street. A sky-blue vintage Ford F-150 pulled up to the curb. "I . . . I can't tell you. I really can't." She twisted the hair above her ear. "If I tell, I'll get in trouble with the dorm prefects. In some ways that's worse than being in trouble with the dean, or even Miss Bee."

"You can't give us any idea how you discovered the dumping?" Susan pressed.

"Let's just say I was in the river on a Sunday and saw it." Mandy pleaded with her eyes. "And that's breaking two rules right there, by the way. If Mrs. Bailey hears about that, I'm totally screwed."

"She won't," Jake said. "As a former Saint Mike's covert weekend river swimmer, you have my word. But the way you say 'in the river' sounds like it might not have been a voluntary dip."

"It wasn't . . . exactly, but please, that's all I can tell you."

"You've been great, Mandy. Can't thank you enough. Your knowledge of fracking is outstanding," Susan said. "Now we better get you back to class."

Jake hailed the waiter for the bill. Mandy frowned and sighed. She put her cup to her lips and thrust her head back—the bottom of her cup pointing at the ceiling—trying to capture the last drops of chocolate foam.

On the way back to school, with the browning Pennsylvania hills rolling past the car, Susan made Mandy promise one more time.

"Your mind is too good to be distracted from your studies. You're going to do great things someday, but for now, you've got to let us pros focus on the oil well and your scary experience." Susan said. "Promise?"

"Scout's honor," Mandy said. "Miss Bee put a catch-and-kill order on my Beauford story, so there isn't much else I can do on that. Plus, I've got a major paper for English due Monday."

"Who knows, when our investigation is complete, it might turn out to be catch and release. Your pics and article might still get printed. What's it on? Your paper," Jake asked.

"*A Separate Peace,* the novel. I plan to lay low and focus on that assignment. Usually helps if I actually read the book."

"Smart girl. The opposite never worked for me. Doesn't mean I didn't try it several times," Jake said.

That evening as they drove up to the school's guest duplex, they saw several deer browsing in the dimly lit forest understory just behind the building. A light was on next door, and one of the school's maintenance pickups was parked in the driveway.

Later, lying in bed, they quietly compared notes about meeting

Mandy. Since she knew there was a man working next door and she might be overheard, Susan sent Jake a text saying there was little reason to return to the Beauford well until the weekend when they might see illegal dumping into the river. Jake read the text, nodded his agreement, and then deleted it.

Jake switched off the light; forest-filtered moonlight produced a lattice pattern on the bedroom floor.

They made love—no longer the grappling of the desperate and ravenous, but rather the communion of the familiar and confident. Gentle touches, gentle coupling, leading to gentle releases.

Was it the presence of the school employee burning the midnight oil working on the other side of the duplex? Or was it the beginning of a new phase as a married couple?

Regardless, soon after, they slept soundly surrounded by the sylvan quiet of Penn's woods.

Beauford's man, Lester, who had been listening at their bedroom wall, waited until he was pretty certain they were asleep and his arousal had subsided, then left quietly.

November 9
Wednesday

Early Wednesday morning nodded more toward winter, with colder temperatures and intermittent rain. Susan and Jake agreed their time would be best used indoors doing online research into local mining and drilling. They also needed to catch up with Amy.

The school library, a two-story, redbrick building, had excellent Wi-Fi and several private rooms. Joan had offered them a small one dedicated to Ralph Waldo Emerson. It was to be "command control" for the Goddard Consulting Group, aka Jake Goddard and Susan Brand.

After setting up their computers and perusing email and Instagram posts, they spent the rest of the morning and early afternoon online while snacking out of their backpacks. When they saw that classes had ended for the day, they headed over to the athletic complex to attend Amy's first JV basketball game.

Susan and Jake sat on the opposite side of the gym from the home team and waved at Amy so many times while she warmed the bench that she frowned and stopped waving back.

When Saint Mike's had a healthy lead just before the final buzzer, Amy got a few minutes of playing time, missing her only shot from the top of the key. She did, however, manage to land a few shots with her elbows in the ribs of her opponents.

Jake and Susan waited for Amy outside the locker room. She finally appeared, tall for a freshman, slender, and sporting blown-dry, blonde hair in a short, stacked bob. She was dressed in a Saint Mike's windbreaker over jeans.

"Hey, Amers," Susan said, pulling her daughter into a hug and then steering her toward Jake.

"Good game, champ," Jake said, putting his hands on her shoulders and pecking her on the cheek. She looked skeptical. "Seriously, you made JV as a freshman. That's a great start."

"I miss you guys so much," Amy said, hugging them both at once.

"We miss you too, sweetie." Susan studied her daughter up and down. "But *my stars*, how you've grown. I swear you've shot up six inches since you left Utah."

"In two months, Mom? I don't think so."

"Can we walk with you? We need your opinion about something."

"Sure. You know I'm always ready to offer an opinion. I've still got an hour before dinner. Let's walk to my dorm."

They headed down the hall past the fitness room. Behind the door, shoes slapped, machines whirred, and weights clanked. They pushed through the double exterior doors and went outside. Although water had pooled in places, the rain was holding off for now. The wind gusted and leaves swirled about.

Jake pulled up the collar on his trench coat. "There is no colder air than wet Pennsylvania air," Jake said.

"That has been an adjustment. The humidity," Amy said, walking between them.

Susan fluffed the back of Amy's hair. "Great for the skin and the *do*, though."

"Yeah, Mom, like you, I constantly worry about my hair. You didn't even fuss that much for that *sweet little outdoor wedding* you two had last spring."

"What? Wait. I had flowers in my hair."

"Yup. Looked like you had fallen asleep dead drunk in a mountain meadow. Your handgun gets more loving attention."

"Ouch," Jake said.

"A girl can't be seen out in public with a dirty Glock, now can she?"

Susan put her arm around Amy's shoulders. "That's my little straight-shooter. Tells the truth even when it hurts." She gave her a squeeze and kissed the side of her head. "I love you, you little turkey. Now tell us about your friend, Mandy Fry."

Jake split off to avoid a puddle on the asphalt and rejoined his wife and stepdaughter on the other side. They passed a brick building housing the dining hall in a swale off to their left. The school's loop road wound through a short stretch of tall conifers before opening out onto the edge of the quad.

"Oh, so that explains the unscheduled visit. Doing a little sniffing around, are we?" Her eyes darted from one to the other. "Hired by the Busy Miss Bee to snoop on poor unsuspecting freshmen? What's the crime, uniform violations or excessive tardiness?"

"A transgression you apparently know a bit about," Jake said. "We are looking into something a little more pressing, but unfortunately, we have to keep you on a need-to-know basis," he added.

"So what else is new?" Amy said, rolling her eyes.

"So, your friend, Mandy?" Susan asked.

Amy stopped, faced them, and spoke in urgent hushed tones. Students in casual attire passed by them in clusters. The sun, close to setting, broke through striated clouds behind the mansard roof of the student center.

"First of all, Mandy is not my friend. As far as I can tell, Mandy has no friends."

"What? She seems like a good kid. Very knowledgeable—"

"That *knowledge* thing is part of the problem. Mandy is a know-it-all. Can't be told anything by anyone. Barely pauses long enough for the teachers to tell her anything. And she's manipulative."

"How so?" Jake asked.

"Mandy will go from one teacher to the next until she convinces someone to fight her battles. Adults find her very charming and convincing. Kids see right through her."

"Wow, honey. That's not what I was expecting to hear, but thanks for sharing. Very helpful . . ." Susan trailed off.

A handsome, athletic-looking boy of medium height rushed up and stood beside Amy. He brushed a lock of coal-black hair off his forehead. "Hey," the boy said to Amy.

"Hey, hi," Amy said. She turned. "Mom, Jake, this is Will."

"Nice to meet you." Will smiled and shook Susan's hand, then Jake's. Firm handshake. Eye contact. He turned back to Amy. "How 'bout some pong before dinner?"

Amy looked at her mother. Susan slowly nodded.

"Okay. See you later. Love you guys," Amy said.

She and Will ran toward the student center, holding hands and laughing.

Susan looked stunned. Jake looked amused. "She likes boys and boys like her." He fired a look at Susan. "Imagine that."

"That was fast work. I have to say."

"Poor Matthew—my hapless tongue-tied thirteen-year-old son. He thinks if he can just score enough soccer goals while Amy is present, she will feel the love. I'm pretty certain in his heart he believes if he ever actually gets up the nerve to reveal his feelings, she will be waiting for him. Might be a country song in that. *He scored a goal in my heart but tripped on his tongue.*"

"Don't rule Matt out just yet. Amy can be pretty fussy. Will might be a starter relationship. Or at least Will *will be* if I have anything to say about it."

"The hard truth is, Susan, and it seems just about all the parenting books agree on this, after puberty—and even a blind man could tell your daughter has gone through puberty—parental influence diminishes. Whereas the influence of the child's peers—"

"Okay, okay. I get it."

He patted Susan on the shoulder. She was still staring toward the student center. "It's the natural way of things, Mom."

After freshman swim team practice, Mandy Fry, dressed in gold Saint Mike sweats, walked alone back to her dorm on the school's loop road.

Dusk was quickly enveloping the campus; streetlights were blinking on and reflecting off the rain-soaked pavement.

She passed a school maintenance truck parked on the road at a speed bump. A large man wearing a dark jacket and leather workman's gloves was removing metal bollards from the bump. They were inserted during the day for the safety of students walking on the road to class and athletics but were removed at night so faculty cars could come and go directly to the dormitories and residences.

The workman was bending over the last of the three bollards as Mandy walked past the truck and around him. He looked up, smiled, and nodded. Mandy said hi and walked on, thinking how nice everyone at the school was. Or at least the adults were. The older kids and especially the prefects could try a little harder to be nice.

On she walked, along the edge of the quad past the library and the student center toward her dorm.

Something gnawed at the back of her consciousness. What was it about that man? It wasn't his appearance. All the maintenance men dressed like him. It wasn't his manner. Like all the people on staff, he had been friendly. He was just doing a job that was repeated every single evening, nothing unusual about that. It was something else—something fleeting and elusive, teasing her memory. Then it struck her. It was an odor, a familiar one. She worked to pin it down. Finally, in a rush it came to her. The man smelled like the oil rig . . . no . . . the sumps. That was it. His clothing emanated the unmistakable rank odor of the sumps. She stopped and turned just as the pickup pulled away and headed toward the maintenance barn.

But how could she be sure? Based on what she thought she smelled? And he seemed like a nice man.

Knowing she was already on thin ice and fearing that she might be pushing her luck with Mrs. Bailey if she reported her wild hunch, Mandy pushed it out of her mind.

As she neared the dorm, her thoughts switched to the mountain of homework that awaited.

November 10
Thursday Morning

Jake and Susan walked toward the campus entrance, wearing their customary jeans but with matching gray hoodies recently purchased in the school store. Yesterday's rain clouds had dispersed, and early-morning sun glowed above the houses, barns, and pastures that lined the road paralleling Saint Mike's campus.

Jake followed Susan through the low fence surrounding the football field, and they soon caught up with Joan walking on the track. She was decked out in well-worn running shoes, black, capri-length yoga pants, and a blue windbreaker.

"Morning," Joan said. "Beautiful day in central PA."

"Yes, it is," Susan said. "I'm starting to get why Jake has such fond memories of growing up near here."

They rounded the end of the track and passed under the scoreboard. It featured a large window for a digital clock and had two similar, smaller windows for displaying the score below the words "Home" and "Guests." The school's nine-hole golf course stretched away from them to the edge of dense forest; mist drifted above the still-green fairways.

"Thanks for meeting me. Unless it's pouring, this is where I usually start my day." She glanced at Jake, then at Susan. "Many conflicts and concerns have been addressed right here on the school track."

Jake beamed. "Oh, I get it. Nobody leaves until we resolve this issue, or somebody collapses from exhaustion, whichever comes first."

"Something like that, yes. And most of my staff know I can walk all day." Joan smiled and shaded her eyes against the sun. "It's a technique I learned from a mentor. Walking shoulder to shoulder immediately mitigates the tension that can be palpable, sitting in an office across a desk. Also, walking inspires creative problem-solving." She swiped at her brow with the back of her right hand. "So what did you learn from our cub reporter?"

"Great kid," Susan said. "Very earnest about her causes. I sometimes wish my daughter had that sort of passion."

"That'll come, Susan. I sense a budding leader in Amy. Mark my words, she'll make the perfect prefect someday."

Jake said, "That actually brings us to a concern. Can we keep what we learned in confidence? We gave Mandy our word."

"Yes, of course," Joan said.

"No reprisals based on what we are about to share?"

"I'm giving you my word." Several cars entered the campus and passed the field. "Here come our day students."

"She's afraid of the prefects," Susan said.

Jake added, "Unless I miss my guess, there's some hazing going on, and oddly enough that might be how Mandy learned about effluvium flowing into the river on the weekends. Do prefects still make freshmen swing?"

"Swing?" Susan asked.

"I thought I should ask you before I mentioned it to Susan. Being the mother of a freshman."

Joan shook her head with exasperation. "Jump in the river off a rope swing while wearing the school uniform."

"Happened in my day," Jake said. "Not as innocuous as it sounds."

"A tradition we would like to see fade away, but every time we think it is one for the history books, some overzealous alum insists to his legacy student that it's just not Saint Mike's without swinging freshmen."

"Funny; Amy hasn't said anything about that," Susan said.

"Well, the tradition is to surreptitiously work through the freshman class alphabetically, so if it is happening, it has happened to Amy Brand. But after seeing your intrepid daughter on the soccer field, I can imagine her marching out, insisting on going first, maybe doing a swan dive with a half twist off the rope, swimming to shore, asking 'What's the big deal?' then promptly forgetting about it."

Jake and Susan laughed and nodded.

"She has always been tenacious. I'm impressed with how well you know my daughter."

"Leadership material, like I said." Joan glanced at the Fitbit on her right wrist. "If it *is* still happening, and I would be naive to assume otherwise, it is certainly not sanctioned by the school."

"Mandy was hesitant to give us details regarding how she learned about Beauford's dumping, but as an alum it was pretty easy to put two and two together."

"That's exactly why I asked *you* for help. Tell you what: let's expand your purview to include spying on my prefects. Didn't you say in your email last night you were going to go back out to the river this coming weekend?"

"Yes. It doesn't make much sense to go before then," Jake said.

"Then how about informing me if you happen upon any covert swinging activity? Give me the names of the older students," Joan said.

Susan asked, "How will we know who the guilty ones are?"

"Easy. I'll get you a school directory with a picture of every single one of our darling Mikes. And the ones standing on the bank, acting *way* too mature, sophisticated, and cool to jump into the chilly Susky in November—those will be your ringleaders."

"We'll go Sunday, then," Jake said. "In the meantime, can we meet with Mr. Marlowe?"

"Of course; I'll set it up. Is Jim the one who got Mandy all worked up about fracking?" Joan asked. "If so, then let me speak to him first and bring him into the loop on her situation."

"You didn't hear it from us, but yes, she said it was Jim Marlowe. I guess that's why you call the class STEAM," Jake said.

"Our teachers are instructed to remain impartial and present both sides of the issue, but they are passionate, intelligent people, and that has become a very tall order in these politically divisive times," Joan said.

"Which reminds me of a question regarding our initial assignment to research the local Beauford well. Do you anticipate increased problems under Dick Tucker's administration in Washington?" Jake asked.

They passed under the scoreboard again.

"Frankly, I do, and I've even discussed it with my board, which tells you how concerned I am because a head never wants to invite board member involvement in something that is not clearly looming as a governance problem. They have enough to worry about."

"How so?" Susan asked. "I mean, how will your problems increase?"

"You want the facts or the alternate facts?" Joan asked.

"Just the facts, ma'am?" Jake said in his best Jack Webb voice.

"Thank you for that, Jake, or Jack. In my line of work, I have to cherish every chuckle, and that really was a pretty good impersonation. We have reason to believe that what oversight there is now of fracking will be thrown out the window as the industry is deregulated, the EPA is defunded and/or defanged, and states invite oil and gas companies to regulate themselves. They have already attempted to roll back a requirement that the companies provide information on methane emissions."

"I recently read an article about that. If I remember correctly, it said methane is the key component of natural gas and has a global-warming potential more than twenty-five—or it even might have said thirty—times that of carbon dioxide," Jake said.

"Industries regulating themselves conjure up images of foxes regulating the henhouse," Susan said.

"Doesn't it just," Joan agreed. "And when it comes to the 'new' EPA, it's a fox who denies the climate is changing." Joan stopped and faced the two investigators. "I take my job very seriously. And job one is the health and safety of the children in my charge. I'll share with you what is keeping me awake at night right now—right up there with the prospect of our drinking water being contaminated by Beauford. Lorna Matson, our heroic school nurse—a woman who does not have an alarmist bone in her body—is convinced that she is seeing more cases of severe asthma at Saint Mike's, and she believes they are tied to the literally thousands of hydraulic fracturing oil and natural gas wells that surround us here in Pennsylvania. Her concerns have been borne out by a Johns Hopkins University study indicating that sufferers living near hydraulic fracturing wells are four times more likely to have a serious attack." The school head looked from Jake to Susan. "Now I have to get ready for my first meeting of the day. Keep me posted. You can always find me out here in the mornings."

She turned and headed toward the opening in the fence.

"The Marcellus Shale formation, which extends from New York and—just our luck—goes right under us and into Ohio and West Virginia, is believed to be the largest onshore reserve of natural gas in the country. It has even been given a name by the industry, Shale Crescent USA. Drilling deep wells and then injecting water, sand, and *top secret* chemicals at high pressure to break up the rock is needed to release the natural gas." Jim Marlowe, a short, fit, beach-boy blond, had shifted into professor mode when asked about local wells. He stood at the front of his classroom.

"Fracking?" Susan asked. Jake and Susan were sitting on a front lab table, legs dangling.

"Hydraulic fracturing, or fracking, yes," Marlowe said. "Benefits—including energy independence—are many." He adjusted his tie and cleared his throat. "Possible consequences include man-caused earthquakes, contaminated groundwater, and health effects from wellhead emissions."

"Health effects such as asthma and even cancer, right?" Jake said. "Those are pretty serious consequences."

"Could have been worse. In the sixties there was a proposal that actually gained some traction to use nuclear warheads for fracking wells near the Colorado River." Marlowe raised an eyebrow in punctuation. He was leaning with one elbow on a wooden podium. He turned and glanced at the clock above the wall-mounted whiteboard at the front of the room. They could hear movement and laughter outside in the hall.

"I know the kids are due any minute," Jake said. "Just one more quick question. Is there anything you might have said that could have encouraged Mandy Fry to break school rules and put herself at risk snooping around the Beauford well?"

"First off, Mandy is not your typical freshman. Ninth graders usually need a fire built under them. In Mandy's case it's about keeping the existing fire from raging out of control. Her parents are high-profile environmental activists." He picked at some lint on the front of his burgundy V-neck sweater. "They may have done too good a job with their daughter. If anything, Mandy needs reining in. But I've only had this class of freshmen for two-plus months, and I'm still learning what makes them tick and what makes them think."

"And I assume in the case of kids like Mandy, what makes them act foolishly," Jake said.

"Exactly. It's a delicate balance. You want them passionate and engaged. You obviously don't want them acting in an unsafe manner or even doing and saying things out in the community that reflect badly on the school. We need to coexist with our, for the most part, much more conservative neighbors."

"'Clinging to their guns and their religion,'" Jake said.

"I've got to say, 'the previous president'—have you noticed how Tucker never refers to him by name while blaming him for everything—pretty much hit the nail on the head regarding our neck of the woods with that observation," Marlowe replied.

"You're struggling to remain impartial?" Susan asked.

"Yes, like most of our staff, and also our head, by the way. I'm trying every day to remain unbiased in my discussions with students. Plus, this is central Pennsylvania. Some would say 'Pennsyltucky.' Many of our local students are thrilled with the new normal. Mostly because of what they hear at home."

"The new abnormal," Jake said.

"Don't get me started," Marlowe said with a grimace.

"We're two gun-toting, country-music-loving, redneck liberals who have lived as adults in Arizona, Wyoming, and Utah, three very conservative states. So we hear you," Susan said.

"Plus, I think Joan may have told you I grew up near here," Jake said. A bell rang in the hall.

Marlowe smiled, shifted toward the podium, and opened his laptop.

Jake and Susan thanked him and departed through a green-and-gold wave of energetic kids entering the lab.

Susan got permission from the dean, Cliff Hall, to take Amy to lunch. To save time, they headed to the nearest eatery. It was just off one of the main roads that originated at an intersection near campus.

The Hanna Valley Inn was a quaint little treasure tucked in a cul-de-sac at the end of what appeared to be a depressed rural neighborhood.

They drove past a large, peeling Richard Tucker for President poster. Tacked under it, a hand-scrawled sign advertised firewood with an arrow that pointed to a dirt road leading into the trees. Beside that was a No Trespass sign indicating that transgressors might find themselves looking down the barrel of a gun.

Just beyond stood a two-story, ramshackle shack with tractor tires painted white, circling a mailbox pole. The tarpaper and shingle-covered dwelling had a long aluminum ladder leaning on the roof above the blue-plastic-tarp-enclosed front porch and reaching up to the chimney above the second floor. A small trailer parked in the side yard was cluttered with rotting wood pallets, various car parts, and sundry buckets. A satellite dish on the south wall and a late-model sedan parked out front stood in stark contrast.

And beyond that sat the Hanna Valley Inn, surrounded by mature deciduous trees. They parked and entered. The inn was quiet and relatively empty. They chose a booth in the dining room.

Soon Amy was working on her grilled cheese sandwich and tomato soup and answering questions about her classes and sports.

Susan put down her chicken Caesar wrap and changed the subject. "What can you tell us about freshman swinging?"

Amy looked up from her sandwich. "Nothing that can go beyond this room."

"Agreed," Jake said. He reached for his Arnold Palmer iced tea.

"So like the first night in the dorm, I hear about this *really scary* ritual prefects have subjected poor innocent freshmen to for eons." She shrugged her shoulders and spooned some soup into her mouth. "Like all similar crap intended to freak you out, the worry is worse than the reality. I walked out to the river in my uniform on a warm Sunday in September, accompanied by a few of our rule-enforcing prefects—who were breaking the rules, by the way. Swung out over the river on a rope, dropped in, got out. Walked home. It was, if anything, refreshing . . . as well as no big deal—silly and stupid, really."

"Notice anything odd about the river?" Jake asked.

"No floaters, if that's what you mean."

"I was thinking of something a little less dramatic than cadavers, like activity around the well or polluted water," Jake said.

"I didn't see anything out of the ordinary. But then I wasn't really looking either. Just wanted to get it over with and get back to my plans for the day. Actually, something really good came out of it. Will was in the same group and was equally unimpressed. We walked back together in our wet unis."

"Okay, let's talk a little more about Will," Susan said.

"Let's not," Amy said.

Jake and Susan exchanged a look.

"In that department, I'm keeping you two on a need-to-know-only basis." Amy smiled a little mechanically. "And there is really nothing you need to know." She concentrated on the second half of her sandwich.

And that was all the intel re: Will the skilled investigators managed to pry out of their daughter.

Amy got anxious on the way back to the campus when she realized she was late for class. Before Jake had fully stopped at the curb, she grabbed her backpack, jumped out of the car, and ran toward the covered archway leading to the doors of classroom building. An older student wearing a tie and school blazer stood thumbing a cell phone. Without glancing up, his hand shot out and stopped her. Jake and Susan observed the exchange from the car and felt the need to intervene.

Jake killed the engine, hopped out, walked over, and introduced himself. "Hey, so sorry. I'm Jake." He pointed to Susan as she approached. "This is Susan, Amy's mom. We had Amy off campus for lunch. Mr. Hall approved it. I'm afraid it's because of us she's late." He reached out his right hand.

The student didn't look up from his texting and didn't offer his hand. "Jed Beauford, senior prefect. I'm on attendance this afternoon." He glanced up. "Amy, this is a pattern that has to stop."

"It's really not her fault," Susan said.

"I'm a graduate, former prefect myself, and I know what a high value Saint Mike's places on punctuality. I promise it will not happen again." Jake looked at Amy and smiled. "That is, if we have anything to say about it."

Beauford yawned, put his phone in his pants pocket, and scratched the back of his head.

"Too late; I already texted it to the dean's office." He turned disinterested eyes on Jake. "Not sure what the rules were like thirty or forty years ago, but things have changed. Today we emphasize student responsibility. We are, after all, a prep school, Mr. and Mrs. Brand, and our job is to prepare our students to be personally responsible in college as well as *independent* from their parents."

Amy glared at Susan, brushed by Beauford, and entered the building.

Beauford shifted his eyes to Susan. "Your trying to take responsibility is not doing your daughter, who has a tardiness problem, by the way, a favor."

Jake recognized Susan's look. He'd seen it halt charging horses and cause snarling dogs to stop, drop, and roll over.

"Okay, thanks for the important reminder," Jake said, pulling Susan toward the car.

They closed both doors, Susan slamming hers. "Power-crazed punk. Why did you stop me?"

"We're only here for a short time; Amy has to make her own way in the school hierarchy. Every school has its assholes."

"And Beauford's the biggest one I've ever encountered."

"No argument," Jake said. "But we don't want to do anything that could cause older students to have it out for Amy. The best thing a freshman can do is fly under the radar. Judging by how she described her attitude toward the hazing experience at the river, she has already figured that out."

"Jerk!" Susan thrust herself back in the seat. Then sat upright again. "Wait. Beauford. Isn't that the name on the well?"

She sat back hard again. "'Blowhard' or 'Bloated' might be better choices."

Jake turned the rearview mirror for a look at his face. "I can handle being called Mr. Brand, but 'thirty or forty years ago'?"

He readjusted the mirror, started the car, and headed to the library for some research in the Emerson incident room.

November 11
Friday Morning

*J*ake felt like a dismounted rodeo cowboy braced against his taut lariat, trying to bring down a roped steer. He lay on the ground with his back propped against a small boulder and fought the bottom of the jerking rope to eliminate as much slack as possible. His best friend, Eli Finn, grunted his way to the top. Jake gaped up at the soles of Eli's Converses— gripping, releasing, ascending, and gripping again. Considering he had cajoled his roommate into scaling the riverside rope swing in the first place, steadying it was the least he could do. Eli's legs and shoes were now so high they were blurring in Jake's vision.

"Go, go, go!" chanted the boys ringing Jake. "E-li, E-li, E-li. Go, go, go!"

The limbs of the massive oak whirled above as the sun blinked through the leaves, blinding Jake. He felt dizzy and sick with anticipation. It was as if he knew how this would end. "No, no, no."

Suddenly Eli was plummeting toward him, his body rapidly expanding in size. Jake, the rope now slack in his hands, rolled out of the way. Eli's head hit the rock with a thump. Jake twisted around and stared at his friend in horror. Eli's body lay crumpled in a pile of hemp, his hand on Jake's shoulder as if initiating an embrace. Behind the fallen boy's ear, a trickle of blood streamed down the rock. A scream fought to escape Jake's throat.

"Jake!" Susan shook him. "Jake, wake up. You're having a nightmare."

Jake blinked awake and rubbed his forehead. "Oh my God. It was so . . . it was . . . just." He sucked in a breath and sat up in bed. Dim light from the campus road illuminated their room.

"Too late. I should have tried to break his fall. I just . . . I just instinctively rolled out of the way. Then it was too late."

He flopped back against his pillows, heart pounding.

Susan rolled against him. "If you talk about your nightmares, they don't come true," she said.

Jake turned to her with despair in his eyes. "Too late."

They found Joan on the track doing her laps. The sun was trying to break through the fog accompanying the crisp morning.

After exchanging greetings, they walked in silence for a few moments.

Jake cleared his throat and spoke. "You know, Joan, my best friend died at the river in the fall of our senior year. He fell while climbing the swing rope. It broke. I . . . I had never told Susan until I had a nightmare about it last night."

"I do know about that. Although I didn't realize you were involved. Rare as they are, every tragic loss of a student becomes a sad part of school culture and history."

Jake stared off across the golf course toward the wooded hills at the edge of the campus. The fog was starting to thin. "I've always felt it was my fault." He ran the tip of his tongue across his lower lip. "Eli was an incredible athlete. We all envied him. He bragged constantly that he could climb the rope, no problem. I was the one who . . . who dared him to do it . . . to shut him up. I realized later I was jealous of him. I was secretly hoping he would fail . . . but . . . never dreamed he would fall. Eli Finn never fell. He always landed on his feet. But that time, he almost hit me and landed on his back."

Joan stopped and looked into his eyes. "You were kids. Boys seeking adventure. You are not to blame."

Susan put her hand on his shoulder. They resumed walking.

Joan said, "I've read about the accident in the files; all trips to the river were suspended for several years. The riverbank was literally patrolled by faculty on weekends for a time. Ropes on limbs that popped up were removed. But Saint Michael's is not a prison. Eventually it became too difficult to enforce. It is such an attractive hazard—especially for boys. The more the school said no, the more students wanted to go."

"I thought I should discuss it with you." Jake forced down a dry swallow. "We were basically told to just get over it. It felt like it was swept under the rug." His voice grabbed a little. "It has haunted me my whole life."

"You might be interested in knowing John Barrow, the head of school during your time, was strongly sanctioned by his board for creating an atmosphere of machismo and hazing at Saint Michael's School. Shortly after your friend died, Barrow was required to do a sensitivity training course for CEOs, and shortly after that, when it obviously hadn't worked, he was let go."

"Really? I had no idea. I mean, I knew he had moved on, but . . . we were all terrified of the guy, I have to say. Any expression of affection or emotion during Barrow's reign was considered to be a sign of weakness. The students had a saying back then: 'Boy or girl, Saint Michael's will make a man of you.'"

"In case you're wondering if I feel this in any way disqualifies you, don't," Joan said.

"Thank you. Feels good just to . . ." Jake trailed off.

Susan put her arm around Jake's waist. "Let's just say Jake is a work in progress when it comes to expressing his deepest feelings."

They walked in silence for a while.

"So what did you think of Tucker's campaign-like rally in Harrisburg last night?" Susan asked.

"*Ooooff.* The media described it as a fiery speech tossing red meat to his base. A Republican aide to several presidents called it the most divisive speech ever made by a sitting president. He found it deeply disturbing, as did we all."

"I thought of a *Macbeth* line. ''Tis a tale told by an idiot, full of sound and fury, signifying nothing.'" Joan glanced at her Fitbit. "These

Pennsylvania miners, farmers, and small business owners are not stupid, but they aren't worldly or well educated. And our reality TV president has played them for suckers."

"What has that man ever done for blue-collar workers during his self-absorbed lifetime of getting richer?" Jake asked.

Susan added, "I can't believe a single college-educated woman voted for him."

"I just read a column by a local writer this morning. He likened local folks voting for the current administration to chickens voting for Colonel Sanders," Joan said. "The country is as divided as it has been since the War Between the States. And it's like trying to remain neutral during the Civil War. You were either for slavery and its expansion into western American territory or against it. There was no middle ground. You are either for regulations that protect health and the environment or against them. You either believe the science of climate change or you don't. We are, for all intents and purposes, engaged in an internecine war. And I struggle every day to walk the fine line of keeping the battles off our campus. I keep hitting three notes: respect, honesty, and compassion—in short, civility. Those are the qualities of social responsibility that bind society together. How do we as educators hold our students to those standards when they see how little regard the leader of the free world has for them? The truth is, our students are not allowed to act like the president. Case in point: Saint Mike's has zero tolerance for bullying."

"Amen," Jake said. "It has got to be tough."

"Our new, unspoken mantra has become 'Do as we say and do—not as Dick Tucker says and does.' It is very frustrating. But your 'amen' reminded me, Jake, that I'm preaching to the choir, aren't I? I apologize, I'm lecturing. Former history teacher . . ."

"We are definitely on the same page. But it's not like the previous administration didn't play fast and loose at times with the EPA's oversight of domestic oil-and-gas development. There was definitely some fishy EPA reporting regarding groundwater contaminated by fracking in Wyoming," Jake said.

"Fossil fuel is the evil chef who offers a smorgasbord of poisoned choices," Joan said.

"Except one," Susan said. "The one we Americans hate: the choice to tighten our belts, conserve, and go with alternatives."

"That's correct. At least we are trying to do our part and educate the kids in that regard at the school. But regarding the current administration and its joke of an EPA, looks like I'm about to become a covert member of the resistance. I don't dare speak publicly about how I feel, but I can't do nothing."

"You'll look good in a belted trench coat and fedora," Jake said. "That reminds me of something I've been wondering. When you drive off campus on county roads, you can't help but notice that head-to-toe camo is a very popular clothing choice. If I were to, say, accidentally run over one of those guys, do you think I could get off by claiming I never saw him?"

Joan laughed and picked up her pace for a final lap.

After eating lunch with a table full of students in the dining hall, the two PIs returned to the Emerson room.

Jake sat in an overstuffed chair, reading and making notes on copies of articles on fracking he had found online and printed. Susan sat at her laptop, researching Beauford Oil and Gas.

"Did you enjoy our lunch companions?" Jake asked.

"What, those senior boys? They're hilarious."

"Cracked me up with their discussion of the pros and cons of bringing an ostrich on campus as a senior prank," Jake said.

"Did you do stuff like that?"

"Absolutely. It was the only time prefects could just be one of the guys."

"What was your prank?"

"It was brilliant. It was a beautiful day in late May just before finals. When the last bell rang to begin classes and McGregor Hall got quiet, a Tibetan chant was playing throughout the building. When teachers went en masse to find the source, the seniors led every student out onto the lawn to a picnic waiting in the sun."

"Sounds like harmless fun."

"Because the faculty could see we seniors had worked hard pulling the picnic together, and because we invited them to join us, it was over an hour before they got us back inside." He turned back to his article. "What are you finding on Beauford?"

"Only that it looks like it might be a mistake to treat the company like an outlier. Beauford appears to be a small player in a multinational consortium of energy companies, with its American HQ in Texas and deep interests in oil, gas, gold, and battery-metals development all over the US. Including, it seems, in Wyoming, Idaho, and Utah."

Susan's email pinged. "Oh, yay. Just got a message from Jen." Jennifer Wise, or Zullie Jen, was an old college friend of Susan's who spent her summers based in Missoula, Montana, when she wasn't parachuting into forest fires.

"How is she? Read it to me."

"'Hola, Brandy, just finishing up my season, and it has been one long, hot mother. Don't know how much longer, blah, blah, blah.'"

"No, I'm interested, read it all, Susan."

"I am, those are her words. 'Don't know how much longer, blah, blah, blah. Knew you and Jako were frackin' around in PA, so thought you might be interested in this sidebar for me. My cousin Carrie in Southern Colorado has asked me to come down and help her look into a methane hotspot. Imagine that. She's an enviro and a mom, and she worries about her two middle-school kids inhaling benzene every day.

"'Headline: Zullie hotshot jumps into methane hotspot. Not sure how I can help or exactly what I'm getting into, but I love that area and am suffering from severe thrill deprivation right now after my fire season. I'm leaving tomorrow to drive down. I'll be in touch. Probably pick your brains. You're so lucky to be working near Amy. Hug her tight for me. Jake too. Love, Jen.'"

"What's up with benzene?" Susan asked.

Jake flipped a few pages on his legal pad. "Known carcinogen emitted by oil and gas wells." He glanced up. "Bad shit. Both short- and long-term health effects."

"J-Y to the rescue yet again." Susan said. She flashed on the memory of her friend jumping out of a plane, flying in under canopy, and saving her from an armed and dangerous hombre.

November 13
Sunday

Jake had loaded his daypack with water, snacks, and other supplies. The two investigators headed back to the River Trail well before most teens were seeing the light of day. Jake admitted on the walk out that he didn't have high hopes for catching kids at the tree. Such a gray, blustery day would likely dampen the school spirit of even the most ardent upper-class proponent of freshman dunking.

Once they were out of the woods, the first objective was to check the river while appearing to be out for a hike—just in case there were hidden cameras.

Jake and Susan strolled along the riverbank, holding hands like the lovers they were.

One hundred yards downstream from the well site, they noticed a diluted purple plume fanning out into the main flow of the river. Close to the well, the water was brown and opaque. Once they got upstream from the well, the water was more typically blue-gray and ran relatively clear.

"Looks like Mandy had 'em dead to rights," Susan whispered.

Gunshots echoed off the adjacent hills, stopping them cold. But then Jake remembered where he was—Pennsylvania, where hunting was a religion and the first day of fall deer season was a school holiday.

"Probably the hopeful blasts of weekend warriors stalking deer," he said. "I was totally into it, growing up here. Went with my dad." They strolled on toward the rails-to-trails hiking trail upstream from the well. A mated pair of mallard ducks floated in an eddy by the far bank. Gusts of wind stirred up whirls of swirling leaves and blew them over the water, where they were captured by the current and ceremoniously carried downriver.

When the "lovers" rounded a bend and were out of sight of the well, Susan indicated a downed tree trunk they could sit on side by side.

"I've got to say, it looks like a clear case of illegal dumping," she said.

"Or a *murky* case, as the case may be. Must've pissed them off, being busted by a fourteen-year-old," Jake said. "I hate to even imagine what that brown crap is comprised of, but it sure as hell *cannot* be okay to flush it straight into the river. Even under the new Environmental Prostitution Agency's rules."

"Check the polluter box. Now let's see if we can catch some swingers," Susan said, shielding her eyes from windblown debris. "If they even show in this weather." She shifted on the log, placing her back to the wind.

After swigging some water, munching on granola bars, and allowing a decent amount of time to transpire, the pair strolled back down to the River Trail and into the woods to take up a position out of sight off the path.

They found fairly comfortable posts, Jake leaning against a tree with a convenient limb on which he could prop his binos and focus on the swinging tree while Susan straddled a log holding the student directory she had retrieved from Jake's pack. The good news was they were out of the wind. They settled in for what all good sleuths must master: the wait.

After several minutes of silence, Susan spoke. "Is that the tree, Jake?"

Jake shook off his memories. "Which tree?"

"*The* tree."

"The Eli Tree?"

"Yes."

"No, it's up another half mile or so beyond where we turned around. We thought we were being sneaky by installing our very own rope swing in a less obvious location."

"I can't believe you never told me about the death of your school friend."

"I know. I should have. I buried the whole awful memory pretty deep. Being back here, especially being back here on the river, brought it up to the surface."

"I can only imagine how you must have been hurting for a long time after."

He turned to her with wet eyes. "When the rope broke and he plunged toward me, I instinctively rolled out of the way like I was avoiding a hit on the football field. When I rolled back toward Eli, his . . . uh, his face was less than a foot from mine. He was lying on his back. Blood was dripping down the rock under his head. I pushed up on my knees, grabbed his head, and yelled his name. There was no response." He looked down at his opened palms. "His blood was literally on my hands."

Susan got up, walked to Jake, wrapped her arms around him, and pressed her chest into his. She could feel his body shake.

"A senior bloody prefect. What a travesty!" Jake said as they headed back to the campus through the woods. "Making those little kids swing out over the water and then walk back to the school in wet clothes on a cold day. It's disgusting."

"Makes me want to rethink what I said about Amy following in your footsteps. If that Beauford jerk represents student leadership at the school, I'd rather have her join the resistance."

"I never abused my power like that when I was a prefect, nor, to my knowledge, did any of my friends—bellowing at those little freshmen and the derisive laughter and taunts. Funny thing is, as a prefect, I was called a narc. Now I guess I'm fulfilling my destiny, narcing on a prefect, but I imagine once Joan hears what a colossal bully he is, Jed Beauford's leadership days are numbered."

"Maybe there *is* justice in the world, if only in this little tiny world in this remote corner of Pennsylvania," Susan said.

"Let's just hope his parents aren't big donors," Jake said.

November 14
Monday

Joan poured coffee for Jake and herself while Terri, her assistant, brought in a cup of tea for Susan. They were sitting around the table midmorning in front of the fireplace in Joan's office. Terri eased the door closed on her way out.

"I've had a chance to think about what you reported to me on the track this morning," Joan said.

"Sorry to be the bearers of doubly bad news," Jake said.

"I've learned in my short time as an investigator the best news for a client is no news," Susan added. "Your spouse is not cheating; your employee is not skimming; your daughter is not sneaking around with that drug dealer after all."

"Ah yes, if only . . . But I'm certain nothing untoward to report is only too rare in your business."

"Way too rare," Jake said.

"Now concerning Mr. Beauford, the bully. He will be summoned before the student-faculty discipline committee, and the ironic thing about being judged by his peers is they are still idealists and their outrage often makes our jaded adult response look like pique." She lifted her coffee mug and sipped. "My best guess, at a minimum: the hypocrite will be stripped of his prefectship and made to move back to the senior dorm.

He certainly shouldn't be allowed to continue living among the young students he's been harassing."

"I can imagine a dorm-wide celebration at that liberating moment," Jake said.

"Ding-dong, the bully's gone," Susan added.

"And perhaps the greatest punishment of all will be explaining this disciplinary action to the colleges he will be pitching himself to next semester," Joan said.

"Now as to the matter of the oil company dumping in the river, I'll get my school attorneys after them. We will report them to any state and federal regulatory agencies that are still actually doing their jobs. That should serve to turn Beauford's ire toward me and my board and away from Mandy Fry—and any other of our students, for that matter."

"What about Mandy's attack and stolen phone?" Susan asked.

"As much as a part of me wants to pursue that, I just can't see the upside to involving a fourteen-year-old living so far away from her home and parents in that kind of investigation and legal entanglement. Certainly, if the perpetrator is identified and more evidence is presented, I would be in favor of prosecuting, but at this point I'm sure the local police have done all they can, or all they are capable of, and there really isn't anything more Mandy can tell them. I'm going to offer to replace her phone and do my best to convince her parents that this is an anomaly and she really is safe here at Saint Michael's."

"I just don't know—" Susan said.

"Imagine if she were your daughter, Susan. Would you want her concentrating on this mess, or her algebra?"

"How can you be certain she's out of danger?" Susan asked.

"They have what they want—her phone—and we are going to suspend all off-campus hikes for the winter, ostensibly because of the freshman swinging. She is perfectly safe with us on campus. I just can't risk panicking my school community."

Joan drained her coffee and stood. "I can't thank you two enough for the gift of your expertise and services. Stay as long as you like, but by Saturday we will be a ghost town after the kids and many of the faculty leave for Thanksgiving break."

"That ended kind of abruptly," Susan said as they walked across the campus to collect their belongings from the Emerson room in the library.

"You may be too close to this situation because of Amy. To use your example, after you tell a client his wife is cheating on him, you don't demand to know what he's going to do about it."

A stocky Asian boy in a school uniform was exiting the library. He smiled, nodded, and held the door for them as they entered.

November 17
Thursday

Susan suggested, and Jake agreed, that since they were already at Saint Michael's with all expenses paid and comfortable accommodations in the school's guest quarters, the best plan was to wear the parent hat for the reminder of the week. That way when Amy was free to go on Saturday, they could all fly back to Utah together.

The only pressing PI work looming was a find-and-document-assets job, for which an attorney in Salt Lake had retained them while they were at Saint Mike's.

The attorney was advising two parents who were thinking of suing a riding stable after their daughter had been injured, fortunately not permanently, falling from a horse. The job was basically to search public records for registrations of cars, boats, planes, property, etc. Real estate transactions, loans, liens, and foreclosures were helpful also. The goal was to determine whether the business was worth suing, and adhered closely to the old adage cautioning about attempting to get blood from a stone.

That job could be done in the evenings from any computer connected to the internet, including the one conveniently provided with their campus duplex.

They decided during the day to immerse themselves in the life of the school. By Thursday they had—to Amy's great embarrassment—visited two of her classes, eaten several meals in the dining hall (providing a chance to check on the progress of the ostrich caper), and cheered wildly at several athletic events, even while Saint Mike's stalwarts were being buried by the opposition. They had also dedicated one evening to attending a student production of *Arsenic and Old Lace*, in which the laughs piled up with the bodies.

And at Jake's insistence, Susan spent some time with Will in the student center and got to know—and even like—him a little.

In fact, they invited Will to join them for dinner off campus at an Italian restaurant the kids all raved about. Anthony's was a bit of a drive, but Amy had assured her parents the pizza alone was well worth the trip.

After much pleasant small talk about recent events on campus, discussed over dripping slices of pepperoni pizza and side salads against a painted backdrop of rolling Tuscany vineyards, Susan said, "I ran into Mandy Fry on campus today. We're all going to be on the same flight to Salt Lake Saturday."

Amy got quiet. Something Susan had always known, and Jake had learned in his five short years in her life, was not a good sign.

Amy cleared her throat, "So, uh, guys, uh, Will's parents have invited me to spend this weekend at their home." Will smiled blankly and studied the shop-worn décor. Amy barely paused for a breath. "I was thinking it might be okay since I've seen so much of you this week—even in my Spanish class—and that I could maybe fly home Tuesday. I would still have a full day at home before Thanksgiving. Most kids don't even get out until the Wednesday before Thanksgiving. So I really wouldn't be missing anything important."

As is the case with most unsuspecting people who have been blindsided, the parents' initial response was stunned silence.

"So . . . Mom. What do you think?"

Will felt the call to enter the fray in a manly fashion. He glanced at Amy out of the corner of his eye and attempted to put the parents at ease.

"My folks love Amy. We just live an hour from school, and they will be home the whole time, I promise, if that is a concern. And we have a guest house—"

Susan interrupted but tried to keep her voice steady. "Sweetheart, you have a flight to Salt Lake City on Saturday." Amy scratched behind her ear and looked down at her pizza. "Amy, you do have a flight to Salt Lake City, on Delta, on Saturday, right?"

Amy muttered, "Actually, I knew you would hate to waste the money on the change fees, so I do have a flight to Salt Lake City, on Delta . . . but . . . it's on Tuesday."

Susan pushed back in her chair and glared at Jake for help.

Jake tilted his head and smiled—a sign that she should go easy, which she ignored.

"You *what*?" She took a breath. "Sorry you have to hear this, Will. Amy, you will not ambush us like this. You will change that reservation tonight, and you can damn well work over the Christmas vacation to earn the money to pay us back for the change fee."

Amy reddened but remained silent. She stirred her salad.

Susan continued, eyes on low beam. "And you can hand over my credit card in the morning. Which I entrusted you with, by the way. There is no way you are not flying home with us Saturday." She turned her high beams on Will. "Will, please understand, and thank your parents for their kind invitation." And again, focusing her low beams on Amy: "And apologize for us and for our daughter's rudeness."

After a few moments of silence, Jake cleared his throat and said, "I hear the tiramisu is good."

November 19
Saturday

Mandy disembarked from the rear of the plane at the Salt Lake City International Airport. An obese, middle-aged couple, struggling with their many carry-ons as they worked their way down the aisle, slowed her.

Once off, she hurried past the couple she had mentally dubbed Mr. and Mrs. Waddleson and passed through rows of benches with a smattering of passengers waiting for flights. Large green wreaths with red bows adorned every wall. Canned Christmas music filled the concourse.

She walked past several gates, searching for the nearest ladies' room. Because of another complication that reminded her with irritation that she was becoming a woman, with all the attendant inconveniences that brought—including having to dig out the right change for the feminine product dispenser—her visit was longer than expected.

After finishing up, she washed her hands, slung her daypack on her shoulder, and went back out on the concourse. She passed the open-air Stubbs Coffee Shop and was disgusted to note they still offered plastic straws. She exited through security.

Anxious to see her parents, Mandy hurried to the covered bridge spanning arriving and departing airport traffic. The bridge led to the short-term parking garage; two escalators heading down to baggage flanked its entrance. She was alone. All the other passengers had cleared the area.

Just as she was about to step onto one of the escalators, she sensed the movement of a wheelchair behind her. She started to sidestep out of the way when she felt a sharp prick on the back of her neck. Her shoulders were jerked from behind and a large hand clamped her mouth. She struggled briefly and was vaguely aware of being pulled onto the wheelchair, covered with a blanket, and rolled across the bridge to the tune of "Jingle Bells" before blacking out.

A blinking yellow light and the shriek of a claxon heralded the arrival of luggage on the conveyor-belt-fed carousel; oversize bags, many holding skis, clattered through a hatch at the side of the room.

Susan waited patiently at the back of the crowd—her hand resting on the extended handle of her small, wheeled carry-on—looking smug in the knowledge she had packed conservatively and avoided Delta Airline's baggage fees.

Jake recognized his bag when it slapped onto the carousel, slid to the bottom amid a jumble of other suitcases, and trundled toward him. He heaved it up and off and worked his way through the waiting travelers to Susan.

"Nice to be back in the old Beehive State," Susan said.

"Yup. Always good to be home," Jake said. "But please, Christmas music before Thanksgiving?" Jake removed his ball cap and scratched at his scalp with his thumb. "That's extreme even for Salt Lake City."

"At least it's snowing. Ski resorts must be thrilled. I'm anxious to head to Boulder and beat the storm, but I'd like to say goodbye to Mandy," Susan said.

"That'd be nice." His eyes searched the crowd. "And maybe meet her folks."

"Assuming they are even here to meet her. If I had just returned from Asia, I'd be comatose," Susan said. "I didn't see her get off. Did you?"

"All I saw was the sign for the men's room."

The remaining passengers checked bag tags, gathered their things, and headed out the automatic doors to waiting shuttles and cars. The snow had intensified. The faint odor of cigarettes from furtive outdoor smokers wafted into the baggage area.

Eventually only one other couple remained, both dressed in black quilted down coats open in the front. The man, square-jawed and attractive with a full head of thick, premature white hair, eyed the escalators that had just delivered the passengers from the flight. It descended empty now to baggage. The woman, slender with sharp facial features, studied her phone. Between them stood a large green suitcase.

Jake approached. "Are you Mandy's parents?"

"Yes," the man answered cautiously. "And you are . . . ?"

Susan had joined them. "Jake Goddard. This is my wife, Susan Brand. We were on Mandy's flight."

"I'm Ben Fry . . . my wife, Melissa." Melissa glanced up, her face framed by long, thin brown hair. She nodded without smiling and continued to study her phone. She wore no makeup.

"We were just coming from Saint Michael's, where our daughter is also a freshman," Susan said. "Amy is visiting the home of a fellow student for the first few days of Thanksgiving break."

"We lost a battle on that one. You've got a teen, you know how it goes," Jake said.

"Our daughter is coming later, but we spoke to your daughter on the plane," Susan said.

"It's a relief to know she got on. We weren't certain, even though we have her checked bag. We were getting a little concerned," Ben Fry said. "How long does it take to walk to baggage?"

"She probably just got distracted," Jake said.

"Our first stop is always the restroom when we get off long flights, so . . ." Susan said.

Jake glanced at the time on his phone. "We live in Boulder and still have a long drive in the snow ahead of us. But let me give you my contact info." He pulled his wallet out of his back pocket. "Might be fun to get the girls together on break." He slipped out a card and handed it to Ben. "Ask your daughter about how we got to know each other at the school," Jake said.

Ben dug a business card out of his breast pocket and handed it to Jake.

"Have a great holiday with your family," Susan said.

"Nice to meet another Saint Mike's family," Ben replied.

Jake and Susan walked out the doors, pulling their bags, and immediately jumped onto a waiting shuttle bus to long-term parking.

They hauled their bags across the icy asphalt in the parking lot. Yellow streetlights illuminated their steamy breath and cast the lines of snow-covered cars in an orange-popsicle hue. While Susan loaded luggage in the back of their Subaru wagon, Jake started the engine and used the wipers to clear the front window of snow.

Soon they were huddled inside, eagerly anticipating warm air once the defrost had done its job.

"Damn. Cold," Susan said, wrapping her arms around her chest. She was glad she had remembered to pack her fleece jacket.

"Early start to what might be a long winter."

"You didn't mention our involvement in Mandy's assault."

"I would want the green light from Joan for that," Jake said.

"True."

Jake was about to slip the car into drive when his phone pinged with a text.

"Better check it. Might be Amy. My battery's almost dead," Susan said.

He undid his seat belt and leaned against the side window to remove his phone from his rear jeans' pocket. He saw an unfamiliar number and then realized it was Ben.

"Ben Fry is insisting we meet before we leave the airport—says he read my card and he has the jacket I left in baggage."

"Wow. Weird. You didn't leave a jacket." She glanced in the rear seat. "Did you leave a jacket?"

"I don't think so, no. I'm wearing the only jacket I brought along."

"Did he mention Mandy?"

"Nope. Just basically urgently requesting we not leave until they talk to us."

Jake texted their location and said he would flash his lights when he saw them get off the shuttle bus.

Five minutes later, Mandy's parents slid into the backseat of the Subaru. They left Mandy's suitcase outside the car. Jake glanced into the rearview and noticed that Melissa looked shaken.

Without preamble, and with a trembling hand, Ben held his phone up between the two front seats.

"Please read this text. I just received it in the baggage area. It's from Mandy's new phone."

"I'm terrified," Melissa blurted.

We have your daughter. Do as we say, and you get her back. Defy us— you never see her again. No police. We are watching you and monitoring ALL your communications. We will call soon. No cops!

Susan turned in her seat. "Oh my God! Is there any way at all this could be a joke?"

"Our daughter knows better than to joke like this," Ben said. "We live in Park City. We thought—"

Melissa cut him off. "We need help."

Ben said. "I read your business card. I thought I could hire you to help us find Mandy and that since . . . since your daughter attends the same school, it would . . . it would not arouse suspicion if we were seen together. We live just up in Park City. Please come and spend the night while we decide what to do and wait for the call."

Melissa started sobbing quietly.

Jake looked in the rearview and saw a heartbreaking mixture of desperation and despair; he glanced at Susan and knew immediately no discussion was necessary.

"Did you sense anyone following you to our car?" Susan asked.

Ben said, "No, I watched. No one suspicious got onto the shuttle. And as you could see, no one else got off at this stop. No cars followed the bus to this lot."

A white van drove by behind their car, briefly illuminating the interior of the Subaru, and headed toward the exit gates. "I suggest you go home,"

Jake said. He held up a pen and a dry-cleaning receipt he found in the console cupholder. "Jot down your address and home phone number." Ben reached for the pen. "No more texts or calls from your cell phone. We'll spend an hour or so searching the airport before driving up to your house for the night," Jake added. "But I'm not hopeful we'll learn anything."

Melissa's sobbing intensified. "We can't go home without her."

"There's really nothing more you can do here," Jake said.

Susan said, "I recommend we communicate with each other exclusively face-to-face tonight in case the kidnappers really do have a way of monitoring your phones and computers. As far-fetched as that is, in this age of malware and sophisticated hacking, it's certainly possible." She drilled a look at Melissa and then at Ben. "And if they call, for now at least, play along. This may be the hardest thing you've ever done. But for Mandy's sake, you have to stay strong. We will find her."

A shuttle bus was approaching. The Frys exited the car and dragged Mandy's suitcase toward the covered shelter.

It was close to midnight when Jake and Susan pulled off the snow-covered road onto the bare driveway winding up toward Ben and Melissa's triple garage. The house—a log and stone mansion—was cut into tall conifers on the side of the mountain above Park City. Jake switched off the engine. Ben's face appeared briefly in a window above.

They unloaded their luggage from the rear hatch. Windblown snow swirled around them. A lone coyote sang on the slopes above the house. Snowflakes landing on the heated driveway melted instantly.

As the two bumped their suitcases up a wide concrete staircase to the house, Ben opened the front door and held it for them. "No word so far," he said.

"I'm sorry, Ben, we didn't find anything either," Jake said. "But before we come in, do you happen to have an open bay in your garage?"

"Yes, my Audi's in for repairs until Monday in Salt Lake. Why?"

"Just an extra precaution. It's one thing to claim you're placing someone under surveillance; it's another to pull it off logistically. But on the remote chance they're going to be watching your house, let's get our car out of view."

"I'll meet you downstairs in front of the center bay," said Ben.

After parking the car in the garage, Ben led Jake and Susan up a set of interior stone stairs into a cavernous two-story living room. The walls were comprised of thick logs. Massive lam beams crisscrossed above. A fire burned on the far wall in a fireplace large enough to stand in. When Jake saw Melissa, he shook his head. "Sorry, Melissa. No sign of her."

Melissa sat rigid on a long L-shaped leather couch in the middle of the room, working her wedding ring on her finger. In front of her was a copper and wood coffee table that ran half the length of the couch. An untouched glass of white wine sat on the table. Susan sat down beside her. Ben crossed and paced in front of the fireplace beneath a chandelier made from elk antlers. Jake handed him a small shrink-wrapped box.

"What's this?" he asked.

"A Walmart phone. We picked it up before we left the city." Ben looked confused. "It has prepaid minutes and no contract. Can't be easily traced or hacked." Ben turned the package over in his hands. "It's a burner phone," Jake explained, smiling. "All the drug dealers on *The Wire* had them."

"Oh, okay I'll need to repay you for this."

"We'll get all the money issues sorted out later. For now, let's concentrate on your daughter." Jake put his hand on Ben's shoulder. "When they call, let them talk. Let them feel like they're calling the shots and you are complying with their every wish, but when I signal you, insist on speaking with Mandy to determine that she's okay. It will help her as well as you."

"And might provide some valuable information about where she's being held," Susan said. "Listen to the background noise as much as possible while reassuring her."

"Joan told us about Mandy's assault in the woods by the school. She said you two were very helpful. I didn't put that together until I saw your card at the airport. I wonder if this could be related."

"All we did was confirm what Mandy had already discovered about the well and dumping in the river. We were very impressed with your daughter's passion and courage," Susan said.

"Thank you. It can be a little over the top," Ben said.

"She recently joined a youth group called One Degree that is fighting inaction on climate change," Melissa said. "Greta Thunberg is her new hero."

"Greta Thunberg is my new hero," Jake said.

"Joan mentioned you were a police officer before joining Jake's firm." Ben said. "That's reassuring."

There the conversation stalled. Jake sat on the couch with the two women. Ben added two logs to the fire.

After an awkward hour of mostly silent waiting, Jake suggested they all go to bed and try to get some sleep.

Ben turned to his wife. "Honey, please show Jake and Susan to their room."

Melissa sat and stared straight ahead as if she hadn't heard until Susan placed her hand on her arm.

November 20
Sunday

The two investigators and their clients hunched over coffee around a breakfast table in a nook off the kitchen. Outside the snow was blowing sideways, a small drift building on the protected sill of the window. The nearby fir trees stood like phantom sentries in the snowstorm.

"Were you able to get any sleep at all?" Susan asked.

"I drifted off around two to two thirty, only to be jarred awake with nightmares about Mandy," Ben said.

"I have to ask an awkward question," Jake said. "Do either of you have any reason to think someone might be out for revenge by abducting Mandy?"

"This has to be about money. Why don't you think it's about money?" Melissa demanded.

"Chances are good this is kidnap for ransom, but we should consider all possible angles," Susan said.

"As environmentalists, we've made some enemies in the rural ranching communities," Ben said. "I've been in a few standoffs at public hearings with members of that state's rights group, Sage Use . . ."

"Jake and I have history with Sage Use," Susan said.

"Then you know their rank and file disagrees with any federal jurisdiction over lands within their state or, for that matter, over any

RARE AS EARTH • 65

species, endangered or otherwise," Ben said. "I've even received a few death threats but never took them seriously."

Melissa said, "We recently attended a protest of a proposed frac sand mine near Kanab—"

Ben's iPhone buzzed. It was Mandy's new cell calling. He stared wide-eyed at the device and then at Susan. Jake pulled scratch paper and a pen out of his backpack.

"Go for it, Ben. Remember what we discussed last night," Susan said. She reached across the table and took Melissa's right hand in both of hers.

"This is, uh . . ." Ben wet his lips with his tongue. "This is Ben Fry." He put his phone on speaker.

"Good morning, Mr. Fry." It was a man's voice. "Mandy had a pretty good night, considering. She is fine and will not be hurt as long as you and Mrs. Fry do exactly what we ask."

"We would do anything to get Mandy back." He glanced at Jake. "But promise me you won't harm her."

"Again, if you cooperate, I assure you no harm will come to her. And speaking of that, I trust you haven't contacted the authorities."

"No. Just as you asked."

"Well now, that's being a good soldier, isn't it?"

"How much do you want?" Ben asked.

"This is not about how much we want, but more about what we want from you."

"Anything to get our child back safe. Just tell us what you want," Ben said. His eyes darted at Susan.

"You're the president of the board of the Outdoor Clothing and Equipment Company, correct?"

"Yes, but—"

The caller cut Ben off. "And you and your wife are large donors to, and your wife is president of, the board of Southwest Wild, the environmental organization?"

"Yes."

"Excellent. What we want in order for you to see your daughter again is simple. Those two organizations are, along with several Indian tribes, fighting a legal battle. We want both organizations to quit that legal action."

"What are you talking about?"

"The legal battle to prohibit the reduction of Bears Ears and Grand Staircase-Escalante National Monuments in southern Utah. We want it stopped."

"What? You want what?" Ben said.

Melissa blurted, "We're only one voice on those boards. We can't dictate policy."

"Good morning, Mrs. Fry," the man said. "Oh, I think you're being modest. You two have great wealth and great influence." His voice hardened. "You have two weeks. I'll send you a message from this phone with a separate number. You will text that number every day, reporting on your progress toward the successful completion of our demands and your girl's safe return."

Ben looked at Jake with confusion and fear. Jake nodded his head and formed an emphatic but silent "yes" with his lips. He held up a piece of paper with *Mandy* scrawled on it.

"Okay, we agree to *try* and do what you ask. But I want to talk to my daughter," Ben said. "Can we FaceTime?"

"I'm sorry, I can't let you see her, but I can let you hear her." There was a pause and some rustling.

"Daddy, I—" Mandy cried, and the line went dead.

Melissa stared in horror at the phone. "I want my daughter." She buried her face in her hands. "I want my daughter home."

"What if we can't . . . ? Oh God." Ben's lower lip trembled. "Please help us find her."

"Let's take a breath and review what we know," Jake said. "We know that Mandy is alive. If we can take the kidnappers' word, we have reason to believe she's not been harmed. Honestly, there is no upside to them hurting her. Let's find hope in that."

Susan added, "We know whoever has Mandy stands to gain more from the reduction of two isolated national monuments than from a ransom demand."

Jake got up and stood by the window. "We know at least one of the kidnappers is an English speaker who is most likely North American. He speaks as if he is well educated but with no discernible accent."

"That may not sound like much, but any detail could be important," Susan said.

Jake crossed back to the table and sat. "Okay, folks, we need you to tell us about your boards and everything you know about this battle over the national monuments."

Melissa swiped at her tears. Ben cleared his throat and swallowed. The pair eventually regained enough composure to comply with Jake's request, starting with explaining the American Antiquities Act of 1906 and the designation by President Theodore Roosevelt of the nation's first national monument—Devils Tower in northeastern Wyoming. They explained the current reduction controversy was centered around much wild, archeologically important terrain, some of which was considered sacred by local tribes and which included Garden of the Gods, an area, like most of the two endangered monuments, that was rich archeologically but also rife with minerals and gold, and both oil and gas.

Reciting chapter and verse of the American Antiquities Act seemed to help Ben and Melissa collect themselves.

"From the Devils Tower to Garden of the Gods. Interesting," Jake said.

"Okay, tell us about your boards, and then let's discuss next steps," Susan said.

Melissa reached out for Ben's hand, inhaled, and straightened her back.

November 21
Monday

After the phone call from the kidnappers Sunday morning, Susan and Jake had driven the five hours home to Boulder. Just before departing, they had informed the Frys that, barring an emergency, they would not be returning to Park City until Monday night when they would be watching the house but staying nearby. They explained it was imperative they limit their visits to the Frys' house.

Jake reminded them Amy was flying in Tuesday afternoon. He said they would communicate with the burner phone and would only come by the house after they had picked up Amy.

The night at home gave the couple a short time to unpack, do laundry, repack, and check in with their neighbor, Mike, who was boarding Cinder, their aging black lab. Mike owned the small farm contiguous to their property. Cinder, though wag-happy to see them, exhibited no urgency about returning home. Proof that, contrary to their wishes, Mike was spoiling her again.

They also checked on their vintage Airstream stored in a lean-to attached to Mike's barn. Susan noticed the third tire—the spare on the rear bumper of the 1957 Flying Cloud they lovingly called Majestic—was a little low and needed air. They borrowed Mike's air compressor and filled the tire.

They decided they would head back up north in Susan's Toyota truck.

That way, from a vehicle that had not been seen in the area, they could watch for the bad guys who claimed to be watching the house. If they caught a break and spotted the kidnappers, they just might be able to follow them back to where Mandy was being held.

With the Rocky Ford Reservoir stretching blue and cold on their right near Sigurd, Utah, and just before crossing I-70, Jake was preparing to call Ben Fry on his designated cell.

Before dialing, he said, "Amy is going to hate being jammed in this small back seat."

"Given her current residency in the doghouse, she's lucky I don't make her ride home in the bed."

He put the call on speaker. "Ben, Jake. How are you two holding up?"

"This is torture, Jake. Melissa is inconsolable. She is pressuring me to call the police."

"Hi, Ben."

"Hello, Susan."

"Please reassure Melissa by telling her that as a former police officer, I'm treating this like it is my own child. Like it is Amy who has been taken. And my gut tells me it is in Mandy's best interest to handle it this way."

"Especially based on what we have learned so far about the kidnappers," Jake added.

Susan leaned toward the phone. "You and Melissa should begin to concoct ways to stall them."

Jake agreed. "It is imperative you convince them that progress is being made toward meeting their demands. But we will help you slow-walk it as much as possible."

"There is one major flaw in their thinking that screams 'amateur'; they really have no way in the short run, except to assume that you are so traumatized that you will do exactly as they ask, to prove you are complying," Susan pointed out.

"We need you to do two things: stay at your home in Park City except for routine activities so you don't arouse their suspicions, and give them a slow drip of information and reports of progress toward their demands. We can help you create a game plan for that," Jake said.

Silence.

"If at any time we feel that it is best to alert the authorities, we will tell you immediately. This is not about us having a job. We do not operate that way," Susan said.

Silence.

"Ben, you still there?" Jake asked.

"Yes. Sorry. Still here. Just thinking." Another pause followed by a long exhale. "Okay, I'll tell Melissa what you said. See you tomorrow, then." He ended the call.

"God, he sounds exhausted. Poor Ben. Poor Melissa." Susan put on her left signal in preparation to pass a slow-moving farm tractor. "I can't wait to hug my child, even though I'm mad at her and it has only been a few days since I saw her," she said.

When they reached Park City, Susan parked her truck down the hill from Ben and Melissa's house on Silverthorne Drive, the winding road that led up to and past the driveway to the Frys' log mansion.

All the dwellings on the mountain were on large tracts of land. The investigators had a clear view between two lower houses. But dusk was making an early appearance as the Earth hurled toward the year's darkest day.

Jake dug his binos out of his pack behind Susan's seat. Just as they settled into their individual watch-and-wait slouches, they noticed a red Jeep Grand Cherokee stop on Silverthorne below the house. Two people were in the front. A short blonde man in a ski sweater and stylish wool vest got out of the passenger side and appeared to be taking photos on his phone before jumping back in the car. The Jeep sped away.

Jake and Susan snapped to attention. Without speaking, Susan cranked the motor and they pursued.

The Jeep accelerated and climbed the road contouring higher on the mountain above the Fry house. It was going at breakneck speed, considering the snowpack.

Susan tried to close the gap, but her light truck was already fishtailing by the time they passed below Ben and Melissa's house.

"Damn, I wish I had put on my studded snows," Susan said, wrestling the wheel.

"A little creative fishtailing can't hurt," Jake said. "Just be careful as we climb these switchbacks. Looks steeper and more exposed the higher you go."

"Not to mention deeper snow," Susan said.

"Steep and deep. Great for skiing powder. Not so great for car chases," Jake said, flashing a tense smile at Susan.

The Toyota still had two switchbacks to go when the Jeep stopped at the top of the mountain. Susan braked, causing Jake to stiff-arm the dash. The truck slid toward the edge, putting one front tire into the packed snow passenger side berm. An expanse of white fell away below Jake's window.

The same man got out and snapped pictures down the mountain toward the Frys' house. Or was it Susan's truck he was taking pictures of? After a few seconds, the Jeep was off again and disappeared over the top of the mountain. Jake reached into his pack, removed his Browning nine-millimeter pistol, and cradled it on his lap.

As Jake and Susan spun up the final ascent, they noticed fewer houses. However, several realtor signs advertising steep properties dotted the hillside. The high lots had no trees; clumps of wet snow clung to sagebrush bushes. Snow-covered mountains rolled away to the darkening horizon. Lights were beginning to blink on in the town below.

On the back of the mountain, the way got rougher and the snow got deeper. A set of fresh tracks twisted down the mountain road. On the inside bank, snow was piled deep by plows. The exposed side revealed six or seven hundred feet of drop to a switchback below. A slide off the edge would most likely be fatal.

The SUV was putting more distance between them. Susan pressed the gas and charged roughly one hundred yards to a slight turn where her little truck lost its grip, resulting in a slow and graceful, totally out-of-control pirouette in the snow. First the sage-covered mountain flashed by the windshield, and then they were staring out over the abyss.

"Lay off the brakes, steer against the spin," Jake shouted.

Susan complied, and after completing a full circle the truck lurched to a stop—deep in the snow against the hill.

Susan puffed out air. The Jeep was gone.

Susan got out and grabbed the shovel she always carried in the bed of the truck. Fortunately, they had dressed for what they had thought would be a long, cold surveillance.

One hour and fifteen minutes of digging in the dark later, they headed back up over the mountain from the direction they had come, at a snail's pace. Lights down in the town were on full and illuminated patches of the snow-covered streets.

Several additional dark hours of watching the house yielded nothing but cold asses and frayed tempers. They couldn't agree on when to run the engine for heat. Susan voted for more. Jake, always keeping the environment foremost in mind, urged her to tough it out. After all, he said, she was the one from the Arizona desert who complained all summer about the heat in Boulder, resulting in constant battles with Jake over their fans.

Jake wanted to find a fast food restaurant for dinner. He said they could warm up over some burgers. Susan feared they would miss something important. She accused him of always thinking of his stomach. Said it might do him some good, going into the holidays, to skip a meal or two.

Most importantly, they discussed Amy. Her behavior regarding her visit to Will had been rude and inconsiderate. And they, of course, were somewhat embarrassed that they had ultimately caved. They argued over the proper consequences. Jake wanted to go easy, suggesting the upside was that Amy was becoming independent. Susan just saw her daughter's actions as presumptuous and thoughtless and deserving of punishment.

Also, Susan felt it would be a mistake to tell Amy that her classmate had been abducted. Jake felt Amy was mature enough to handle it just fine. How else, Jake asked, would they explain their presence in Park City two days before Thanksgiving? And how would they concoct activities to keep Amy occupied and in the dark while they did their jobs?

At midnight, they checked into the Best Western in Park City where Jake had reserved a room. Susan complained it was too expensive.

Susan piled every blanket she could find on one queen bed and slept like a rock. Jake tossed and turned in the other.

November 22
Tuesday

A band of dazzling light transected the mountains. The sun reached the town in the valley and reflected off the snow-covered slopes, illuminating Jake and Susan's east-facing motel room. After a hasty cookie-cutter breakfast, they went back to watching the house from a safe distance. Nothing. Not even the red Jeep.

They returned and checked out of their room at 11:00 a.m. with the intention of heading to the Salt Lake Airport just over an hour away. Amy wasn't due in until 3:15, but Jake always liked to arrive at the airport early. He could get a shoeshine and buy a paper, as he liked to say, even though he rarely wore leather shoes and mostly got his news online.

Jake was driving. Snow covering open lots glowed like polished silver. Businesses were open but in general the town was quiet. Susan checked in with Ben on the burner. She put him on speaker.

"We have sent two texts so far relaying false information about contacting fellow board members for an important unscheduled meeting."

"Good. That's good. Any response?" Susan asked.

"No. No response."

Susan decided the red Jeep incident was not conclusive enough to worry Ben about it.

"Okay, we're going to get Amy. We'll be back in touch soon. Be strong," Jake said. Susan ended the call.

"Is the phone off?" Jake asked.

"Yes. Why?"

"I would never say this to Ben. But this situation would be so much better if the kidnappers were seeking a ransom."

"Why?"

Jake bore a look at Susan. "Playing devil's advocate, how, after their demands are met, can the kidnappers risk leaving any member of the Fry family alive?"

"Frys know too much." Susan stared out the side window. "And once Mandy is out of danger, they'll have nothing to stop them from telling what they know to the FBI."

"Scares the shit out of me." Jake said.

They were leaving Park City heading for I-80 when Susan noticed a log building standing alone in a large lot with a circular drive of plowed snow. A rustic sign said PC PROPERTIES. Parked in front of the building was a red Jeep Grand Cherokee.

"You see that?" Susan said as they drove past.

"Looks like it could be our guy," Jake said. "I'm going back." He pulled into a side street and through a Shell station. "Hand me that slip of paper with Ben's address."

They parked in front of the log building and went in. A bespectacled receptionist greeted them. The man they had seen snapping pictures sat in a glass-encased office behind her. He had short-cropped hair and Germanic features. He was wearing the same charcoal-gray wool vest as the evening before. When the receptionist learned they were interested in property, she ushered them into the office and introduced them to Rick Fenstermacher.

Twenty minutes later, they were back in Susan's truck.

"You buy it," Jake said.

"What? That he was only taking pictures because people ask about that house all the time? Yes." Susan picked up her phone off the console. "And what he said about being aggressive in a seller's market and approaching homeowners even if they haven't expressed interest in selling." She glanced at her phone. "I buy that too." A loud snow machine with a man driving and a small child on board passed behind the real estate office.

"Yeah. Rick's not guilty of anything except being a smarmy salesman in a ski sweater. When I asked specifically about the Fry address and he immediately showed us his pictures of their property on his iPad, I ruled him out of any foul play," Jake said. "Jeez. What happened to the concept of privacy?"

Susan made an imaginary gun with her thumb and index finger and pointed it at her phone. "This is what happened."

"And to think we almost slid off a mountain chasing a frickin' realtor." Jake turned the key, backed up, and pulled out of the driveway.

Fenstermacher stood at his office window taking pictures of their truck with his phone when they were driving away.

As they descended Parley's Canyon through the Wasatch Mountains toward the Salt Lake Valley, Jake was thinking how if it had been at least a month later in the year, a sunny winter day in Park City could portend gloom and doom below. Mid-December often marked the onset of the winter inversion.

"When I lived in Salt Lake, I skied Park City a lot. Often while driving down after a beautiful, sunny day on the slopes, a gray sea of bad air would initially loom and then encase me—the dreaded Salt Lake Valley inversion. It sometimes lasted for weeks before a front blew it out, only to return again and again."

"I can't imagine living in such a polluted bubble," Susan said.

"Bowl is more accurate. Polluted bowl. The mountains on the east and west come together to the south to form a bowl. That's a big part of the problem."

"Does it go on for most of the winter?"

"Yup. Smog gets trapped in the cold air below by the warm air above, squatting between the Wasatch Mountains to the east and the Oquirrhs to the west." He passed a semi on the steep descent. "I wrote the mayor once with a suggestion for a solution."

"I'm sure that was interesting," Susan said.

"I thought so. I told her, 'The Oquirrh Mountains have already been partially removed by one of the largest copper pit mines in the world. A simple solution to the pollution would be to remove the rest of the

Oquirrhs so the bad air can move out over the desert to the west.' Never got a response."

"Probably just tossed your letter in the 'Wackos—Do Not Respond' file."

"You think?" Jake looked at her with mock surprise.

They spent the rest of the drive discussing how to inform Amy of Mandy's plight.

At the airport, Jake parked in the short-term parking garage. They crossed the enclosed bridge above several lanes of airport traffic to enter the terminal and rode the escalator down to wait in Delta baggage.

They had books and online news on their phones, so waiting was never a problem. In fact, in their line of work, it was often required. They sat along the wall, oblivious to passengers coming and going. Except for one gaggle of giggling teenage girls that was impossible to ignore. They waited with great enthusiasm at the base of the escalator to greet a returning missionary. Elder Simmons was his name, based on the signs his admirers held welcoming him home.

The Delta app on Susan's phone indicated Amy's flight was on time. Soon Susan's phone pinged with a message from Amy saying she was on the ground.

A few minutes later, Amy came down the escalator. She was wearing her daypack over a green Saint Mike's sweatshirt. She walked over to greet her parents.

Watching her daughter approach, Susan mused that it was as if Amy had grown and changed since they last saw her just a few days prior in Pennsylvania. Or was it that so much had transpired with Mandy and her family? Regardless, she was relieved to have her home safe. Susan's hug was tighter and lingered longer than usual. "Have you had lunch?" Susan asked.

"If you call two tiny bags of pretzels lunch?" Amy said.

"Not for an extreme athlete like you," Jake said.

"Extreme bench warmer, you mean," Amy said, pushing him in the chest.

They chose an eatery near the main baggage area and settled at a table.

Christmas music filled the hall. Their small table had a red plastic candy cane attached to the wire basket holding the condiments.

After ordering, Susan said, "So how's Will?"

Amy blurted, "Will's great. His parents—who were there the whole time—say hi. Am I forgiven?"

"Oh, no. Not even close. Penitence will be paid in the form of extra holiday domestic duties, extra Cinder walking duties—especially that, since it's one you love so much. Just before bed in the dark and cold—"

"But, Mom—"

"Don't 'But, Mom' me. You totally set us up."

"Whatever, Mom."

"Oh, I can't tell you how much I missed that blow-off, sweetheart."

"Open and fair communication and compromise is always recommended, Amy," Jake said. "No one likes to feel cornered into a major decision without having a say. And especially with your friend present."

"Unfortunately, we will not have much of an opportunity to administer the required lashes," Susan said.

The parents' demeanor turned serious. "Something really troubling has happened," Jake said. "We have a job we never dreamed of and that we wish had never come up."

The waitress brought their food. Caesar salad for Jake. Burgers for the two women.

"Pass the ketchup, Jake," Amy said lifting the top half of her bun.

He did and said, "Mandy Fry was kidnapped here in the airport Saturday night. Just after our flight arrived."

Amy stopped the ketchup bottle in midair. "Kidnapped? Here? Are you sure?"

"I'm afraid so," Susan said. "Her parents have heard from the abductors. As far as we know, she is fine. Ben and Melissa hired us to help after being threatened with . . . Mandy being harmed if they contacted the police."

"Oh my God. Poor Mandy." She put the bottle back on the table unused. "How terrifying. Is there anything I can do?"

"Well, since this is going to cut further into your Thanksgiving break. And this involves a schoolmate. We discussed deputizing you." Jake had a bite of salad.

"For instance, the bad guys claim to be monitoring all communications of the parents and watching their house," Susan said.

"You got them a burner, right?" Amy asked.

Jake and Susan exchanged a glance. "Somebody has been watching too many crime shows in the dormitory," Susan said.

"Mostly in the student center. *Special Victims Unit* is a favorite. But, you did, right?"

"Yes, actually we did," said Jake. "But we're worried about being identified coming and going from their house, if indeed it is being watched."

"So you can give us cover," Susan said. "Parents visiting with a child Mandy's age makes much more sense than us visiting alone."

"Another bonus of this unplanned time in Park City and the Wasatch Front. Maybe we can squeeze in a visit with my sons," Jake added.

"I would love to visit Tim and Matthew," Susan said. "Wouldn't you like to see Matthew, Amy?"

Mandy lay in the bed under the covers, curled up like a baby. She was scared. And she was cold. Deeply chilled. Her kidnappers had thought of everything except proper heat. She had a single bed in a wood-paneled room, a dresser full of clothing, magazines and books stacked on built-in shelves, and a minimally stocked bathroom with a stall shower.

In the few moments since her capture that she had been able to think clearly, she determined she was in a basement because there were no windows and she heard footsteps above. But she begged *them, whoever they were,* while pounding on the door, to let her go, or at least to turn up the damned heat. Spending all day under the covers was just not her style. She needed room to move. Space to pace and plan.

After the first terrifying, tear-filled twenty-four hours since being carried from the trunk of a car to the room—her hands and feet freed, and the tape removed from her mouth—she was feeling a little less afraid. After the initial fog from whatever they had drugged her with had lifted, she had steadily gained strength and focus. She was even reacting with less trepidation now to the occasional visit from one of her kidnappers, usually around mealtime.

Mandy struggled to keep the longing for home and ache she felt for her parents at bay. She needed to keep that focus. She knew her parents were frantic and doing everything possible to find her, but still, if she didn't fight it, fear would consume her.

Although her captors made her put a blindfold on when they brought in and gathered up her tray, she sensed they didn't want to hurt her. In fact, she came to believe the blindfold and the time that had elapsed since her capture meant they had no intention of harming her.

Mandy cranked her investigative journalist persona into high gear and began looking for clues of whom her kidnappers were and how she might escape. She noticed, judging by the voice, the same man came in each time. He said little and ignored her questions and requests. He was not the one who had instructed her to talk to her dad on the phone and had cut her off after a few words. There was little she could discern from the voice of the food guy. Poor English for sure, and a familiar accent, but still one she couldn't place. But since all she knew of him was his few utterances, she began to refer to him as the Voice.

She listened intently to the footsteps on the floor above her, trying to guess how many people there were and learn anything she could about them. She could hear a muffled TV playing constantly.

In an attempt to warm up and stay focused she threw off the covers, jumped out of bed, and did push-ups and sit-ups on the carpeted floor. She danced wildly around the room while singing "Come & Get It," her favorite Selena Gomez song. And she sang it loud to show the bastards they hadn't won.

Then she chanted. She needed her mantra now more than ever as the seconds, minutes, and hours crept by.

"Who am I? Amanda Fry. Fight for Right and Never Say Die!" Over and over, louder and louder, twirling around the cramped space until she collapsed on the bunk and stifled her sobs in the pillow.

Jake called Ben on the way up from the city and asked if they could stop by and bring Amy. Ben said Melissa had taken a sleeping pill earlier in the day, but he would find something for dinner for all of them.

He was grilling steaks in the fireplace when they arrived. They ate in silence, sitting around the round dining room table in a space off the living room. The fire provided warmth to what would otherwise have been a large chilly room—the chill perhaps due as much to circumstances as the season and weather.

Melissa had roused herself and microwaved a few potatoes but only picked at her meal while working on a bottle of red wine. She and Ben sat with their backs to the fire. Jake, with Amy on his right and Susan on his left, sat across from them.

"This is a guilty pleasure. We've been lobbied heavily by Mandy about the impacts of animal agriculture on climate." Ben held up a fork with a speared piece of rare meat. "These are some of our last ones. We've promised our daughter to quit consuming meat starting in January. I'd be lying if I said I wasn't going to miss a good steak every now and then."

Jake filled them in on their surveillance. The realtor caper brought a slight smile to Ben's lips.

"Fenster is known for his hard-sell tactics. He wouldn't be my first choice in agents, but I'm pretty sure he's harmless." He took a sip of wine. "He almost got punched out a few years ago after getting caught taking pictures of a man's license plate so he could do an internet search on him to determine his potential as a client. His brother is a deputy sheriff here in Summit County. They're in cahoots."

For a spell, the only sound was cutlery clattering on china.

"This is déjà vu for me," Susan said. "And I trust it will turn out as well." Jake smiled, seeing where she was going with this reassuring memory. "Five years ago, when I was still on the force for the Jackson, Wyoming Police Department, Jake and I were trying to find a missing young woman named Lyn Burke. Long story short, I found her but only because I was in as much jeopardy as she was—the criminals abducted me too. We ended up dumped together on the top of a butte in Nevada."

"You can imagine by this time, I was getting pretty frantic," Jake said.

Ben's gaze was riveted on Susan. Melissa wiped at her nose with a tissue and stared at the table.

"After the kidnappers proved their stupidity by dropping my backpack to me on the butte with my phone inside, I managed to get a partial text message off to Jake. Then Lyn, a college rock climber, and I climbed down, relatively unharmed, and headed toward Lake Mead."

"My mom scrambling down a butte and surviving is right up there with the guy who climbed El Cap with no ropes," Amy said.

"Unfortunately, their triumph was short-lived," Jake said.

"Very short. When the bad hombres saw we had escaped, they sent a lackey out to watch the place every desert creature must ultimately go, a rare seep and a pool of water in a canyon adjacent to the butte. We were immediately recaptured."

"Where were you at this time?" Ben asked Jake.

The fire popped. Melissa jumped.

"I was trying to decipher the partial message I got from Susan and wildly guessing where they were heading," Jake said.

"As I look back on it, I don't call it a wild guess," Susan said, smiling at him. "Jake had discerned where we had to be and was coming like the cavalry."

"More like a foot soldier; I had high-centered my Subaru on a boulder and was jogging up the canyon two-track."

Susan continued. "But when we turned a corner—with the moron driving the truck with one hand while jamming a pistol around Lyn's shoulder and into my skull—guess who's blocking the road?"

"It was the best I could come up with in a pinch," Jake said, grinning.

"Bad guy slams on the brakes and the three of us overpower him. Including Lyn, by the way; while I was wrestling the loser for the pistol, and Jake was trying to break his window, Lyn soccer-kicked him in the jaw."

"That was a good day," Jake said.

"I tell you this because your daughter reminds me of Lyn. She's going to come out of this. I just know it."

Melissa looked a little buoyed up by Susan's tale. "Oh my God, that would just be the most wonderful thing," she said.

"Mandy is known at school for her guts. I'm betting on her," Amy said.

"Let's discuss our next moves," said Jake. "We have very little to go on, but just as Susan and Lyn's kidnappers screwed up, we have to hope Mandy's will too."

Susan said, "It's important to keep demanding that you speak to her, and better yet, see her, even as you are feeding them false information about meeting their demands."

"Stay focused on any hint that can help us. Background noise, décor, whatever might help," Jake added.

"We also need to try and connect the dots between this situation and what happened to Mandy at Saint Mike's. Seems too unlikely to be a coincidence," Susan said. "Melissa, could you research Beauford Oil and Gas in Pennsylvania and look for connections to the kidnappers' demands?" Again, Jake glanced at Susan, knowing where she was going with this request, mother to mother.

"I would do anything to help," Melissa said.

"I've got an idea," Amy said. "Mandy and my folks got pretty tight at school, what with her interest in investigative journalism. The next time you talk to her, you might drop a clue that Mom and Jake are on the case."

"Like what?" Ben asked.

"Any ideas, Jake?" Susan asked.

"Ah . . . nothing that immediately comes to mind. Just mentioning something about the school might be too vague," Jake said.

"Oh, I know. How about, 'People who live in stone houses shouldn't throw glasses,'" Susan said.

Ben looked confused.

"That's a Jake original and Mandy loved it," Susan said. Ben still looked befuddled. "You have to know my husband."

"Take it from me," Amy said, putting down her steak knife. "Just because you know Jake and love Jake, doesn't mean you *get* Jake."

Melissa smiled for the first time since they had met her.

Later, Jake, Amy, and Susan drove to their inn. The town was alive with activity. The trees lining the sidewalks sparkled with white holiday lights. Three young women all bundled up hurried across the street in front of their truck, talking excitedly, their breath steaming in the cold night air.

Amy was sitting side-legged in the cramped rear seat of the pickup, texting. They had chosen different digs on purpose. Just to mix things up. This one was more of a lodge and sat right in the heart of the old mining homes in Park City. Jake pulled into the parking lot of the Prospector Inn.

"Sweetheart," Susan said to Amy. "Seeing as you can't escape until I open my door, I want to discuss a change in plans with you. Forget everything I said about domestic chores and late-night dog walks as your punishment."

"Thanks, Mom." She looked up from her phone. "Guess I'm out of the *doghouse*." She patted Jake on the shoulder, hoping he would appreciate the pun, and then went back to her texts.

"Not exactly," Susan said. "Just a new assignment, since we're spending so little time at home this vacation and now that we have deputized you. That was a great suggestion, by the way, about Mandy getting the message that we are involved."

Amy glanced up again. "Thanks. But what's this about an assignment?" She was leery.

"I would like you to thoroughly investigate the reduction of Bears Ears and Grand Staircase-Escalante National Monuments and the energy development interests in those areas." Susan turned to look over her shoulder at her daughter. "We'd like you to produce a report Jake and I can use to support our search."

"What? I'm on a holiday. What is this, school on wheels?"

"If it's good enough, you might be able to submit it in STEAM class next semester," Jake said. "And it could help us and the Frys a lot."

"Aw, come on . . ." Amy whined.

"Channel Mandy. She would eat this up. Plus, this could contribute to her rescue," Susan said.

"When's it due?" Amy asked.

"Tomorrow night," Susan said.

"What? The day before Thanksgiving?"

"Yeah, this is real world, Amers," Jake said. "Think of the vacation Mandy is having."

"And to keep you from getting distracted, I'll take your phone until your time has been served and your assignment is complete. Tell Will we said happy Thanksgiving and fork it over." Susan held out her hand. "Don't worry, I won't spy, I promise."

Amy rolled her eyes and exhaled audibly, pressed a few more letters, hit the send icon, and relinquished her phone.

Jake and Susan opened their doors.

November 23
Wednesday

Students in all manner of dress thronged the capitol's steps. Their bright outfits and multihued signs added color to an otherwise austere setting on an overcast day. The capitol building perched on a bench above Salt Lake City was a large domed gray stone structure with wide sidewalks and marble steps leading up to massive, closely spaced granite pillars.

The surroundings were spectacular—the foothills ramping up to the Wasatch Mountains that towered over the city.

The snow in the city was gone, the snowline having receded to above eight thousand feet, but the slate sky augured more snow.

Vans from all four of the local television stations, with their communication arms and dishes extended, waited in anticipation of the One Degree event about to unfold. A microphone on a stand stood at the top of the steps with wires running to a stack of speakers. Barricades controlled the movements of the crowd, and three police cruisers were parked on the perimeter. Seagulls soared above, their call simulating raucous and derisive laughter.

There was a sprinkling of supportive adults, but most of the participants were students, some too young to have driven to the event on their own. The kids held homemade signs and banners of all stripes and descriptions. DON'T FRACK WITH MY FUTURE, read a cardboard sign held up by a slight girl in a red down vest. A lanky boy in a bulky black snowboard jacket was carrying a sign reading, SAVE THE POLAR BEARS, AND OH, YEAH, ALL OF HUMANITY. All the signs communicated one basic but urgent message: students demand climate justice.

The guest speaker, Henry Trent, was a survivor from a shooting incident at an East Coast high school. He had witnessed his best friend being gunned down in cold blood in the library. The shooter was later identified as a disgruntled former student. A kid everyone would have said was nobody had suddenly, sadly, and infamously become somebody. His glum visage had been splattered all over the national news.

Henry channeled his grief and anguish into action on two issues: gun control and climate change. His goal was to organize a million youths for each. His mantra was, "Adults are not solving these problems. It's our future. We must."

Today's rally was for the One Degree organization, focused on achieving a goal of zero carbon emissions by 2030. The organizers hoped this first Utah event would result in recruiting more student activists. It was also intended to highlight the Utah National Monuments reductions to promote fossil fuel and mineral extraction.

The students were chanting, "One, two, three degrees, a crime against humanity!" A large red-and-white banner strung between two pillars behind the podium read STUDENTS DEMAND CLIMATE ACTION (@ CLIMATESTRIKEUT).

Henry was the first to speak. He took the mic while trying to still the tremor in his hand. He swallowed hard and cleared his throat to keep his voice clear and steady.

He was tall for sixteen, slender and wiry—a silky tuft of down adorned his chin. A chestnut ponytail sprouted from under a blue wool watch cap that matched his hoody sweatshirt.

"My name is Henry Trent." His voiced echoed across the plaza. "Friends call me Hen. Last May, I watched my best friend die fifteen feet away from me. A deranged loser with a deadly military weapon, *purchased legally,* attacked our school. My friend's name was Charles Sherman. This gathering today is not about gun control, but I dedicate my activism and all my speeches to my bro Charlie's memory." A quiet murmur rippled through the crowd below.

"Charlie was an activist before I was. He used to say, 'If adults won't act, who will?' Then he would smile his killer smile and say, 'Guess that leaves us.'

"That leaves us, my friends. So let's get our act together, recruit one million kids, and kick some ass."

A cheer went up, and a few chants renewed and faded when Henry raised his hand. "This is a great turnout. Thank you for your responses to our rally's Instagram, and please push us out to *your* personal contacts on Instagram, Snapchat, and WhatsApp." Henry pumped his right fist in the air and then looked down at his notes. "So good to see so many of you here up from Moab."

Cheers.

"You guys traveled a long way."

Someone shouted, "Go Red Devils!"

Henry cleared his throat. "Many species are facing extinction. We are choking on our fossil fuel emissions. Because of *the one-degree difference* between thirty-two and thirty-three degrees brought about by the actions of mankind, our glaciers and ice caps are melting at alarming rates. Yet we continue to open up sensitive natural areas, like Utah's national monuments, for coal and mineral extraction and fossil fuel exploration, drilling ever deeper oil and gas wells, causing polluted groundwater and destructive earthquakes."

Boos erupted from the crowd.

"And what are adults doing to prevent this? They idle their SUVs, turn up the heat in their homes rather than put on another sweater, and fly when they could take public ground transportation.

"They have the technology and the intellect to turn this crisis around, yet they continue to bury their heads in the sand." He licked his lips and took a sip of water from an aluminum bottle sitting on the step beside him. "Although many adults do support our efforts—such as the former UN climate chief, who said, 'It is time to heed the deeply moving voice of youth' in support of the student walkout in England—too many are still in denial. Ten thousand students walked out of classes to protest inaction on climate." He paused and waited for the crowd's applause and cheers to die away. "Now it is time for adults to follow our lead." More shouts.

"To quote Greta Thunberg, 'We can't save the world by playing by the rules because the rules have to be changed.'"

A brief chant rippled through the crowd, "Greta, Greta, Greta . . ."

"Don't tell us to be patient! Don't tell us to be quiet. Don't tell us to wait our turn. The forest is on fire, and your *adult* solution is to blow on it like a candle. The time to act is now—"

Henry stopped speaking. Three huge pickup trucks roared up to the base of the capital from separate accesses. The trucks, two black and one red, riding above massive tires, crushed barricades and spewed black diesel exhaust, inking the fleeing students while honking their horns and blasting patriotic music. Three cops jumped out of their cars and drew their weapons.

The red monster truck, a Dodge Ram sporting yellow and orange flames at the wheel wells, parted the crowd, spewing kids in every direction, and bounced up the Capital steps toward Henry. He stood his ground as the driver in a red ball cap and black ski mask stopped ten feet short of him, leered, threw the truck into reverse and bumped back down the steps. On the plaza below the driver swung the truck's tail end around to make his escape, scattering students. A boy in a yellow parka who couldn't get out of the way was knocked down and backed over.

The truck sped off with one police car in pursuit. The two black trucks split up and went in different directions. A terrified girl knelt beside the injured boy—who lay face down—and screamed for someone to call 9-1-1. The whole assault had taken less than three minutes.

Susan had gone to the lodge's fitness room. Jake was sitting alone on his queen bed, reading. There was laughter in the hall. A vacuum cleaner hummed next door.

Amy worked away on her report at Susan's laptop set up on the desk by the window. Jake's phone on the bedside table trilled with the special ring for Ben's burner.

Without prelude or greeting, Ben told Jake to turn on the TV to any local station and hung up.

He and Amy sat on the bed transfixed, watching a report of the events at the capitol building. The voiceover mentioned that Henry Trent, the person speaking at the time of the assault, had in his remarks drawn attention to climate change and the reduction of Utah's national monuments. When the video recorded at the event showed the truck backing over the teen, Amy turned her eyes away from the TV.

"Oh my God. Those are kids," Amy said.

"High school kids like you, Amers."

"That was disgusting," she said. "The bastard ran over him like he was garbage."

"It was pretty hard to watch," Jake said. "I want to believe he'll survive and recover."

"I sure hope so."

Jake turned to Amy. "That was a painful way for you to see it. But this is really why we wanted to involve you. You just witnessed a battle in what has become your generation's war. Those kids would probably much rather be shooting hoops or hanging out playing video games, but they are filled with passion and commitment, like Mandy, laying their beliefs on the line."

"But it's not fair. We're just . . ." Amy's eyes filled with tears.

"No, it's not fair, but your generation is not the first to be forced to fight for your future before being old enough to vote. My grandfather enlisted in the marines at the age of seventeen and fought against Germany during the Second World War. That was a world war worth fighting. I suppose you could say fighting for the Earth is a world war worth fighting also. My grandfather didn't really have a choice. Sad to say, but you don't really have a choice either."

She walked back to the desk and sat down. She stared at the monitor. "Goddammit!"

The door clicked open and Susan charged into the room. She saw the flat-screen TV was on. "Have you seen it?" She asked.

"We've seen it. Ben called," Jake said.

The talking woman's head mentioned that police had been afraid to discharge weapons near such a large crowd and that all three trucks had escaped. Their plates had been obscured with mud. The young man who had been injured and whose name was being withheld was being treated at LDS Hospital. He was in critical condition.

Susan stared at the screen. "Goddammit!" she said.

Jake went to the fitness room for his workout. It was identical to most motel fitness rooms, with the exception that the lodge had provided a basket of fruit and a cooler of ice-cold power drinks. He was alone.

He got up a pretty quick pace on the lone treadmill. His best activity for thinking was walking outside. Second best, walking on a treadmill.

The reports of the attack at the rally played over and over on the two flat-screen TVs. After twenty minutes nothing new was being reported, so he paused his machine and crossed to a stand beside the water cooler. It was essentially a box on end that held clean towels in the opening. He grabbed the remote off the top of the towel stand. He clicked off one screen and was aiming the remote at the second when the footage of the red truck climbing the capitol's steps played again. He paused. Something about the truck was hauntingly familiar.

He picked up his phone and asked Susan if she could join him in the lobby.

They sat shoulder to shoulder in front of a gas fireplace and chatted quietly. The front door opened, and a mother with a baby in a front pack entered and climbed up the carpeted stairs toward the rooms. The receptionist was away from the desk, in an office behind it. They had the privacy they needed to discuss what was on Jake's mind without disturbing Amy.

"Amy was pretty fired up by this turn of events," Susan said.

"She was really upset watching that poor kid get run over. It seemed to motivate her."

"I'm just glad she's safe with us. Oh my God, if I was in the Frys' situation, or was the parent of that boy, I would be beside myself."

"Beside yourself and ready to commit murder. That combination of empathy and killer is one of the reasons I love having you on my team."

Susan shook her head and smiled sorrowfully. "So why did you call me down?"

"I was watching the footage of the attack on the One Degree rally, and I thought I recognized the truck that climbed the steps."

"What? Monster trucks are not exactly your thing."

"No, but they are Timmy's. Thanks to neighbor Mike, who lets him ride on his 'way cool' Massey Ferguson tractor, and Rachel, his mom who lets him watch too much TV. Remember last time I visited? He talked me into taking him to a tractor pull in Tooele that he had seen advertised. They had monster truck events too, and he was hooked. And I thought I was raising enviros. Matt had a soccer game. Rachel covered that."

"Pays to advertise—especially targeting children. What makes you think you've seen the truck before?"

"The color and the flags are identical. The truck I saw was a red Dodge Ram with flames and had both a checkered flag and a Confederate flag on the rear window, just like the one that attacked the student rally. It was parked outside the arena. I remember thinking, 'What does a truck with Utah plates have to do with the Confederacy?' Utah wasn't even a state when that little disagreement down south was decided. And get this: we had to go back because Tim had left his jacket in the stands. That truck was still there. Might be a regular or even an employee."

"And the connection to Mandy?"

"Maybe I'm just desperate for a lead, but that attack was coordinated. It wasn't just a couple of Mormon rednecks a few Diet Cokes over their caffeine limit. There appears to be a directed effort to stop action against the monument rollback.

"I checked the Tooele website. There's an event Friday night. I've been meaning to call my ex anyhow. I'll see what Rachel thinks about us taking Tim and Matt to that event."

"What could be better? An American dad bonding with his boys while witnessing the enchanting sound and smell of excessive fossil fuel consumption."

"Kind of ironic, don't you think?" Jake said.

"Off the charts. Looks like we're going to Tooele. First Mandy, then Amy gets involved, and now maybe we get a lead thanks to Timmy. This is like Bad News Bears PI."

November 24
Thanksgiving

The Brand/Goddard trio had wrangled a last-minute invitation to Thanksgiving dinner at Jake's ex-wife Rachel's place. Rachel had chosen to live in Spanish Fork because it was affordable and within commuting distance of her job in the accounting department at Brigham Young University in Provo.

Considering the spontaneous nature of their request to join Rachel, Matthew, and Timmy for Thanksgiving—not to mention the awkwardness inherent in Jake bringing his new wife and stepdaughter—it all went pretty well.

Jake brought the wine and apple cider and made his famous garlic mustard smashed potatoes, while Amy and Susan helped Rachel with the rest of the cooking.

After eating midafternoon, Jake and Amy kicked a soccer ball around with the boys in the backyard. Susan and Rachel looked on from the kitchen and made safe small talk around the table. The wine helped.

Matt, demonstrating his newfound cool as a nascent teen, showed nothing but disdain at Jake's suggestion that they drive to Tooele for a Monster Slam monster truck extravaganza on Friday. Younger brother Tim was ecstatic.

Amy asked if she could hang out with Matt while her parents and Tim went to Tooele. Everyone seemed pleased with that suggestion, especially Matt, who was caught momentarily dropping his stoical cool and displaying a full-blown blush.

Susan agreed on the one condition that Amy get up the next morning and finish her report on the monuments before they dropped her back at Rachel's house.

Jake, Susan, and Amy left around 7:00 p.m. and stayed at a nearby Super 8.

November 25
Friday

There were at least three ways to get to Tooele from Spanish Fork, but only one, which headed west just north of Utah Lake near Lehi, minimized time on congested I-15 along the Wasatch Front and maximized time in the desert. Jake preferred that route and he took it.

When they pulled into the packed dirt parking lot for the Tooele Fair Grounds in their Toyota truck with Timmy in the back seat, they immediately felt dwarfed. Huge trucks surrounded them. Obviously, the fans of Monster Slam were living the monster truck dream, even if they couldn't compete.

The parking lot was ringed by a chain-link fence covered by banners and signs advertising things such as auto parts, auto insurance, various and sundry motor-head products, and energy drinks, including, of course, Monster.

Kids, mostly boys, filled the lot, chattering excitedly, some pulling their parents by the hand to hurry them inside. Jake stood in the truck bed and scanned the lot. He didn't see the red truck with the flags. He did, however, see many red ball caps on males that could fit the vague description of the driver.

Jake climbed out of the bed and said to Susan out of earshot of Timmy, who was taking in the surrounding trucks, "Red ball caps are apparently de rigueur in this redneck of the woods."

"They certainly appear to be the men's head cover of choice," Susan said.

"That pretty much renders that aspect of the suspect's profile unhelpful," Jake said.

They paid and went inside the massive metal arena. Stands lined the walls. The trucks in the parking lot seemed small in comparison with the ones lined up inside waiting for the competition to begin.

There was one common thread throughout the evening: noise—kids shouting, the PA blaring the next event/heat/competitors, and above it all, engines revving and tires squealing. It was a constant racket, and fifteen minutes after the start of the competition, Susan leaned in to complain in Jake's ear. "This is all giving me a monster headache."

Two trucks emblazoned with the names "Smasher" and "Death Throws" respectively were competing on two short, identical dirt tracks. Smasher had just slid around a hairpin turn on its huge tires suspended well below its neon-yellow body. The all-purple Death Throws ran up a dirt ramp and flew over several smashed cars, landing with its hind wheels on the furthest but bouncing down and racing on, undeterred, to the finish line and a first place in the heat, winning advancement to the next bracket. The races were single elimination; Smasher left the track and headed toward the arena's overhead warehouse doors to depart.

Jake said close to his wife's head, "Susan, how about taking a break from the fun and seeing if you can bat your eyelashes at Smasher's driver and learn if he knows anything about my suspect truck."

Timmy was oblivious, bouncing up and down beside his dad in the bright-orange Monster Slam T-shirt he had successfully wheedled out of his stepmom when they entered. The next heat had started.

"Dad, Dad look at those two," he shouted. The two new competitors had both chosen shark's teeth for a motif.

"That would be a welcome break from the noise," Susan shouted. She unwrapped a stick of chewing gum and popped it in her mouth. "Gum. The great seducer," she said, patting Jake on the shoulder and rising to slide in front of other fans on the bench and head toward the door.

When Susan plopped back down twenty minutes later, the timed freestyle event had started. She reached across Jake and handed Timmy a bag of caramel popcorn.

He grinned. "Thanks, Susan."

Jake smiled at his son and ran his hand over his bristly blond crew cut. "Susan's spoiling you."

Timmy hunched forward over his popcorn and nodded his head vigorously without taking his eyes off the action.

In this event one truck at a time did jumps, wheelies, doughnuts, and sometimes even backflips in an attempt to impress the judges and take home a cash prize.

All black with magenta highlights, "Drag-gone" exploded off a ramp. The driver danced the truck triumphantly on its rear wheels, landing the best wheelie of the night and bringing the crowd to its feet, applauding and shouting. Timmy was the most appreciative superfan of them all.

After the event, the revving engines still reverberating in her ears, Susan drove Jake and Tim to a McDonald's just two blocks from the fair grounds. The hubbub in the fast food restaurant was tame by comparison to, and a welcome break from, the high-octane activity in the arena.

Timmy wolfed down his burger in record time and headed off to the adjacent play area.

"That shirt you bought him will be the coin of the realm around here."

"Guaranteed instant status in Tooele," Susan said.

"What did you learn?" Jake asked.

"I gotta say, the kid, the driver—sweet guy. Total opposite of what I expected. Never once hinted about anything. Course, I could be his mom."

"But what a hot mom," Jake said.

"Thanks for that, lover." She sipped her decaf. "He didn't recognize the description of the truck. He said he wasn't from here but suggested I speak to Betty at the concession stand. That's when I bought the popcorn. I told Betty the guy had helped me change a tire at a recent event and I wanted to thank him."

"Good call."

"Anyhow, when I described the truck to Betty, she immediately mentioned Blake Wilson. Wilson appears to be our rebel Utahn. She was surprised he wasn't around tonight. Said he is one of the event organizers. Works at, guess where, NAPA Auto Parts here in Tooele."

Jake pushed back from the table. "I think we have enough on Blake to offer an anonymous tip to the Salt Lake City PD, don't you?"

"I do." Susan beamed. "I definitely do."

"Better get my monster jammin' kid home," Jake said. "I'll drive and you can call from the road. Give them as much specific detail as possible. Contrary to the stereotype, I've always felt they take women more seriously."

"Maybe that's because they all had mommies."

They went to collect Timmy.

November 26
Saturday

M andy was startled awake by a hard knock on her door. The Voice commanded her to put on the hood so he could bring in her breakfast.

She jumped up, pulled an oversize sweatshirt out of the dresser, and put it on over her underwear.

She sat on the bed with the black hood over her head and called out that she was ready.

She listened to the sounds of the door being unlocked and her tray being placed on the dresser. True to form, the Voice said little, only that it would be back in thirty minutes to pick up the tray. He went out. The door lock clicked.

Mandy removed her hood and stared at . . . the usual—a red plastic cup of orange juice, one hard-boiled egg, and a piece of white bread. There was no silverware and no napkin.

She wolfed down the egg and bread. Then she chugged her orange juice and—turning the empty cup in her hands—got an idea.

When the Voice returned for the tray, it demanded to know where the cup was.

Mandy, again hooded and sitting on the edge of the bed, said, "I put it in the bathroom. I'm feeling thirsty and would like to drink more water."

There was a pause. "You can keep it for today. Tonight, I'll bring you a bottle of water and I'll take the cup."

"I want to go home. When can I go home?"

Mandy heard the door close and lock. She removed the hood, went into the bathroom, rinsed the cup, and dried it on a towel.

She came back out to the bedroom, cleared her books and magazines off the top of the dresser, and pushed it a few feet away from the wall.

She climbed up on the dresser, placed the rim of the cup against the ceiling, and turned her neck to flatten an ear against the bottom of the cup. After a few adjustments, the voices from above came in loud and clear.

Two men were talking. She recognized them as the Voice, who brought her meals, and the Jerk, who had been so rough with her when she was first dragged into the basement. A third man, the one who had told her several times to speak to her dad on the phone and had cut her off after just a few words, did not appear to be upstairs. Or if he was, he was not speaking. She thought about the clue from her dad the last time she was on the phone with him. As soon as the Jerk had put the phone to her ear, she had heard her father say Jake's "throw glasses in stone houses" line. It had to mean Amy Brand's parents were looking for her. That had given her hope and encouraged her to get off her butt and get busy.

Above her, the two men were discussing a news report currently airing on TV that Mandy caught pieces of during their many silences. The report was about a man who had been arrested early that morning for running down a teenage protester at a One Degree rally at the capital earlier that week.

The Jerk was clearly pissed off at the man who'd been arrested. "If he'd half a fuckin' brain he'd be dangerous." He said things were getting too hot. Added something about moving the girl. The Voice mostly responded with grunts indicating agreement. Then Mandy was shocked to hear what the Jerk said next—it nearly knocked her off the dresser. "We need to hide this little bitch deep in the desert where no one can find her."

Mandy jumped down, pushed the dresser back against the wall, and placed the cup on the bedside table. Although terrified, she had a slight advantage now, which was the knowledge of what was to come.

Action was the only thing that could keep her fear at bay. She studied the room for anything that could help her escape during the impending move. She lifted the mattress and studied the slats under the box spring. No way she could pry one up. She ran her eyes over the room: bed, dresser with semicircular metal handles (no help there), books, magazines, shoes, and dirty clothes on the floor. Not so much as a lamp or anything that could be used as a bludgeon, not that a bludgeon of any size could be hidden in her clothes.

She rushed into the bathroom, breathing heavily. No furniture of any sort in there. She opened the doors covering the space below the sink. Nothing under the sink. She noticed one of the two cabinet doors had a knob. She twisted the knob out with both hands.

She sat on the toilet lid, holding her prize while trying to slow her breathing. The knob had an inch-long bolt sticking out the back. The diameter was small enough on the end that it was actually sharp. If she held the knob in the palm of her hand and let the bolt protrude between her index and middle finger, she had a small weapon that could cut skin.

She stared at the toilet paper roll. That gave her an idea. Mandy removed the spring from the toilet paper holder. She stood up and wrenched one of the towel racks sideways so she could wriggle the crosspiece free. The bar was made of solid metal, was about eighteen inches long, and had some heft. None of these items—or for that matter not even all three used together—was going to seriously wound a grown man, but they could surprise and distract. She did her best to cover the results of her search for weapons with towels and dirty clothes.

She then closed the bathroom door, hoping her two captors would be in a hurry when they came for her and wouldn't check there.

Mandy went to the dresser and rifled through the clothes. She decided to pair some cargo pants with low side pockets with the oversize sweatshirt she was already wearing. She purposely chose loose-fitting item, because she planned on hiding her weapons in her clothes—the spring in the cuff of the left sleeve of the sweatshirt, the knob in her right rear pocket, the bar under the waist of her pants and up her back, tucked in the back of her bra under her shirt and sweatshirt.

She sat ramrod straight on the bed and waited, heart pounding in her chest.

After discussing Blake Wilson's arrest on the burner, Jake and Ben had decided to risk meeting in Provo at a coffee shop called The Coffee Shop. Melissa stayed in Park City in case the kidnappers called. Susan remained in Spanish Fork with Amy and the boys at Rachel's house.

"Anyone follow you?" Jake asked.

"Don't think so," Ben said and puffed out air. "It's been a week. Melissa is saying if I don't agree to involve the police, she is going to take matters into her own hands, whatever that means." He stared balefully at Jake over his coffee mug.

"You two must be going crazy—any parent would be. But you have one advantage. Your kidnappers stand to gain nothing if Mandy is hurt. As long as they can demonstrate to you that she is fine, and you can convince them you are working toward meeting their demands, then we are at a stalemate that keeps her safe and buys us more time. How did she seem when you spoke to her yesterday?"

"Scared. Tired. But okay, I guess. I don't know. They only let her say a few words."

The Coffee Shop was near Brigham Young, a university comprised for the most part of folks for whom drinking coffee was at best anathema, and at worst a religious taboo. This being Saturday, the place was virtually dead.

Jake and Ben were alone except for one clean-cut polo-shirt-clad male barista who ran the grinders and manned the counter.

"Let's give it a few more days, Ben."

Ben cradled his cup and stared out the window.

"We *can* find her; I just know it." Ben was fighting back tears.

"The four of us working together are flying under the radar. Your first instinct to hire us was correct because Mandy's abductors may have some way of knowing if you go to the authorities. They could get scared. Scared or cornered criminals are dangerous criminals. Hell, they could even have someone on the inside of whatever agency you went to."

Ben shook his head and bit his lower lip.

"Look how quickly we tracked down Blake Wilson."

Ben cleared his throat. "We really appreciate the work you and Susan did helping the police nail Wilson."

"That is a good example of when the cops work the most efficiently—and when there is the least likelihood of the bad guys being tipped off. When the police are presented with irrefutable evidence and you point them in the right direction, they can move quickly—like with Wilson."

Ben nodded and swiped at his eyes with his napkin. "I'll talk to Melissa."

"Can you make any connection between Blake Wilson and anything or anyone involved with the monuments?" Jake asked.

"An auto parts and monster truck guy from Tooele seems like someone of lower rank to me, and I have no clue who he's working for."

"I would like you to call anyone connected in any way to the monument movement and see if you can find links to Wilson."

"Why do I say I'm calling?"

"Tell them the attack on the One Degree rally is very disturbing, and you are trying to help insure more such violent incidents are prevented."

"I guess I can do that. The good news is Colby Janes, the kid who got run over by the truck, is out of the ICU. He's expected to recover."

"That is great news," Jake said. "And we are going to get you even better news, Ben. We are going to find Mandy. Now please go home and make those calls. And remember if you are using your home phone to give no hint about your real reason for calling—trying to connect Wilson to Mandy's abduction. Just in case they are listening in, you cannot afford to slip up."

"What are you going to do?"

"I have to get Amy and Susan to Boulder tonight so Amy can have at least two nights at home before flying back to school Monday. I'll come back up to Park City alone tomorrow."

The mention of Amy returning to Saint Michael's in two days seemed to pull Ben up short. "She seems like a good kid, Jake. You and Susan need to keep her safe."

Ben stood, shook Jake's hand, and quietly left. A few minutes later,

Jake walked out of the coffee shop, zipped up his jacket, and watched as Ben drove out of the parking lot in his brown Audi.

The Wasatch Mountains to the east had a new layer of snow. Above them the sky was a gray flannel blanket.

Amy sat glued to her phone in the back of the truck at the start of the drive to Boulder, which began with a stretch on I-15 South from Spanish Fork. Susan had returned the phone when Amy announced her assignment had been completed.

Long views of sagebrush flats rolling away to foothills filled their windows. Low clouds truncated the Wasatch Mountains to the east.

"Are you ready to stand and deliver, young lady?" Jake asked.

"Standing is pretty much not happening," Amy said.

"Then how about just delivering so you and I can enjoy our two nights at home unmarred by further consequences," Susan said. She reached down to the pack between her feet, slid out her laptop, and passed it back to Amy. "Enlighten us, my love."

Amy fired up the laptop and began to paraphrase from her notes. "The president's decision to cut the two national monuments took effect on February 2, 2018."

"Isn't that Groundhog Day? Maybe he was frightened by his shadow," Jake said.

"Uh, Jake, if you want me to read this report, you will have to stop the stupid jokes and drive."

"Yes, ma'am," Jake said, putting his hands at "ten" and "two" and staring straight ahead at the road in mock compliance.

"Good boy. Now where was I before . . . hmm, let's see. Bears Ears, the previous president's baby, is now down to sixteen percent. Slick Willy's love child—"

"'Slick Willy's love child'? Talk about stupid jokes," Jake said.

"Will you two children just stop? Go on, Amy."

"Okay, Bill's *monument,* Grand Staircase-Escalante, is a little over half its original size."

"Two gorgeous and sacred places that deserve all the protection they can get," Jake said.

"Jake!" Susan said.

"Sorry, go on, Amers," Jake said.

"The land no longer under national monument protection has been reopened to claims under the General Mining Law of 1872."

"Add that to the list of assaults by the Environmental Prostitution Agency," Jake said, pounding the steering wheel. "New mineral, oil, and gas leasing opportunities in protected lands such as the Arctic National Wildlife Refuge—check. Easing drilling regs and rolling back habitat protection for endangered species—check. Now this monument reduction bullshit—check."

Amy slammed closed the laptop. A black pickup pulled even with them, trying to pass. They were gaining elevation, and it was starting to snow.

"Amy, I'm sorry. I'll shut up, I promise. You're doing a great job. Please keep going." The truck signaled and pulled over in front of them.

Amy exhaled her frustration and opened the laptop.

"This has only happened on a large scale once before. President Wilson in 1915 reduced Mount Olympus Nat Mon by half. That was not challenged in court. This rollback has been."

"Right on!"

"Mom!"

"Sorry."

"Five Indian nations and several conservation groups have filed suits to protect the monuments." Amy scrolled through her pages. "Oh, and I found this great description of Bears Ears in a *Nat Geo* article. 'The massive acreage descends from the pine forests and high meadows of Elk Ridge and the Bears Ears, twin buttes held sacred by local tribes, through fissured sandstone canyon systems and pinion-juniper desert notched with bladed ridges and packed with ancestral Pueblo artifacts.'"

"That is a beautiful description," Jake said. "What did you learn about mining potential? That's critical."

"That was surprising. I expected to find lots of evidence of get-rich-quick crap as incentive to cut the monuments, but then I found this: 'Bears Ears has lucrative oil and gas fields on the northern and southeastern boundaries, but terrain is rugged and remote and archeologically sensitive.'"

Jake added, "And we know there are rich coal reserves on the Kaiparowits Plateau near Grand Staircase-Escalante, but that is deeply buried, hard to reach, and complicated to transport to a now nonexistent market. So it would appear large-scale extraction on the whole is not viable right now. Interesting." They had gained elevation and were passing through a forest. With the fresh snow, the conifers looked like frosted trees in a Christmas diorama. Jake turned on the wipers and the headlights. "Maybe Tucker's incentive was as much about reversing the previous president as about economic advantage. Of course, there is always political advantage at play. For instance, his base revels in this stick-it-to-the-lefties crap."

"And of course, we are left with the most pressing question of all: what do Mandy's kidnappers gain from the reduction going forward without interference from conservation groups and local tribes? Amy, solve that one and you can go straight to college without passing high school," Susan said. "Anything else?"

"Not much, no," Amy said.

Susan turned and squeezed Amy's leg. "Bravo, sweetheart. That's very helpful. Thank you."

"So I'm out of trouble?"

"For the moment, yes." Susan smiled at her daughter. Jake carefully guided the truck over the increasingly slick mountain roads.

"Flesh that out a bit and you'll have a damn good science paper," Jake said.

"Oh, I almost forgot; I found one scary threat to Grand Staircase." She read from her notes. "A hard-rock mine that shut down when the Grand Staircase-Escalante National Monument was established in 1996 could soon be back up and running. A Canadian-based mining company has purchased the rights to it. The Pony Butte mine has deposits of copper and cobalt, along with zinc, nickel, and molybdenum." Amy stumbled over that one, pronouncing it molly-be-denim. "High Mountain Resources, Inc., based in Vancouver, BC, announced that it had acquired the property that is *not far from Boulder, Utah*." She looked up at the parents before continuing. "There is strong backer interest in the battery metals: cobalt, nickel, and copper. Surface exploration work will start next summer on the Pony Butte property, and drill permitting will be initiated shortly."

"Unless . . . unless litigation delays that start date. Damn, how did that slip by us?" Jake said.

"We should encourage some of our activist neighbors in Boulder to look into High Mountain," Susan said. "Assuming they haven't already."

They drove in silence and darkness over towering, fire-scarred Boulder Mountain toward Boulder. Their town—once innocent, isolated, and protected by proximity to Grand Staircase-Escalante National Monument—now felt threatened and endangered.

Several hours had passed. Mandy guessed her captors were waiting for nighttime before moving her. She eventually fell asleep on the bed. There was a sharp knock. "Put the hood on now," the Voice demanded. Mandy sat up and scrambled for the hood.

"It's on." The door opened, and a few seconds later her arms were jerked behind her back.

"Hey, you're hurting me," she cried. A zip tie tightened on her wrists. She felt the plastic compress the hidden spring in her sleeve.

"Let's go." She was led up the stairs and out the back door of the house to a waiting car. This time for some reason, perhaps because the trunk was full of their personal belongings, they chose to place her in the back. She was shoved across the seat against the far door and covered with a blanket.

She could feel the presence of the Voice beside her and assumed the Jerk was driving.

She took all this as a good sign, made better by the fact that the hidden spring had worked. On the way to the car, she had managed to work the spring up above the zip-tie in her sleeve, creating some room for her hands and wrists to maneuver.

They started to move. External noise flooded the car, but none helped Mandy get oriented. Conversation between the two men was limited to the occasional question regarding directions. But fortunately for Mandy, the ride was bumpy, perhaps because of potholes, and the route involved many turns. She took advantage of each bump or turn to work her wrists against the plastic constraint before settling her body down as the car leveled out.

Soon she gave up on trying to count turns. There had been too many, plus she had no idea where they were coming from, let alone where they were going. Instead she focused her energy on her wrists and strained to hear anything that might prove helpful.

External sounds included diesel engines running up through the gears after full stops and the occasional distant siren. At one stop a deep base pounded out a salsa beat, but that soon faded as the kidnappers' car got back up to speed.

"Fuckin' beaners," the Jerk muttered from the front seat.

Mandy was sweating under the blanket. That was a good thing. She had managed to work the sleeves of her sweatshirt out from under the zip tie, and her wrists were slick with perspiration.

The driver hit the brakes hard. Exactly what Mandy had hoped. She exaggerated the effect and pitched forward against the rear of the front seat while jerking her hands against the plastic strip. She was immediately grabbed by the shoulder and forced back into the corner.

But she had accomplished the desired effect. Her hands were free. Her next task was to work the metal pipe out of her pants and shirt. After about twenty minutes, she clutched the pipe in her right hand. She reached in her pocket and retrieved the sharp knob. She was ready. She waited. The driver was bound to stop for gas or the bathroom eventually. When he did, she would make her move.

Mandy calculated that the car had been traveling for several hours without a stop. She was certain her time was at hand. They would have to pull over soon.

After approximately twenty more heart-pounding minutes, while pretending to be asleep, she heard the words she had been waiting for.

"Need gas," the Jerk muttered.

The car slowed, turned, and stopped. The doors unlocked with a click.

Mandy threw off the blanket and thrust herself toward the Voice, raking the sharp bolt in her left fist across his cheek. He clutched at his wound and grunted. The Jerk's head turned in the front seat, and she clobbered his ear with a backhand from the pipe. When he bent forward in pain, she dropped her weapons and tore at the door handle.

The door opened and she was out, blinking against the bright lights of the truck stop. She ran behind a large blue pickup truck parked unattended at a pump but immediately realized that she was too exposed as the two men got out of the car and approached, gesturing at each other to each take a side. The Voice pressed a handkerchief against his cheek.

Mandy, in a panic, briefly considered and then rejected the thought of seeking help from the few people she could see through the windows of the store. Her captors could claim she was insane or something equally as ridiculous.

She sprinted as fast as she could across the asphalt and around the side of the building. The men had thus far not made a sound, but they continued to stalk her silently. As she rounded the back corner of the building, she was suddenly staring up into the huge grill of a departing semi. She dove out of the way toward a stack of old tires by the wall close to the compressed air hose. The semi driver never saw her. She considered the tires as a hiding place. Too obvious. She crawled, kneeled, and when another departing semi provided cover, ran toward the truck parking area behind the store. She stopped—sucking in frenzied breaths—between two idling big rigs whose loads were covered with tarpaulins. Her eyes searched the parking lot frantically, uncertain about what to do next.

She heard footsteps behind her and ducked between the wheels of the loaded trailer to her right.

The two men stopped and spoke in breathless whispers. She could tell they were trying to avoid attracting attention and wondered how she might use that to her advantage. Maybe scream "sex slave" as a last resort.

Mandy crouched in the shadows under the chassis behind the truck's huge tires. She could see four legs from the knees down. When the legs moved toward the front of the truck, she crawled toward the rear. Then the legs reversed, and she worked her way toward the front. A flashlight, perhaps from a phone, clicked on and illuminated the asphalt at their feet. It was only a matter of time before they peered under the rig. She scrambled out and up and quietly pulled on the passenger's door of the cab. It opened, thankfully with no interior lights. She eased in, gently closed the door, and ducked between the seats burrowing into the bedding in the sleeper unit.

She could hear the two men searching around the truck and cursing in low tones. The door to the cab opened.

An unfamiliar voice shouted, "Hey! Get the hell away from my truck!" The door slammed closed.

An older, brown Chevrolet sedan stopped in front of a defunct business in a mostly abandoned strip mall. Two men slowly climbed out of the front. They shaded their eyes against the intense glare from a parking-lot light pole. The driver was tall and slim and wore a faded yellow polo shirt, brown cargo shorts, and a floppy, wide-brim khaki fishing hat. His shorter passenger sported a wrinkled Hawaiian shirt and a washed-out denim Colorado Rockies ball cap with a threadbare brim that matched none of the colors in the shirt. They exchanged a glance that communicated dread and resignation. It was late. Very late. They were in deep shit. Very deep.

Inside the dank building, they crossed the dimly lit floor of what was once a medical supply store, working their way around empty shelves and stacked boxes covered with dust. They knocked on the door at the rear. A grunt told them it was time to face their fate. They entered.

"Boss," said Fishing Hat, looking at the ceiling.

"Boss," said Ball Cap, staring at the floor.

Beauford sat in a La-Z-Boy chair. He had been reading a *USA Today*, which he tossed on a side table. He leaned to look around them.

"Boss, bullshit!" He jerked his red tie's knot away from the dingy white collar of his shirt, exposing a tuft of steel wool at the neck. "Where's the girl?"

"Um," said Fishing Hat. "You see . . ."

"We lost her," Ball Cap blurted.

"You lost her? You *lost* her!" His face raced to match his red tie. "You two geniuses were outsmarted by a what? Fourteen-year-old girl?"

He pushed up from his chair, grabbed his 7-iron from against the wall, and stared in disbelief at the hapless pair. They recoiled as one. A sneer split his lower jaw. He charged and cracked Fishing Cap on the right shin, bending him over in pain, then slashing the club across his back. He turned and hit Ball Cap in the crotch, buckling him, groaning, to the floor.

"Fore!" Beauford formed a visor with his right hand and feigned staring into the distance before laughing and putting his club back against the wall. "Stand up, you pussies." Both men struggled to stand erect. "Turns out it's your lucky day." He walked behind his chair. An ancient, red velvet curtain covered a portion of the wall.

"I was planning on letting the girl go today anyhow. You two jagoffs saved me a lot of trouble. Look who arrived on a Greyhound bus?" He yanked on a cord, and the curtains jerked apart.

"Girl's mother arranged for an exchange."

Melissa Fry sat behind a thick pane of glass at a table that was bolted to the floor, her hands chained to the legs. "Meet Melissa. Melissa Fry." He turned to the men and grinned. "Now we've got bigger fish to fry."

Melissa sat hunched over the table—her long, thin face lowered and registering more exhaustion than fear. The cuffs had been removed. She rubbed her wrists to relieve the chafing they had caused. The chair across from her was empty.

Beauford stood in front of the table, practicing his swing with the 7-iron. He dropped the club head by his feet but held the grip in his left hand.

"So, I'm curious. How'd ya find me?"

Silence.

"You realize if you don't cooperate, I can make things very uncomfortable for your daughter," he lied.

Melissa looked up and glared into his eyes. "That was not our arrangement. Our arrangement was my daughter for me. If you want any, *any* cooperation from me, Mandy goes free. Unharmed."

"Whoa, missy." He leaned on the table with his free hand. "You're not in charge here, sweetheart. I know that's a radical change for you. You're *abaut* going nuts not being in control of the situation."

"You're from Western Pennsylvania, aren't you?"

"And just what makes you think that?"

"Flat vowels. About becomes *abaut*."

"You can go to the head of the class, smartass."

She stared at the table and said quietly, "You will get nothing from me until Mandy goes home. Nothing."

He walked behind her with the club head gripped in his hand and tapped her on the shoulder with the grip. She shrugged away.

He came around in front of her and sat, leaning the club against the table. "Okay, mama bear, what if I told you we've already let her go?"

She looked sideways at the wall. "I'd need proof."

He pulled a cell phone out of his pants pocket and slid it across the table.

"You have thirty seconds to call your husband." He looked at his watch. "Go!"

When he wrestled the phone from her grasp and ended the call, Melissa sat back looking drained but relieved. Ben had quickly confirmed Mandy was home, healthy, and safe, and sleeping in her own bed. He started to ask why she had placed herself in such danger but was cut off.

"Just so you know, we can get your daughter back anytime we want. And this time she will not survive. Now. How did you find me?"

"I need water."

"Just full of demands, aren't we? Used to being waited on there in Park City? Kind of ironic for a tree hugger."

Beauford hit a button on a brown box on the table. "Bottle of water in here. Now."

Fishing Hat delivered the water immediately. Beauford sat across the table from Melissa, resting his right hand on the golf-club grip.

After drinking deeply from the plastic bottle, Melissa answered Beauford's question. "We did exactly what you demanded. We didn't go to the police or FBI, but—"

"*Buuut.* Yes, go on."

"We did ask parents of Mandy's school friend—"

"You talking about Goddard? Ha! We've known about his involvement since we picked up his sorry ass on our cameras near the oil well by the school."

"You knew they were helping us?"

"Oh, shit yes. They pose absolutely no threat. Next time you hire a PI, get one that can shoot straight. I can probably hit more with this 7-iron than Jakey can with the best 9 mm. Asshole screwed over my nephew at the school, too."

"His associate asked me to research your oil company, and while digging as deep as I could, I, of course, discovered a lot of violations and shady dealings with zero regard for anything but profit. And I determined how to get a message to you." She turned and stared at him. "It worked."

"Why not just do it in one of our check-in calls?"

"My husband would have tried to stop me. I didn't want him to know."

"Now you're going to tell me how those boards of yours and Ben's are going to Rambo the effort to stop the reduction of Bears Ears. And I'm all ears." He leaned in, grinning. "As with your daughter, all I'm asking for is a tit for a tat."

"Please, just let me sleep for a few hours first, and then I will tell you everything."

Beauford stared up at the ceiling, scratched at the hairs in the opening of his collar, and exhaled his impatience.

November 27
Sunday

Susan and Amy were perched at the kitchen table, sipping morning coffee. Jake, standing in the living room, ended a cell call, looking perplexed. "This may be the most extreme example of good news/bad news I've ever heard of."

"Oh, damn. I'm afraid to ask," Susan said.

"That was Ben. Mandy escaped unharmed at a truck stop near Beaver, Utah. She rescued herself with the help of a kind truck driver."

"*Yaaa-hoo!*" Amy crowed, throwing her hands in the air.

"But yesterday Melissa, in a bizarre twist of fate, handed herself over. She was intending to exchange herself for her daughter and had no knowledge of Mandy's escape."

"Oh my God." Susan sat back in her chair.

Amy slowly lowered her hands and dropped her head into them.

"Now what?" Susan asked.

"Same crime. Same criminals. Same game plan. Different victim." Jake paced over to the living room window and looked out at Mike's pasture. "Wow. That's a first."

Susan got up, walked over, and hugged Jake from behind. "Well, I've got some news that's all good."

"I could use some of that. What?" Jake asked.

"Thrill junkie J-Y texted me while you were over at Mike's picking up Cinder." The black-and-white-around-the-muzzle black lab lifted her head on the other side of the coffee table in the living room.

"Apparently she feels like she had so much success getting the officials in southwestern Colorado to consider the deleterious effects of benzene on children's health that she is now volunteering to join us," Susan said. "Arriving late tonight."

"Jennifer Wise coming to visit?" Amy said.

"Uh-oh. I'm in trouble," Jake whispered.

Susan turned him around and stared reassurance into his eyes. "Sweetheart. Looks like we need to bring the Airstream over from Mike's and set it up as a guesthouse." She walked over to the table and picked up her coffee cup.

"Of course, Jen doesn't know we're investigating anything other than the dealings and transgressions of a fossil fuel company because that's all the information I shared with her."

"Sweet, Jen's coming," Amy said, perking up and then deflating again. "Great. Just when I have to fly back to school tomorrow."

"Actually, there is something Ben suggested." Jake turned toward Amy. "Mandy is clearly in no condition to return to Saint Mike's right now." Jake went over and stood in front of Amy. "How would you feel if we appealed to Mrs. Bailey to let you stay home until second semester? Both as our deputy and as emotional support to Mandy. Ben has offered to pick up the change fee on the flight."

"Yeah, baby!" She jumped up and ran in to sit cross-legged in front of Cinder, taking the dog's massive head in her hands. "You hear that, Cinds? We're going to get some quality time together. And we're going to find Melissa." She buried her head in Cinder's neck fur, but then her head snapped back up. "Oh, crap, what about Will? I'll miss Will?" She stared into the dog's black eyes. "Oh, well, he better wait for me. And if he doesn't, it'll be his loss, right?"

Jake winked and nodded at Susan.

November 28
Monday

After the breakfast dishes were done the next morning, Susan got organized to drive to the NAPA store in Tooele. She invited Jen, who had arrived the night before and stayed in Majestic, their Airstream, to accompany her. Jake and Amy, accompanied by Cinder, had already left for Park City in Jake's Subaru.

In the first few miles out of Boulder, Susan assessed her friend with a series of side glances. Jennifer had not changed. She was still the same shapely, compact beauty.

Susan took a few minutes to fill Jen in on the case and concluded by saying, "Now that Blake Wilson is out on bail, the idea is simply to have a chat with the accused monster-truck felon."

"If you say so, Susan. But you've never struck me as the chatty type," Jennifer said.

Slanting winter sun irradiated the sagebrush flats west of the Oquirrh Mountains. The recent snow of several inches, which had covered Salt Lake City and the rest of the Wasatch Front, had not touched the desert terrain to the west.

Between small isolated towns, the tallest objects viewed from the car were utility poles and billboards, some advertising plans for the proposed Tooele Valley Mormon Temple. The trip presented the two friends a great chance to catch up.

"You look fit, Jen."

Jennifer flexed a tanned left bicep beneath her form-fitting gray yoga top. "Thanks. We call it end-of-fire-season fit. Not much to do between fires but party, read, and work out. And then every fire is like going through boot camp all over again. And, of course, with climate change we are fighting more and longer fires than ever. Upside—assuming you don't become a Roman candle in a fire—fitness."

"You might even call it survival of the fittest," Susan said.

"You got that right." Jennifer pulled her long brown braid out of her coral, sleeveless down vest collar and fiddled with the thick brushy end. "It was great to see your little family looking so good."

"Thanks, friend."

Jen beamed a perfect smile at Susan. "Damn, that girl has grown up. Last night it was all Will, Will, Will."

"Too much to hope that it would be all math, math, math, I guess. But she seems to really like the school, and early reports are all positive."

"That's great!"

"In fact, if I can brag just a bit on my baby girl, the school head, Mrs. Bailey, said she could release Amy from the rest of the semester because she was in such good shape academically. And, I thought to myself, the JV basketball team is not going to miss her butt on the bench.

"Miss Bee is going to pitch it to the faculty as a field science project about climate change and the national monument reductions and ask the teachers to email her homework assignments."

"Our girl will keep up for sure," Jen said, squinting into the sun out the passenger window. "But what about Mandy? I just can't believe what that poor child has been through."

"The head said Mandy has legitimate recovery issues related to the abduction to warrant time at home. She just doesn't plan to go into specifics with the staff about what caused her stress."

"I know Amers will be a great support to Mandy while she recovers."

"Pretty tough on a fourteen-year-old, but that's the life kids are living today. Growing up fast in a scary and rapidly changing world."

They drove past a dirt road leading off toward a distant ranch house surrounded by trees. The intersection was marked by a dead snag with dozens of pairs of old shoes hanging by their laces from the branches.

"How you like private dicking?" Jen asked, suppressing a smile.

Susan glanced at her and grinned. "Okay, I guess. It can be frustrating having to use my wiles when my persuader of choice when I was a cop was the Taser. Used to be my badge meant something. Have to be subtle now. Not my strong suit."

"Taser's quicker, that's for sure."

"Speaking of Tasers, any stunners chasing you around the Montana mountains these days?"

"You mean like men?"

"Yeah, exactly. Like men."

"Same old adage seems to hold true. Make a dinner date—get the call for a fire. Never fails."

Susan turned to Jen with a guileless smile. "Women?"

"Women! Now that's a loaded question." Jen blushed and cleared her throat. "Nope." She lifted her left wrist and fiddled with her braid, whisking it up and down her forearm. "You always have been and always will be—the one—and *only*." She reached over and squeezed Susan's arm. "Sometimes late at night in the Zullie dorm in Missoula I remember our drunken 'date' and that deep kiss good night you planted on me."

Susan swallowed. "Yes, well . . . I love my husband. Jake's a great father." She adjusted the rearview mirror. "I plan to spend the rest of my life with him." She glanced out her side window. "And he's a great lover. Sure, it's not as hot as it once was, but . . . but . . . if I was ever . . ." She gave Jen a long and loving look before having to jerk the wheel to prevent the truck from drifting onto the right shoulder.

Mandy and Amy walked, with Cinder panting behind, up the snow-covered road above the Frys' house. Amy had a green school fleece tied around her waist. Mandy wore an old gray Harvard sweatshirt belonging to her dad.

Ben knew better than to try and tie Mandy down.

He agreed to the walk but insisted she carry a cell phone and a canister of bear spray they used on mountain hikes in bear country.

The sun was brilliant, the air warm, and rivulets of water from melting ice created a matrix on the road. The snow crunched under foot.

They stopped to catch their breath and take in the surrounding subdivisions tucked in rounded and white mountain slopes and valleys and dotted by trees on north-facing slopes.

Mandy pointed to the houses below them. "I hate these McMansions. Total excess."

"When you visit, you will love our little cabin in Boulder. It would fit inside most of the garages here."

"Kind of hypocritical for Ben and Melissa, but our house is about as environmentally friendly as you can make a mansion these days. Mostly repurposed materials. Low VOC off-gassing." Cinder caught up and licked Mandy's hand. Mandy knelt to pet her back and chest. "I love this sweetie. Melissa's allergic, or we would have one."

Amy looked at her with concern.

"Oh, Mom. What have you done?" She cried softly and buried her face in the back of Cinder's neck.

Amy knelt down and put her arms around Mandy's shoulders.

"Okay, missy, you've had your little nap, now report." Beauford sat in the folding chair across the table from Melissa. He held his 7-iron between his gapped knees.

Melissa pulled her hair back with both hands and glared at him. "I don't know what you want."

"Geez Louise! I want proof you and your hubby have been doing what we asked."

She sighed. "You don't just tell board members what to do. Even as the chair. And especially if they have already chosen a direction on an issue."

"True. I've served on one or two myself. Total waste of time. I get that it's complicated to alter the group think. But you two are huge donors. You own those boards."

"No one *owns* nonprofit or even corporate boards. Outdoor Clothing and Equipment Company is a co-op. If anyone owns it, it's the members."

Beauford leaned in, looking angry. "Oh yeah, bullshit. Huge donors have huge influence and you damn well know it!"

"Yes. Up to a point."

"What did you do?" he shouted, causing her to recoil.

"You don't have to yell." Melissa pulled her shoulders erect. "Ben with the Outdoor Clothing and Equipment Company board, and I with Southwest Wild, decided our best strategy was to convince the rank and file our efforts should be applied elsewhere." Melissa surprised herself. She never knew she could be such a good liar.

"And just how did you do that?"

"It wasn't completed yet exactly when we, you and I, agreed to the exchange, but Ben and I had laid the groundwork."

"Fill me in. I'm dying of curiosity."

Melissa's gears were churning. "We met with our respective boards, suggesting that the reduction of the Utah monuments, although in our backyard, had significant support already from wilderness advocacy groups and Native American tribes. We then proposed a larger legal action against the EPA in general for the unlawful deregulation of corporate environmental protections and degradation of basic human rights to fundamental values like clean air, and for rewriting the rules of the Clean Water Act—all, of course, to benefit a few powerful corporations. We suggested that, especially with the climate changing so rapidly, our newly proposed initiatives would be a better use of our resources." She took a breath and then a sip from her half-full plastic water bottle while gathering her thoughts. "And Ben and I offered to fund half the cost if the organizations' donors would match it."

"Brilliant. Nicely played." Beauford stood and took a practice swing. "We will be watching your organizations' communications for proof of the change in direction." He took another swing and then rested the club on his shoulder. "What with your prominent tree-hugger Dems suggesting a ban on fracking—a ban on fracking! That's like spitting on the American flag—we in the industry need all the help we can get."

He dropped the club head to the floor. "Who knows; maybe your enviros can help out my industry the way you did when you blocked all those western dams."

"What do you mean by that?"

"Simple. When your granolas blocked or busted up dams, coal moved in."

"That's ridiculous."

"No, missy, not really. At several of those protested dam sites, fossil fuel plants were later built using river water to cool them. I read recently in an industry paper that loves to stick it to snowflakes that fossil fuel plants that were built at blocked or removed dam sites have produced 11 million tons of CO_2, or the equivalent of 2.4 million cars on the road. Thanks for helping boost our business." He took another swing. "But it's not just coal-fired plants, gas-guzzlers, and fuel-suckers. Oh, no. Your green-weenie thirst for electric cars, solar panels, and wind turbines is a great boon to our industry as well. Gotta go where the wind blows and adapt, right?"

"Oh, and one other thing."

"What's that, missy?" He lined up another swing.

"We proposed as a part of our legal action to strip fly-by-night and corrupt bastards like you of all power to operate—and to prosecute you despoilers of the land, air, and water to the fullest extent of the law."

Beauford checked his club mid-swing.

The Toyota truck bounced up a washboard dirt road through gnarled and naked aspen trees. Fallen aspen leaves, like tarnished coins, lined the way.

The directions the women had been given at the NAPA store to Climax Creek and Blake Wilson's favorite fishing hole on the west side of the Oquirrh Mountains were appearing to be accurate. At least Susan and Jen were paralleling a good-size stream, which looked promising for the sort of trolling the two women were doing at the moment.

"Is he, like, poaching these fish or what?" Jen asked. "It's almost December."

"Fishing season never closes in Utah. But I'm sure if it had closed, it would not slow down our man with the monster ego for a minute."

At a pullout on the left, they saw the small blue truck Blake was said to be driving while his monster was impounded.

Susan parked beside the truck and the women got out. They could hear the rushing water. The air was late autumn, mountain brisk. There was no sign of Wilson, but Susan figured he might have worked his way upstream. They stood briefly shoulder to shoulder beside the Toyota, and Susan gave Jen's hand a firm, reassuring squeeze.

With Susan leading, they pushed through the willow branches toward the creek. A large brown mass exploded away and clattered across the river cobbles.

They froze, startled, and then burst out laughing. They had surprised a young cow moose, and she appeared to be as frightened as they were as she charged off into the pine and spruce forest on the other side of the water. Jen held her hand over her heart and puffed out air in relief.

They stood on the bank of a twisting, rushing current approximately ten yards across. The water gathered in eddies behind boulders and flowed through natural shoots. The stream ran clear across a bottom covered with grass and leaves.

No sign of Wilson. Susan called his name, the rushing water the only answer. Beautiful setting—sinister overtones, Susan thought. She could almost hear the banjo from *Deliverance*. She felt, then tamped down, the desire to collect her Glock from under the truck seat. Jake had warned her that excessive brandishing of weaponry could cost her license and even land her in jail.

Susan pointed upstream, and they began to pick their way around boulders along a faint trail.

"Mandy, we can stop anytime you say, okay?" Jake said.

"Okay," she answered quietly.

Ben sat on the couch beside his daughter with Amy perched on her other side for moral support. Cinder lay at Mandy's feet. Jake sat across the room, gently interrogating her.

"What can you tell us about the two men who held you?"

"I can tell you they are nowhere near as scary as a one-degree increase in average global temperature." Mandy wore her most determined face. "Never Say Die."

The two men sat back and smiled. Amy shook her head in admiration for the girl she was beginning to see through a new lens.

Mandy shared what she recalled, and Jake teased out as much detail about those recollections as he could. When he sensed he had mined her memory on one point, he skillfully moved on to the next.

After an hour of questioning, it was clear Mandy was tiring, and the two girls were invited to go to the family room downstairs to watch TV.

After they left, Jake said, "What a remarkable young woman. You should be very proud."

"What did you learn that can help us, Jake?"

"For starters, she described the faces of two of her abductors. That makes her the only one who can identify anyone involved with this crime. That could prove very valuable." Jake stood to pace and think. "Seems like her captors were low-on-the-totem-pole henchmen. Not the sort to have a refined accent like the man who was on the calls."

"My thought exactly," Ben said. "I'm convinced Melissa's being held in Southern Utah or Southern Nevada since Mandy escaped in Beaver, but that's a huge area."

"Yes, huge, but with few metropolitan centers. There are fewer than a half dozen cities of any size, even including Vegas. Based on what Mandy remembers hearing when the two men took her out of her basement prison, I sense these hombres need the reassurance of concrete and city lights."

"Sounds right, " Ben said.

"Have you found anything on Melissa's devices that might help us?"

"I found evidence of searches into Beauford and their multinational consortium, leading all the way to Canadian and Russian mining companies, but no evidence of her attempts to make contact," Ben said. "She must have done that on her phone, which she took with her."

"Well, given their pattern, you should hear from them again soon, asking for an update on your progress with their demands," Jake said. "And maybe Jen and Susan will have some luck with Wilson helping us narrow it down."

"God, I hope so, for Melissa's sake."

A wedge of geese flew, honking, overhead and soon disappeared behind the high, conifer-covered terrain on the far side of the stream-cut valley. The trail along Climax Creek was not steep but was covered with leaves, sticks, and driftwood and wound through large boulders, making it a challenge for Susan and Jen to follow. The water was swirling and pooling more now as the terrain flattened.

Susan saw what appeared to be a recently crushed Marlboro pack lying between two sticks just off the trail. "Monster Man smokes Marlboros." Susan picked up the empty pack and slid it into her jeans pocket. "And he's a litterer. Are either of those things a surprise?"

"Coffee is calling, sweetie. Looks like the Ladies' is right over there behind that log. I'll catch up." Jen veered off the trail toward a massive, horizontal tree trunk. As she walked, she unzipped her down vest.

Susan continued to pick her way upstream. She scrambled around a bend in the creek and soon was out of sight of Jen. The water seemed perfect for fishing at this point. Susan wondered how far Wilson could have gone. A stocky gray dipper doing deep knee bends on a partially submerged boulder just offshore winked a white eye and ducked into the current in search of lunch.

A neon-green flash caught Susan's eye. Fifty yards ahead, approximately ten feet from the water and propped against a standing dead tree snag, was a fishing rod with green line attached and with the lure hooked to the rod's bottom eye.

As Susan neared, she saw an orange tackle box left open on a rock and then a blue jacket with the NAPA logo tossed on the ground. A half-empty pint of Jack Daniel's leaned against a driftwood limb. Susan looked into the woods and then upstream as far as she could see. There was no one around.

"Blake!" Nothing. "Blake Wilson!"

She peered into the tackle box—shiny lures, spools of line, and jars of colorful bait.

As Susan bent to pick up the jacket, something grabbed her from behind, jerking her up and back. She realized with horror that a very powerful person was dragging her by the throat toward the woods. She kicked backward but missed. Her hands grasped at the forearm around her neck. It felt like a thick rope compressing her larynx. She could smell the stink of sweat, tobacco, and liquor and discern a blur of ink on the arm choking her. Her attempts to yell came out as a garbled squeak. As she was dragged, her hips and legs banged painfully against boulders. Susan tried to launch herself off rocks when she felt them underfoot but to no avail; she was pinned. The right leg of her jeans caught on a short, jagged limb. She felt the flesh on her calf tear. Her heels skidded in the dirt between the rocks. Susan struggled frantically to get her feet under her and fight back. Instead she felt herself losing consciousness—her body going limp.

Beauford's two henchmen jerked Melissa out of her chair and dragged her down the hall. She was shoved into a small, windowless closet, the door slammed and locked, the light extinguished.

Melissa used her yoga breathing to get her heart to settle and keep panic at bay. In time she could see dim light under the door. That was somewhat reassuring. She held her hand in front of her face and could make out her fingers. She flipped off the closed door and all the malevolence on the other side. That provided a modicum of relief.

She slid her hands around the floor. The closet was empty. She rested her back against the wall and closed her eyes. In time she fell asleep.

An indeterminate amount of time passed.

Footsteps approached, and a heavy object smashed against the door, causing her to jump.

"Just practicing my swing, missy."

Silence. She was determined to not give him the satisfaction of showing any fear.

"You know, sweetheart, we can all work together here. It's in your best interest."

She bit back bile and a desire to tell him to go to hell.

"Not ready to apologize yet?" The iron struck the door again. "Well, okay, then. We'll see what effect solitary has on you. And don't even bother asking for food and water, darling."

The footsteps receded, accompanied by an additional tap after each step, which Melissa assumed was the club head hitting the floor.

Susan heard a grunt and felt an explosion of breath from behind. There was a thump like a bat hitting a melon. Saliva splattered the back of her neck. The grip on her throat released. She went down on her butt in the dirt and then pulled herself up against a boulder, gasping for air.

When her vision cleared, she saw Jen standing over Wilson, holding a limb like a baseball bat that ended in a hefty burl.

As soon as Susan could stand, the two women dragged Wilson to a skinny pine and propped him against it. Jen pulled his hands behind the tree and pinned them while Susan grabbed a spool of line from his tackle box. She tied his hands together with dozens of wraps of line while Jen snapped pictures with her phone.

Susan snatched up Wilson's NAPA ball cap, knocked off by Jen's home-run swing, and carried it to the stream. She cupped some water and quickly washed her wound through the tear in her pants, then dipped the hat in the rushing water.

She crossed back over to Wilson and dashed the water from the cap in his face. She followed with a hard slap that ratcheted his face to the side. His eyes blinked open. He gingerly rolled his head on his neck. Both women stood over him.

"My head," he groaned. "Oh my God, my head. You coulda fucking killed me."

"Still might. Depends on how things go," Susan said.

"And my back." He tried to stretch it away from the tree. "Did you hit me with that thing in my back?"

"This thing?" Jen picked up the cudgel. "No. This thing is what hit you on the head. The shot to the kidney was delivered with this bad boy. My size 9 ½ smokejumper's boot." She picked up her right foot and thrust the thick-soled boot in his face. "Ideal for stomping on hot ashes and assholes."

Wilson pulled his face away from her foot. "Jesus Christ." He glared at Susan. "I saw you going through my stuff. What do you insane bitches want from me?"

Susan held his face in her hands. He averted his eyes. "Let's start off with an understanding. This is not about what we want. That implies there is some chance of not succeeding." She tightened the grip on his face with her nails and leaned into him. "This is all about what we are going to get."

"Who . . . are . . . you?" His words slurred through pinched cheeks.

"What did you say?" She released her grip on his face. "I can't hear you with your face looking like a flounder."

"Who the hell are you?"

"That is irrelevant. But this is what we know about who you are." Susan stood. "You are Blake Wilson. You are facing time for felonious reckless endangerment. You are out on bail. A report of assault and battery on a helpless woman out hiking will not only land you immediately back in jail but also keep you jammed up for a long, long time."

"But you were going through my shit."

"A, you can't prove that. B, it doesn't mean you get to attack me and drag me into the woods."

"Got it all right here on my phone," Jen said. Well, not the attack per se, Jen thought. She had been too busy working her way around behind him in the woods to take pictures, but he didn't need to know that.

"See?" Jen held up the phone depicting Wilson tied to the tree.

"So. What. The fuck. Do you. Want?"

"Just some information, Blake," Susan said. "The right information. This all goes away. You go back to fishing. We go back to hiking. Never happened."

"But," Jen added. "If your information turns out to be incorrect." She shook her phone at him. "I'll still have these candid shots to share."

Wilson shot his foot out at Jen's knee. She jerked her leg out of the way just in time.

"Near miss," he said, leering.

She kicked her boot at his head. He rolled it away, and the metal toe whipped by his ear and slammed into the tree with a thud, spraying bark.

"Near miss," Jen said.

Wilson blanched and sucked in air.

Amy blinked awake on the leather couch. She'd dozed off while watching *The Avengers* with Mandy, and now Mandy was gone. The light outside the ground-floor window dimmed toward dusk. Amy reached down to pat Cinder's haunches and then stood, stretched, and yawned. She led Cinder down the hall in search of Mandy and found her in her room hunched over her keyboard.

"What up, girl? Feeling any better?"

"Feeling focused. Feeling like I have to keep digging until I figure out what these mining bastards want."

"I get that. Mom had me research the monument reductions, and all I could come up with was some metal extraction for batteries near us in Boulder."

"Doesn't seem like the sort of thing that would cause even greedy corporate extraction types to break the law so blatantly," Mandy said.

"That's what I thought," Amy said while scratching Cinder's ears. "Gold, silver—precious metals maybe, but *battery* metals?"

Cinder, sensing this was not going to be a quick conversation involving any treats, stretched out on the carpet.

"Wait a minute. You said metals for batteries?" Mandy asked.

"That's all I found, yeah. My research said the rest of the gold and fossil fuel stuff near the monuments is too hard to reach and transport."

"That gives me an idea." Mandy turned to her computer and typed into her browser "rare earth metals in the US."

Susan and Jen conferred and decided not to release Wilson after all but to leave him hog-tied by the river. Just before departing, Susan dug Wilson's phone out of his jacket. Although the autumn sun was holding the thermometer in the warm mid-sixties for now, the temperature could easily drop forty degrees by midnight. The two women stood in front of Blake just far enough away to be out of kicking distance.

"Hey, Blake," Susan said, shaking his phone at him. "Who do you know, if anybody, that is likely to be sober enough to respond to a text before it gets dark and you freeze to death?"

"What? That's bullshit! You said you would let me go if I cooperated."

"Yeah, well, we changed our minds," Susan said.

"Haven't you heard—women will do that?" Jen said.

"You have ten seconds, or we walk away." She looked at the time on the phone. "Don't make us late for our pedicures."

"Okay, okay. My brother. Rob Wilson."

Posing as Blake, Susan typed a simple text to his brother asking for help with an emergency at Climax Creek and hit the send arrow.

She walked to the stream, tossed the phone into the current, and watched the device bob downstream before sinking. Jen draped Wilson's jacket over his shoulders, and they left.

Wilson's ranting followed them downstream for a few hundred yards until his execration as they neared their truck was finally drowned out by the sound of the rushing water.

Jen drove. Susan's nerves were still jangling, and she was a little amped on adrenaline.

This time they chose the Salt Lake City route. They watched the sun descending toward the mountains on an island in the center of the glistening Great Salt Lake. Susan called Jake.

"My girl Jen saved me from the bad guy." She squeezed Jen's shoulder with her left hand. "She used her superpowers like in Tucson."

Jen smiled and waved off the compliment.

"J-Y kicked ass yet again, but this time it was from the ground, not swooping in from above. We will tell you all about it when we get home."

She held the phone away. "Jake says he owes you big-time." And then put it back to her ear.

"You owe her big-time? I owe her big-time. I could kiss her." She flashed her eyebrows at Jen. "Yup. As we suspected, Wilson admitted to being hired to disrupt the One Degree rally. He says they no longer want anything to do with him since he injured that kid. Not in the plan." She listened. "He's says he's going to rat out the other two drivers as part of a plea. Blake's a really honorable guy."

"Claimed to be totally out of the loop and to know nothing about abductions of any sort. That is until Jen threatened to dropkick him in the face and flatten his nose with her steel-toed boot. Then his memory suddenly improved. Although he was adamant that he never knew the name of the person who hired him."

She listened for a second to Jake's next query.

"Saint George. He said he overheard something about Melissa being held in an abandoned strip mall in Saint George."

As soon as he heard that Melissa might be in Saint George, Jake was anxious to meet Susan in Boulder and come up with a plan. He first had to convince Ben to remain in Park City. If by chance he was being observed, staying behind upheld the appearance of doing nothing against kidnappers' wishes. Jake also suggested that he take both girls with him.

Ben was reluctant at first to let Mandy go. Jake reminded him she was the only one who had seen and could identify two of the captors. He assured Ben that she would not be placed in harm's way. Mandy said, without hesitation, that she was up for it.

As soon as everyone had returned to Boulder and after a hasty late dinner, Jake and the four women worked until midnight packing the trailer.

Amy and Mandy walked Cinder to her second home next door. Then Mandy slept on an air mattress on the floor in Amy's room.

November 29
Tuesday

Using the northern route intersecting with I-15 South, the drive to Saint George from Boulder was approximately four and a half hours. That made it a little longer than heading straight south through Escalante, but Jake preferred, at least while towing Majestic, to go the more moderate way in terms of topography.

The Escalante route was one of the most scenic in the American west, with the road initially surrounded by sandstone buttes and eventually following the top of a hogback offering amazing views. But it was also extremely narrow and exposed. One colorful local referred to it as a "real sphincter puckerer." In fact, it was Susan's concern about Amy riding the school bus that way twice each day to and from the high school in Escalante that led to Susan deciding to send her daughter to Saint Mike's.

The crew jammed into Jake's maroon Suburban tow vehicle well before the sun topped the buttes. They left Jen's pink Jeep Wrangler parked at the house.

After leaving Boulder, Jake's headlights illuminated aspen, piñon pine, and juniper trees peppering the hills along the road.

"We should call this the female posse," Jen said from the seat behind Jake, who was driving.

Amy, sitting beside her in the middle seat, nodded. "Yup. Girl power on the move with one token man at the wheel."

Mandy, sitting by the window behind Susan, said, "I don't even want to ask what kind of miles per gallon this old Chevy gets."

"Yes, Mandy. That weighs heavily on my conscience these days. She's the only vehicle we own that can haul the trailer and all of us and our stuff, but I can see the day coming soon when Majestic will be put into full-time stationary guestroom service."

"Or at least until Tesla comes up with a powerful enough electric tow vehicle," Susan said from the front passenger seat.

"But what a shame retiring her would be." He glanced in the rearview. "Just look at her, all lit up and with her gleaming mirrorlike lines, tracking us proudly and effortlessly."

"Jake finds Majestic's aluminum beauty *riveting*," Susan said. "He's really just trailer trash underneath all that faux sophistication."

"Ah yes, living in aluminum. Hard to beat. I slept like a log last night. I'll take Majestic over a bunk in a Forest Service tent any day," Jen said.

Amy would have normally complained about the adult banter, but by this time she was too deep into exchanging texts with Will to comment.

Mandy stared out the window, lost in thought. Amy noticed she looked worried.

Amy put down her phone and made a suggestion. "Mandy, tell these Airstream cult members what you learned about Bears Ears."

"It was nothing definite," Mandy said, turning toward Amy.

"Still worth sharing, I think," Amy said.

"What's the scoop, Mandy?" Susan asked.

"I just got to wondering about these bad hombres playing such a dangerous game for such high stakes. Then Amy mentioned metals for batteries being mined again near Boulder since the reduction of Grand Staircase. I was pretty sure there was no gold or silver in marketable quantities to speak of in the Bears Ears region, so I Googled rare earth metals."

"That's a brilliant thought. Even the US military is worried about China's corner on that market. What did you learn?" Jake asked.

"No smoking gun, unfortunately. But there are rare earth metal mines in Montana and Idaho. And there is a business dedicated to their extraction based in Salt Lake City."

"Wow," Susan said.

The car fell silent.

The sun was now up and providing enough light for Jake to turn off the headlights. As they neared the major routes connecting with I-15, traffic was picking up.

They parked, unhooked, and leveled Majestic at trim-and-tidy Temple Time RV Park in Saint George.

Jake and Susan offered Jen the dinette that converted into a bed by the door of the trailer, but she opted to share a tent with Mandy and Amy.

The girls and Jen struggled to pitch the tent next to the trailer, getting tangled up in the long, segmented aluminum poles and laughing hysterically. It was the first time they had heard Mandy laugh since her escape.

It was a pleasant day—warm and sunny. The red and vermillion cliffs above the city were brilliant in the high desert's fall sunlight. The Mormon temple, not more than a half a mile away, glowed pure white.

Susan warmed some leftover pasta in the microwave Jake had installed above the fridge. It was the Airstream's only equipment that wasn't original.

Once camp is set up, most folks in RV parks have one major source of entertainment: watching and eavesdropping on their fellow RVers, who are invariably parked very close. The crew ate inside so their discussion of next moves would be private.

Susan and Jen sat on one side of the dinette with the girls on the other side. Jake pulled up a folding chair to the end of the table. During lunch, Jake mentioned that he and Susan had decided they should find a realtor to help them comb the city for places that matched where Melissa might be.

After Jake cleared the lunch dishes to the galley, Susan fired up her computer and searched for real estate offices. Century 21 didn't prove promising, nor did Sotheby's Realty. One named Southern Utah Contours popped up. She glanced at a few positive Yelp reviews and studied the pictures of personnel. The headshot of a partner named Nannette Odell caught her eye.

Jake turned at the sink. He had a dishtowel thrown over his shoulder. "Here's what I'm thinking. We're a family from Boulder. It's always best to concoct stories that run close to the truth. Mandy and Amy are sisters. It occurred to me to try and cast Jen as my second wife, this being Utah and all, but let's go with her being your younger sister, Susan."

"*Younger* sister?"

"'Fraid so, sweetheart," Jake said.

"I think I would rather she was my *older* sister wife." She tugged playfully on Jen's braid. "*Okaaaay*, Jen is my *slightly* younger sister."

Jennifer threw both arms in the air. "*Yeessss!*"

"And we are looking for a . . . what? A location for some kind of business. Ideas?"

"We all love the outdoors," Jen said. "In my case especially anywhere outdoors that is not on fire."

"An outdoor clothing and equipment shop?" Mandy said. "My dad can advise us since he's on the board of the Outdoor Clothing and Equipment Company."

"That's it. We want to see all available mall spaces for our proposed Outdoor Shop," Jake said.

"And we have an investor in my sister, Jen, and we want the girls to work in the shop during summers and school breaks and—"

Jake interrupted Susan. "Someday take over the business."

"What're our names?" Jen asked.

"That's easy. Same first names and in your case, same last name. Goddard might pop as suspicious, so we will be"—he looked out Majestic's window above the dinette and saw a red truck towing a huge fifth-wheel trailer making a tight turn into the park—"the Turners."

"Okay, here goes. Susan Turner is calling Southern Utah Contours for professional help searching for a location for a family-owned outdoor store," Susan said.

"Contours. Outdoors. Sounds like a good match," Amy said.

"Everybody pack some water and snacks. Might be a long afternoon,"

Jake said. "And bring parkas and warm clothing." The girls looked at him quizzically. "I know it's a warm day. But have you two teenage sleuths noticed that everywhere we go we seem to be accompanied by the same brown car?" Blank looks on both. "I didn't think so. Jen?"

"Uh. Nope."

"Not to worry. This stuff comes with a lot of practice and an unhealthy dose of paranoia. Susan and I *have* noticed, and we have developed a plan to deal with that little inconvenience."

The girls slid out from the table and banged through the trailer screen door. Susan reached for her cell phone to call Nanette Odell but then punched in the numbers and handed it to Jake. Might be better considering the plan they had concocted if Jake Turner did the talking from the start.

Melissa spent a miserable night in the closet with little sleep, her thirst resulting in a pounding headache. By the time the dim light of dawn crept under the door, she had to admit Beauford had won. Anything was better than this torture. The morning hours crept by with no offer of water or food. Her body ached.

Midmorning, she had been startled by a rap on her door. She then agreed to behave and cooperate if only she could have something to drink.

She sat at the interrogation table, clutching a half-empty bottle of tepid water in both hands. Beauford was perched on his chair a few feet back from the table across from her. He rolled the grip of the 7-iron in his hands, tapping the clubface back and forth on his black leather shoes. He wore a dirty white golf glove on his left hand.

"Got a *raund* in this morning. Got to get there early to beat the heat even in November. Two birdies and three pars. Good day for me. Love the damn game, but I'm no Tiger."

"What is it about Bears Ears that is so important?" she asked.

"Bears Ears? REM. Rare earth metals, sweetie. The gold of the future. Thar's rare earth metals in them thar hills."

"Rare earth metals in southern Utah?"

"Yup. Current administration would kill to get their hands on more domestic rare earth metals. They're desperately needed for everything electronic from cell phones to weaponry. Even tried to buy Greenland." He chuckled and shook his head. "Right now, China has the upper hand with REM—fucks us two ways, on national security and on trade negotiations. They use it as leverage with the dealmaker-in-chief. But that will all change when we start digging the wax out of the ole Bears Ears."

"Why have I not heard of any such resources in that region of southern Utah?" Melissa sipped at her water.

"Because within forty-eight hours of the discovery the government stepped in and declared it a matter of national security. Slapped a cap on that story like a leaking well. Top secret. Few weeks later, the reduction was announced."

"How is it that you know anything about it?"

"Well, you see, dearie, Uncle Sam isn't much good at making anything or doing anything practical. No clue about mining. Couldn't extract a rotten molar. That's where we come in, and that's why we were brought in early on. Or at least the large companies were, and I got wind of it." He propped his club against the table, stood, and faced the glass, finger combing his thin hair over his balding pate.

"That sleepy backwater is going to see a boom that will make the Dakotas seem like a small-town amusement park. We are talking Disney squared—roads, railroads, towns, mines, processing plants. The whole works." He turned back toward her. "And I intend to have Beauford Oil and Gas positioned for a large portion of the pie."

"That explains why you want to remove any roadblocks to the reduction, but why are you telling me all this?"

"Isn't it obvious?" He spun his chair and straddled it. His belly bumped the chair's back.

"No, not really."

"Well, hon, with all you know already I can't let you live, so telling you more ain't a problem. In fact, the whole crew of you is going to have to die. Did you know Goddard, your daughter, and a few other extraneous and expendable females are here in Saint George, staying in an old aluminum trailer?"

Melissa looked shocked.

"Yup, figured you didn't. The moron hasn't even noticed we've been tailing him. They all eat and meet inside. One door. Block that, add accelerant, and it's Jiffy Pop time. I'll bring a video. And believe me, sweetheart; we have a deep bench and a long reach. We'll get your hubby at the same time."

He leaned in. "So, like I said, in the long run, I can't let you live, but if you continue to cooperate and you and Benny continue to provide evidence of your boards taking a new tact regarding fighting the reduction, I will let you live a little longer. But in order to even do that, I need your help with another matter. My partners and I want intel on the key players who are fighting the reduction; contact info, business connections—anything that can help us develop profiles."

"You claim you have lots of people, but I've only seen you and two others."

"Hmmm. Is that so? You could say I'm in the building stage poised to expand and take my place at the table with the big mining companies. Thanks to your daughter."

"What does Mandy have to do with your corrupt plans?"

He started to get irritated. "Shit, she gimme me the idea. When my man on the inside at the school grabbed her, we thought she was just a snoopy kid. But then he did some sniffing *araund* at the school and discovered who that little girl's parents were." He pointed at her. "I hatched this whole idea. Ticket to the big-time in the industry."

"Why didn't you abduct her in Pennsylvania?"

"Goddammit! My well is *abaut* a mile from the campus. Do you think I'm stupid?"

"But you—"

Beauford stood and slammed his 7-iron on the table, denting it. "That's enough. No more questions. Call your husband!" He pulled a cell phone out of his pocket and slid it across the table. "I want to hear you ask for that information on the enemies of the people you conspire with."

Melissa's shoulders slumped with defeat. There could be no more stonewalling. This newly requested information was too easy to verify.

He jerked his belt up under his belly. "Keep feeding me, babe, and you live. That is, assuming Goddard and company don't find us here, unlikely as that is. And that's only until the whole crew has a tragic accident. Nice thing is, they will have a lovely view of the temple while popping."

Tears rolled down Melissa's cheeks.

"Your tears are wasted on me, missy; you're standing in the way of progress. And that's damn near un-American. Dial!"

Jen stood by the trailer door, chatting with Jake.

"Let's go, girls," he said.

Amy and Mandy crawled out of the tent, wearing their school hoodies. Their green-and-brown four-man tent, reflected in Majestic's mirror finish, was dwarfed by the surrounding RVs. The park was bustling. Snowbird season was in full swing.

Jen got in the back of the Suburban and slid to the middle. The girls loaded up on each side of her, Mandy on Jen's left, behind Jake. Susan emerged from the trailer wearing a colorful fleece wrap around her shoulders and carrying a large brown cotton shoulder bag.

Jake cranked the air-conditioning on high and assured the girls they would soon see what was up.

Exactly one hour later, the last thirty minutes being diversion driving, which included circling the Saint George airport twice, going full circle on two roundabouts on Bluff Street, and several laps across a bench loaded with houses overlooking the city and with an amazing view of the distant columnar red rock cliffs—all intended to drop the tail—Jake drove by the back entrance to the Shoppes at Zion Mall and stopped. Susan cast off her wrap, jumped out of the passenger seat, and hurried into the building.

Jake raced for five blocks, glancing regularly in the rearview mirror.

When he was sure they were still alone, he pulled into the alley leading to the back door of Southern Utah Contours, stopped the car, and slid out.

Soon he emerged with a woman in tow. She climbed into the passenger seat and immediately turned toward the back and smiled. She was pretty and of medium height with an athletic build. She had dirty-blonde hair, which would have fallen to her shoulders if the AC hadn't been blowing it across her face. Amy noticed immediately that Nanette looked a lot like her mother.

"Nanette, I'd like you to meet my daughters, Amy and Mandy."

"Hello, girls. Welcome to Saint George."

"And this is Jen, my sister-in-law. Jen, this is Nanette Odell."

"Nice to meet you, Nanette," Jen said.

"Unfortunately, my wife, Susan, is feeling under the weather, perhaps because the darned air-conditioning is stuck on in this old clunker. I apologize for that inconvenience."

"Oh, I'm sure it will be fine," Nanette said, turning and putting on her seat belt.

"Please don't hesitate to put on that fleece wrap Susan left on your seat." Jake stated the engine. "This cool air would probably be perfect here in July, but late November, not so much." Jake steered down the alley past several parked cars, dumpsters, and piles of flattened and stacked cardboard boxes.

Driving normally again, he turned out of the alley onto Main Street. He glanced in the rearview mirror and nodded and smiled at the three women bundled up in the back.

After a few minutes of getting blasted by cold air, Nanette worked the shawl around her shoulders.

"Okay, Madame Realtor, tell us about our first potential business property," Jake said.

"We'll take a right up here in four blocks at the light, and then it is just three blocks to Christensen's Mall. It's a really nice location for a small-to-medium business."

"Okay, but this will just be a drive-by to get to know the lay of the land. We won't be stopping or getting out of the car today," Jake said.

"And you know what, let's drive by Shoppes at Zion first just for the sake of comparison."

He abruptly turned at the next light and headed toward the large mall. He noticed within a few blocks that, as he had hoped, the brown car once again fell in behind them.

A woman with a similar build to Susan but with long, soft brown tresses, a lavender headscarf, and large dark glasses, carrying a brown canvas shoulder bag, walked out of the main mall entrance and slid into the back of a blue Dodge Caravan with a man sitting in the driver's seat. It was the taxi the woman had just ordered with her phone.

She said hello to the middle-aged, barrel-chested Hispanic driver and asked him to wait a few minutes while she sent a quick text. Soon a maroon Suburban with five heads inside drove by, followed a few seconds later by a brown Chevrolet with tinted windows.

Susan looked up and smiled. "Follow that brown car, please. Don't get too close."

After Nanette led Jake and company past Christensen's Mall and one other that was on the south side of Saint George, Jake said, "Forgive me, Nanette, I'm just so worried about Susan, and we're all just about half-frozen thanks to this darned AC. Can I just drop you at your office and reschedule?"

Nanette looked as relieved as if she had just sold an entire shopping mall. They drove back toward the center of town—Nanette spouting the chamber-of-commerce spiel on why Saint George was ideal for a new business, especially one that is outdoors oriented, and why Southern Utah Contours was the right, indeed the only, choice of realtor—and a few minutes later drove up to the real estate office and stopped, this time in front.

As Nanette climbed out, Jake thanked her again and said he would be in touch. She hurried in the office door.

After pulling away from the curb, he turned off the air and smiled in the rearview mirror.

"With any luck, when we get back to the RV park, our constant companions will break off and hurry to base to report our strange behavior and one missing person. And that missing person will be in her cab, hot on our tail's tail."

The trailer door banged open. Susan, face flushed with excitement, was staring at four anxious and eager people sitting around the dinette—Jake and Jen on one side and the girls on the other.

She quickly entered, closed the door, and pulled off her sunglasses, head scarf, and wig and tossed them on the bed. "It worked! It was a long shot, but it freakin' worked!" She shook her hair loose and then tucked it behind her ears. "We counted on the bozos not being particularly bright, and it proved to be true."

"Where is Melissa?" Mandy asked.

"I can almost guarantee your mom is being held in a now defunct medical-supplies store in the Red Rocks Mall on Brigham Street. That's where they went, anyhow. I only stayed long enough to see two men get out of that brown car and go inside."

"Great work, Susan," Jen said.

"Bravo, sweetheart," Jake said.

Susan slipped her video camera out of the brown bag and dropped the bag on the couch. "The taxi charge is like to break us, but Caesar, the driver, had the time of his life. He guessed I was trying to catch a cheating husband and I made no attempt to alter that notion. In fact, I may have added to the intrigue when the two men got out of the car and I said, 'It hurts the most when it's with another man.'"

Everyone laughed except Mandy.

Susan brought the camera to the table and pulled a chair up to the end. On the GoPro viewfinder she played the footage of the two men leaving their car. She had zoomed in as they were entering the building.

Mandy shouted, "Those are the two jerks who had me. What are we waiting for? Let's go get Mom."

"Okay, okay. Listen, everybody," Jake said. "This is where it can get dangerous. I'll sleep with the two girls in the tent, and I'll be armed. Susan and Jen, you guys can have the bed. And Susan will have her Glock nearby. Tomorrow, Susan and I will case the mall in a different car. Jen, you will spend the day with the girls here at the park in public places where the bad guys will be afraid to approach because of the danger of being witnessed. The pool and adjacent rec room would be one good option. The Suburban will need to be parked here. Maybe we can fool them again, but most likely not. It is critical that they never spot us anywhere near Red Rocks Mall."

"But Jake, by tomorrow—"

Jake cut off Mandy. "We can't outgun them or outman them. We must not go off half-cocked. Our only chance is to outsmart them. We've got a pretty good start in that regard. It's also your mother's best chance."

"Mandy, watch and learn for your future career as an investigative journalist," Susan said. "We have a critical advantage, which we cannot risk. They know where we are. By now they have probably guessed they've been made following us, and that we know they know where we are. But they don't know that we know where *they* are."

"Can I please at least call my dad?"

"Yes, of course. I need to talk to him too," Jake said.

"Let's get dinner now and try to get some sleep later," Susan said. "Amy, did you bring cards?"

"Two decks, ready to go." She got up and hugged Susan. "You're awesome, Mom."

November 30
Wednesday Evening

Jen and the girls spent the day hanging around the RV park in plain sight. Jen kept, deep in the side pocket of her cargo shorts, the bear spray Susan had loaned her, just in case she needed to repel unwanted visitors.

It had been a quiet day. The most exciting thing that happened was when two earnest young men in white shirts and ties—Mormon missionaries—approached them in the rec room while the girls were playing foosball. After a few minutes, Jen told them, "Thanks, but not interested," and shooed them away.

Jake and Susan returned from surveillance and, after making certain they weren't being followed, parked their white rental van among the other vehicles in the temple's large parking lot. They walked to Temple Time.

It was evening now and already dark. They were all gathered inside Majestic. Amy and Mandy had just cleared away Chinese takeout, which had been delivered right to the trailer door.

Susan, Jake, Jen, and Mandy sat at the dinette talking. Amy was on the couch, playing with her phone and only half listening.

All the blinds were drawn. Jake and Susan reported about their day of watching and filming the Red Rock Mall.

"Did you spot that brown car?" Jen asked.

"We saw it coming and going, like around lunchtime, but it was never gone long," Jake said.

"The only other activity was a fat, mostly bald guy who left with golf clubs at 8:00 a.m. in a gold Buick and was back just before noon," Susan said. "When we have time, we need to see if we can get an ID on him from the GoPro footage."

"They didn't spy on us at all today. What's up with that?" Mandy asked.

"Hard to say. You said you guys were approached by two young men?" Jake asked.

"Yeah, but seriously, Jake, those kids were as innocent as lambs," Amy said.

"And believe me, I had my hand on my bear spray in case they made one suspicious move," Jen said.

"That would make for a great story at the missionary training center. I'm sure LDS missionaries have been sent away in many awkward and embarrassing ways, but getting a blast of bear spray in the face would have probably taken it to a whole new level," Susan said.

There was a sound just outside the trailer. Jake put his finger to his mouth. The group fell silent. He got up from the table and switched off all the lights at a control panel by the door. Park lighting dimly illuminated the interior. Susan leaned against the metal wall and pulled the blind out a few inches for a view outside. She shook her head at Jake, indicating she saw nothing unusual. He walked to the closet near the rear bed, removed his lock box, lifted out his Browning 9 mm pistol, and shoved in a ten-round magazine. He grabbed the elastic band of his headlamp, switched on the light, and slipped it on his head. He walked quietly to the door near the front of the trailer, the beam of the headlamp shooting lasers of light around the aluminum interior.

Mandy jumped and grabbed Jen's arm at the sound of a can being dropped on the concrete outside.

Jake eased the trailer door open, pistol hidden at his side. He moved his head from side to side, probing the exterior with his light.

The picnic table seemed undisturbed. He eased down the two steps onto the concrete patio. The noise was coming from behind the trailer.

He lifted his pistol and moved slowly to the rear with his side plastered against the aluminum skin. When he had a clear view of the area behind the trailer, he saw something scampering away into the shadows under the motor home parked next door. Tipping his head down, he saw what had attracted the animal.

He laughed. "There's a masked bandit out here. A raccoon got into our recycling bin. What a mess."

Inside the trailer, everyone exhaled. Susan flipped on the lights. They heard Jake cleaning up the cans and bottles. Susan looked at Amy.

"I know, I know, Mom, I was supposed to dump the recycling by the office."

"Best I can remember, that was all I asked you to do today," Susan said.

Jake returned, stowed his pistol, and sat at the end of the table. "Let's talk about tomorrow. Can you guys all sit so we can discuss quietly?" After they complied, he continued. "Susan and I are pretty sure there are only three of them."

"Are we going in?" Mandy asked, flushing.

"Mandy, girl. I love your courage and enthusiasm. Your unassisted escape still amazes me, but no, *we* are not going in. Susan and I will go in when we see one or more of them leave tomorrow. We need Jen to drive the van in case we have to make a quick getaway. What I can't decide is what to do to keep you two safe."

"We can't even consider this unless we are certain you are completely out of danger," Susan said. "Ideas, girls?"

"I don't suppose they have any bars in Saint George that are open all day," Amy said.

"Ha, ha," Susan said.

"Hmmm. If hanging out in bars is out, those cute boys in shirts and ties invited us to a young adult Bible study class followed by a picnic tomorrow. I kept the flyer. The whole thing takes from like 10:00 a.m. until 4:00 p.m. at the ward near the temple. Think that would cover it?" Amy asked.

Susan nodded and smiled at Jake. "I think that just might do it. And who knows? Maybe you will learn something, about, say, God or Jesus," Susan said.

"Or, *Mom,* maybe I'll learn something about brainwashed and oppressed women," Amy said.

Jen laughed and said, "Speaking of brainwashing, don't sign anything. Those guys work on conversions like they're selling magazine subscriptions."

December 1
Thursday

Surveillance, yuck, what a drag, Susan thought. Watch and wait. Mostly wait. Wait for hours. She had her feet propped on the dashboard of the van in the front passenger seat. She had already gobbled down the lunch Jake had packed that morning, and it was only eleven thirty. Jen didn't really have a view from the rear, so she was curled up, napping in her seat.

Fortunately, the sun on the van was warming it, eliminating the need to run the engine and the heater. Jake was in the driver's seat, tapping the keys on his computer perched on the console and humming some off-tune ditty. The GoPro sat on the dash on a freeze frame of the rotund bald man they had observed and filmed on their last visit. Beside the camera sat Jake's cell phone. He was using his phone's hotspot to connect to the internet.

They were the only vehicle parked outside Pets Place, the only extant—but obviously dying a slow death—business in the mall. Pets Place was situated at the far end of the U-shaped cluster of one-story retail locations hunched under a continuous sloping shed roof. The store had the advantage of being diagonally across the cracked and weed-strewn parking lot from—and offering a good view of—the dirty display window and faded, peeling green door of Desert Home Medical, the defunct business they suspected held Melissa.

As discussed, they were waiting for one, or better yet two, of the three men to leave. Then Jen would park in front of the medical supply store, leaving the van running. Susan and Jake would somehow get through the door, overpower and restrain the remaining man or men, grab Melissa, and go. Simple. Except that no one had come or gone from the store all morning. The wait was excruciating.

Susan sat upright. The round, balding man exited the store and, while walking to his car, unlocked it from the key fob. She slumped down again when all he did was retrieve a golf club from the trunk of his Buick, relock the car, and go back inside, swinging the club by his side.

Susan sighed, sat forward in her seat, and pulled her Glock out from under it. "Screw it. Let's go in. What's one or two extra scumbags going to matter?" she muttered.

"Uh, Susan. No. We have no clue what sort of danger these men pose. We need a level playing field," Jake said, glancing from the GoPro to his computer and back.

Susan returned the pistol and slumped back in her seat.

"This waiting is driving me nuts!"

"I think I've got him," Jake said.

"Who is the dickwad?" Jen asked from the rear, yawning and stretching her arms.

"If I'm right, it's Raymond Beauregard Beauford. Your instincts were right on, Susan. Found our Raymond on the corporate page of Beauford Oil and Gas. Graduated Derry Area High School, Derry, PA, in 1989. Two years at Indiana University of Pennsylvania, Indiana, PA. Short stint in the military. Went to work for the old man in the family oil biz. Took the reins in 2008. It's a little hard to tell from the GoPro footage, but Raymond Beauford *just might be our guy.*"

Jake closed down his computer and switched off the hot spot on his phone.

"That could connect the dots to Mandy's initial assault," Susan said. "But what the hell is his interest in Utah?"

Ball Cap and Fishing Hat walked out of the defunct store, putting everyone in the van on high alert. They got in the brown car and drove out of the lot and down the street, out of sight. Fishing Hat was driving.

"It's 'go time,' folks." Jake said. Susan grabbed her Glock. Jake reached for his Browning pistol under his seat and then the GoPro off the dash. He squeezed between the front seats into the back. Jen pushed past him and slid into the driver's seat. Jake set the video cam to film. He slipped on his backpack and attached the GoPro to his shoulder strap.

"Susan, ready?"

"Let's do this thing," Susan said, her excitement rising.

"Start the engine," Jake said.

Jen took a deep breath and turned the van's key in the ignition.

"Drive, Jen," Jake said. He switched on the camera.

Jen pulled out of the parking space and headed toward the medical supply store. She braked just in front of the entrance, and Jake and Susan were out and running.

Jake hit the door hard with his shoulder and almost crashed into the room with Susan piling in behind him.

The door had not even been latched. They gathered themselves and stood at a forty-five-degree angle to each other guns drawn and turning as one unit. Gray light angled through the front display window, the fading letters on the glass casting shadows on the floor. Behind a Formica counter they saw metal tables, paper and plastic bags strewn about, dust-covered metal shelves, and boxes—some empty, some half-filled with medical paraphernalia such as braces and IV bags. In the middle of the back wall was a filthy, cracked window looking out onto the alley. There were footprints in the dirt on the floor, evidence that people had walked through the opening in the counter and across the room, but no sign of anyone. And no sound.

To their left was a single door. After they were certain no one crouched behind the counter, Susan walked to the door and tried the handle; it turned easily. She kicked the door, and she and Jake poured through. The external windows had been covered with plywood. There was a beige La-Z-Boy chair, a lamp, and a side table as well as a round kitchen table with an odd assortment of straight-backed chairs. Newspapers and magazines lay on the table; empty bottles and food containers were piled everywhere and spilled out of garbage cans. But again, no one and no sound.

Part of the far wall was covered with a red velvet material. There was a door adjacent to it.

Jake searched for the cords and jerked back the velvet curtain. Vague figures could be made out in the dark behind the glass, like some strange Halloween tableau. Susan found a light switch and flipped it on, revealing a horrible scene.

Beauford was sitting in a folding chair against the far wall facing the glass. He had Melissa pinned with her back to him between his knees on the floor. She was struggling. He was pressing a golf club, an iron, across her throat. His meaty fists clenched the shaft on either side of her jaw—the back of her head was jammed against his belly. Her legs jerked as she clawed at the metal at her neck. Beauford was strangling Melissa in full view of them. Jake grabbed the door handle. Locked.

Beauford's voice crackled through an ancient speaker on the wall.

"Goddard and Brand. We've been expecting you." He breathed heavily from the strain of pulling back on the club. "Took you long enough." He yanked hard, jerking Melissa's head deeper into the folds of his lap. She gasped and fought for a breath. "As you can see, and as I promised, no harm had been done to Melissa, same as her daughter, mind you, until you two came barging in."

"Release her now or we're coming in shooting," Susan said.

"Oh, I don't know, that door is pretty solid. Plus, you come in shooting"—he jerked hard on the golf club. Melissa flopped like a dying fish—"or try shooting through the glass, you are likely to hit her." He yanked her head up higher on his chest. "What is this called now, a Mexican standoff? Or is that not PC?"

Melissa thrashed—a look of terror on her face—gurgling sounds emanating from her throat.

"Oh, well. It was *abaut* time for us to move on anyhow." The rear door to the interrogation room opened, and Ball Cap entered. He jerked Melissa up to her feet. Beauford stood and started to move backward toward the door, dragging her by the club across her throat.

When they got to the door, the fat man lowered the club so it braced Melissa across the chest while Ball Cap placed a black hood over her head. Beauford backed out the door using Melissa, now collapsed in his arms, as a shield. "Next time you come anywhere near us, she dies!" He kicked the door shut.

Jake yanked on the door handle again, but it wouldn't budge. He aimed his pistol at the lock seated in a small metal plate.

"I'm going to shoot it out," Jake shouted.

"No, Jake! Ricochet! I'm afraid she'd be dead by the time we got to them anyhow," Susan said. "Let's go around."

They turned and ran toward the door to the room, only to find it had been closed and locked behind them. Jake stood back and kicked at it several times until it splintered open.

They rushed to the main entrance to the store and found it had been locked also.

"Oh my God, I hope Jen's okay," Susan said.

"I should have armed her," Jake said.

He kicked hard at the front door, but it was sturdier than the interior door. It held.

"We need to break a window," Susan said.

It took several minutes to dismantle a shelf so they had a leg that could be used as a club capable of breaking thick glass. Finally, they smashed through a panel on the rear window frame, cleared the broken glass, and crawled out into the alley.

The back alley was empty except for two blue fifty-five-gallon drums and some rusted rebar. They ran around the end of the building.

The van was still running where it had been parked initially, although the front right tire was flat. There was no sign of Jen. The gold Buick was gone.

They heard a muffled sound from the back of the van. And thumps on the metal panel.

They tore open the double back doors. Jen lay flat on her stomach. She was trussed with zip ties on her hands and feet and gagged with Gorilla Tape.

They holstered their guns, untied Jen, and helped her up. She was a little shaken and mad as hell, but otherwise fine.

They sat shoulder to shoulder between the open rear doors of the van with their feet on the asphalt. Jake switched off the camera on his backpack strap.

"I never saw the assholes coming," Jen said.

"It was a trap, Jen. None of us saw it coming," Jake said.

"At least I managed to get the tall prick in the fishing hat with my pepper spray before they overpowered me."

"Are you kidding? I didn't know you had it with you," Susan said, hugging Jen's shoulders.

"Hell, yeah. I blasted the jackass right in the face," Jen said.

"Poor Melissa. I hope she's okay," Susan said.

Jake shook his head. "That was a total screw-up, and it was my fault."

"At least you got it all on GoPro," Susan said.

"Yeah, let's look at that footage. Should be pretty incriminating. Definitely rises to assault and battery," Jake said.

Jake switched on the camera and found the point where they had entered the building. When he got to footage of the light being switched on in the interrogation room, his jaw dropped. The video of the attack was useless. The camera had only captured a glare of bright light and blurred reflections of Jake and Susan on the glass. They had nothing but audio.

They sat in stunned silence for a few moments.

"What are we going to tell Mandy?" Susan said.

"I suggest we tell her they were gone when we got here," Jen said. Jake and Susan both nodded. "It's like the fat fuck feels above the law. Like he's operating with impunity," Jen added.

"That guy must be Raymond Beauford from Western Pennsylvania—I would recognize that accent anywhere in the world. Some people call it Pittsburghese, but it's prevalent throughout the middle Appalachian area," Jake said.

"If it is Beauford, that makes a connection to the school incident a lock," said Susan.

"I'm guessing when he hears about the attack on Melissa, Ben might want to notify the FBI, but we are living in strange times. Maybe Beauford does have some kind of immunity," Jake said.

"Guess it comes down to how badly the federal government wants to open up drilling and mining in southern Utah," Susan said. "You know,

I've got an old Phoenix PD contact who is now in the higher echelon of the Utah Highway Patrol. According to Facebook, Dwayne is a captain in Section 11, based just north of us here in Cedar City. If Ben is adamant, maybe we can steer him in that direction."

"Even if Ben did contact the FBI, they might kick it to Utah Highway Patrol because they are Utah's state police and it has all gone down in Utah," Jake said, then stood. "Well, let's go see what they left behind. Jen, you're our lookout. Keep the bear spray handy and lean on the horn if they return."

Jen jumped to her feet. "I might as well be useful and change the damn tire while you search."

Jake stood, grasped Susan's hands, and pulled her upright. He headed toward the store with Susan following. They both pulled blue latex gloves out of their back pockets and wrestled them on while walking back around to the rear of the building.

The investigators spent over an hour combing through the rooms connected to the medical supply business. They discovered that, all in all, there were five rooms. Three they already knew about: the front room where business had been conducted, the room with the La-Z-Boy and strange interior window, and the room where Melissa had been attacked. But farther back they discovered a small bathroom and two more rooms. Those two rooms had beds in them that had obviously been recently slept in.

In the hallway between the interrogation room and the bedrooms, Susan discovered a small closet. It was that space that interested them the most. They saved it for last.

Beauford and company, as piggish as they had been, had been pretty thorough in removing anything that hinted in any way at what they were up to ultimately, or where they were taking Melissa next. They had, however, failed to carefully go over the closet Melissa was imprisoned in.

Susan was certain Melissa had been in the closet for extended periods of time because when she first looked in, she noticed the letters MF faintly scratched in the old, unpainted drywall. The letters were approximately three inches high and, taken together, about two inches wide.

When all five rooms had been searched without turning up anything of interest, they returned to the closet.

"There is absolutely no doubt she was held in this closet," Susan said. "Those scratches look fairly new, and the coincidence with her initials would be too great."

"Agreed," Jake said. "But what good do they do us?"

"There are really only two reasons for her to scratch her initials into the drywall: to communicate that she was held in this space, and to send us a message."

"Well, she accomplished the first goal," Jake said. "But I fail to get the message. Why isn't that scratched into the wall?"

"It has to be here." Susan crawled into the closet and began running her hand over the surface of the walls. Jake pulled his headlamp out of his pack and directed the light over her shoulder.

She sat back on her haunches. "Here's a thought. Melissa is a smart woman. Maybe she felt if they found her initials, they would not make a big deal of it. She could say she was bored or something. But if they found an obvious message, it would place her in more danger, and they would simply erase it or destroy it."

"Yes. I like it. The initials by themselves appear innocuous, but maybe indicate we should look further," Jake said. Susan, still on her knees, started to inch her right hand along the top of the baseboard.

Jake shined the light around the interior. Apart from Melissa's initials, all he saw were dents, scratches, and scuff marks typical of a utility closet.

"Damn," Susan said sitting back on her haunches again. "I just ran my finger over something hard."

"What is it? Can you tell?"

"It's metallic and wedged behind the baseboard." She reached in her pocket for her Swiss Army knife, opened a blade, and worked at the wall.

"Careful you don't damage it," Jake said.

"I'm being as careful . . . there it is. It's out." She held a small object between the fingers of her right hand.

"Look just beyond where you found that. Something is reflecting my beam." Susan shifted her fingers over a few inches and saw the edge of the object. It was shiny and small. She carefully pried it out with the knife.

She stood and studied the two objects in the palm of her gloved hand.

"Let's sit down and think about this," Jake said.

They walked into the interrogation room and sat at the table. Susan placed the found objects in front of them.

"What have we got?" Jake asked.

"I'd say we have our messages from Melissa. And I know that because these two metal objects have been tied together with a long strand of hair of Melissa's color."

"Okay, looks like two large, slightly bent staples—the type that are used for molding—tied with human hair," Jake said. "What about the other one?"

Susan unfolded the silvery paper. "A piece of foil chewing-gum wrapper." She turned it over. "And it's been charred, like with a match or stuck in an outlet."

They sat in silent thought for a few moments. "This place gives me the creeps. Let's take these back to Majestic and see what we can figure out," Susan said.

They bagged the found items, switched off all the lights, and left by the rear door.

After picking up the girls at the ward, Team Goddard gathered at the dinette inside the trailer. Jake had filled in some details from the morning at the mall, saying, as they agreed, that the store had been empty when they arrived and began their search.

Now they all sat staring at the two staples tied together with human hair. Amy was assigned the job of recording secretary. Jake had his laptop open and ready for searches.

"Any ideas?" Jake asked.

Susan rotated the staples longwise. "From this direction, it is a skinny and slightly wavy *E*."

Jake brought up a map of Utah and one of Nevada. "*E, E* . . . I don't see a single place in southern Utah or, for that matter, in southern Nevada that begins with *E*," he said.

"But there are a couple in northern Nevada," Susan said. "Amy, jot that down, okay? Consider Nevada cities starting with *E*."

Amy scratched down some notes.

Susan rotated the staples, so the dual openings faced up.

"That makes a big flat-bottomed *W*," Jen said.

"Again, nothing in Utah, but some candidates such as Wendover in Nevada," Jake said, studying the maps. Amy scribbled on her pad.

Since being told the white lie that Melissa and the Beauford crew were gone when Jake and Susan had entered the building, Mandy had sat as if in silent pain, bent slightly at the waist with her arms wrapped around herself. Susan tried to draw her out of her silence. "Mandy. Ideas?"

"I'm trying to get inside my mom's head, but honestly, I'm so frightened for her I can barely think."

"Understandable. But thinking like her is a great idea. Could help bring her home sooner," Jen said.

Susan turned the staples until the openings were facing down.

"A flat *M*. Lots of candidates in central and southern Utah," Jake said, "Manti, Monticello—"

"Wait!" Jake glared at the staples. "What if it is not supposed to indicate a letter? Obviously tied together means they work together to communicate an idea. What if that idea comes from proximity but not a direct connection? Melissa tied them together to indicate that together they are her message, but that doesn't necessarily mean tied together. Nor does it necessarily mean forming a letter or letters. Can you untie them, Susan?"

Susan disconnected the two staples by slipping the knotted hair down the two coupled legs and over the teeth. "Now separate them, please," Jake said. "Free associate. What have we got?"

"Two teeth," Mandy suggested.

Susan periodically moved the staples to a new configuration.

"The letters C C," Jen said.

Susan moved the staples apart.

"How about ears?" Jake said. "They look like squared off ears. Let me find a picture of the Bears Ears buttes on my computer." He tapped on his keypad and smiled. He turned the computer so all could see.

"Swap the two staples, please," Jake said.

Susan did as he asked. The Bears Ears buttes depicted on the computer screen looked not so much like the rounded ears on a bear as like rectangles, or for that matter, slightly bent staples. In fact, exactly like the staples Melissa had apparently shaped and then left for them.

"Wow, Jake, maybe you should consider becoming a private investigator," Susan said.

Jake stood up. "Great work, folks. I need to take a walk and clear my head and think about what we just discovered."

Jake went out in search of a private place in the RV park from which to call Ben and tell him about his wife's assault and about the clues she had left. While he walked toward the deserted park pool area, he thought about the other item they had found, the charred aluminum foil. He and Susan had discussed it earlier and agreed to keep it from the girls. Burned aluminum had ominous implications.

December 2
Friday

"Well, darlin' . . ." Dwayne Williams frowned. "Can I call you 'darlin''?"

"You always have; why stop now?" Susan said.

"What with the 'Me Too' thing and all?"

"Had some sensitivity training, Dwayne?" Dwayne tried his best to look sensitive. "My solution to that workplace problem is called the 'Knee Two.' You've got a knee, girl, use it," Susan said.

Dwayne slammed the knees of his blue chinos together, cracked his trademark grin, and said, "That should work."

Susan realized she had missed him a lot.

They were sitting across from each other in two leather easy chairs in Dwayne's large Utah Highway Patrol office on DL Sargent Drive in Cedar City. Cops and clerks bustled about outside the insignia-adorned glass door to the captain's office.

Susan took in the oak desk with its state-of-the-art computer and accessories, wood shelves burdened with official-looking books and binders, and oak sidebar equipped with Keurig machine and coffee mugs.

"Nice office. Congratulations. You've done well since we sweltered together on the mean streets of Phoenix."

"Yeah, not bad, huh?"

"I'm impressed. Very impressed. And you're still the same buff, good-looking guy—not a day older if you overlook the salt in that mustache you're rocking—with lavender tie and button-down shirt, to boot. Be still my beating heart." She placed her hand over her heart. "Oh wait. Can I say that?" Susan asked.

The grin again. "I'm pretty pleased with how this all worked out. 'Course, even though the chamber calls this area 'Color Country,' brothers are rare as tits on a bull up here." He frowned again.

"It's okay, Captain Williams. You and I are old friends, so it's okay to say 'bull' too." And again, that dazzling grin.

"At least all these white folks here got used to seeing the dark skin of the previous president on TV. And that first lady, uh-huh."

"You always did have an eye for the lookers with brains, Dwayne. Speaking of which, how's your beautiful wife adjusting to Utah?"

"Jada loves it here. In charge of all educational programming at the county library and finding time for lots of golf and tennis. Plus, she rests easier. She seems to think I'm safer here."

"I can't imagine the gangbangers are as bad as Phoenix."

"They're not as bad, but we got 'em. As the city has grown, so have the urban issues and issues related to the I-15 corridor."

"Who would have ever thought your ship would come in, in the middle of the southern Utah desert?"

"That desert part has been a little weird. Lately we don't even get the monsoons like in Phoenix. It has been several months since we had a drop. But you didn't come for a weather report and urban-growth lecture. How can I help you, Brandy?"

Susan filled him in on the details of the Fry case. She told him about Mandy's abduction and escape and about her mother, Melissa, being held captive. She said that when Ben Fry had heard about the attack on his wife, he decided to ignore the kidnapper's threats and insisted they go to the police immediately. He had also called his daughter home. Susan mentioned Jake had dropped her off with her friend, Jennifer Wise, at a nearby Holiday Inn Express early that morning and was driving north with Amy and Mandy now.

"Jen is trying to line up a practice jump with local firefighters."

"Shouldn't be a problem if she's as good looking as you."

"Better. Jen's a babe."

"Really sorry to hear about what that family is going through. And of course, I hope for the best for . . . what's her name again?"

"Melissa. Melissa Fry. At least we're pretty sure that it's safe for Ben and the two girls in Park City. The ringleader seems to have concentrated his small army of three down here; of course, we can't be certain of that. Mandy is doing pretty well, considering. But I wonder if Melissa will ever recover."

"I'll put out a BOLO on those two cars ASAP. But darlin', speakin' of Knee Two, we are balls to the wall around here right now. We have five national parks in southern Utah and millions of visitors every year from all over the world. Seems like there is no off-season anymore. I can't spare a single trooper. I really can't. Especially round the holidays."

"I'm very sorry to hear that."

"But the truth is, I don't have any cops as good as the cop I'm staring at right now."

"Thanks, Captain. But I'm retired. Just a lowly PI."

"Aren't you the woman who once said she would never again wrap her life around some random buck's agenda?"

"Uh, yep, that does sound vaguely familiar—might have been me . . . in another life."

"Here's what I'm going to do: I'm going to deputize you, Brandy."

"You can do that?"

"Hell yes, this is the Wild West. I have the legal right to form a posse if I want to. In fact, it happened recently in the Wild East. Central Pennsylvania. Didn't I see something on Facebook about you and PA?"

"Yes. My daughter, Amy, is attending boarding school back there."

"Boarding school? Preppies?"

"Long story involving a buck named Jake whose random agenda I got wrapped around." She held up her hand, showing her wedding ring.

"Saw that on Facebook too. Congratulations. I'm officially forming the Brand posse of one. Your title will be Investigator, and you will answer directly to me."

"But—"

"Don't thank me yet. You being a good Girl Scout and all, you have no visible tats or outstanding warrants, and a clean driving record, right?"

"Right, but—"

"Great. However, there are some other requirements."

"Such as?"

"Have to pee in a cup." Her face fell. "And boy, am I looking forward to getting those lab results. But that can take weeks, and you need to be in the field immediately." A sneaky little smile returned to her face.

"You have to accompany me to the range this afternoon and prove you still know the barrel from the grip. And I expect you to be here tomorrow morning at 0700 hours, ready to join me on my daily 5K. That will be your fitness test. Sound good?"

"I don't know what to say, Dwayne."

"Damn, Brandy. *You* don't know what to say? There's a first time for everything."

Susan shook her head and chuckled.

"Now, in all seriousness, you can only carry weapons you are legally permitted to carry as a citizen. And most importantly, you can only use force allowed by a citizen, such as in self-defense, but hell, no one was better at using her brains to prevent an escalation than you—if you overlook that woman you shot in her garage."

"She threatened my partner with a pistol."

"Anyhow, keep me in the loop. I know I won't regret this."

"Wow, Captain Williams. I'm honored. And I think Ben Fry will feel reassured, knowing your resources are behind us."

"You tell him I'm not taking this lightly. It's a serious situation involving prominent citizens and a child, for Chrissakes. Way I view it, it's as if I just put my best person on the case." He placed his hands on his knees and leaned forward. "But unfortunately, all I can give you is a badge, a handshake, and my best wishes."

"That's more than we had before."

"Ready to be sworn in, deputy?"

"I guess I am."

He stood up and searched his office with his eyes. "Now where the hell'd I put that damn Bible?"

"I'm a freakin' investigator for the Utah Highway Patrol," Susan said.

Jen crooned, "She's back in the saddle again," and held up her glass to toast Susan with the white wine she had purchased earlier that day with the help of a cab driver who knew where all the booze was in Cedar City. In fact, Mark, the driver, boasted he could drive to each of Cedar City's few state liquor stores blindfolded.

Susan sat on the inside edge of her queen bed, facing Jen doing the same on hers. Susan touched her plastic cup to Jen's and took a long pull. The bottle sat half empty on the table between the beds.

Susan wore jeans and a plain, white V-neck T-shirt over a lacy rose-colored bra. Jen hadn't changed out of her yoga tights and jog bra after her late-afternoon workout in the fitness room. She had tossed on a sheer, fawn-colored, off-the-shoulder blouse that revealed her flames tat in the small of her back.

Earlier they had each consumed a sativa sour gummy bear legally purchased by Jen in Colorado but smuggled over the Utah line. They chased the gummy with a shot of Patrón tequila at a neighborhood bar called the Roundup. But they could barely hear each other over the country music and soon tired of cowboys sniffing around and trying to get them in a lineup—a line-dance lineup.

The two friends decided to carry on the celebration in their room. The room, which had been nothing to write home about initially, was looking cozier by the sip. Prints of the red, white, and orange eroded rock pillars called hoodoos from Bryce Canyon National Park lined the walls. They could hear music playing softly in the next room.

"So before we get too wasted," Jen said, "what's next?"

"As soon as Jake gets back from Salt Lake with some supplies, we move to Bluff, a small town close to Bears Ears. Oh, and when I called to report about our day, he said he's going to text you a list of equipment he hopes you can borrow from your firefighter-sky-jumper new best friends here."

"Oh, okay. Shouldn't be a problem this time of year. Where're we going in Bluff?"

"There's an RV park near the highway, just outside of town."

"We'll stick out like a sore thumb?"

"That's the idea," Susan said. "We're convinced the baddies were planning to take Melissa to somewhere near Bears Ears. The twin buttes' resemblance to the staples is too exact to be coincidence. And we are just as certain her captors will be watching every spot nearby where a trailer can be parked. Unless they changed their plans, Majestic will shimmer like a shiny lure on the end of a one-hundred-pound-test fishing line and draw them in."

Jen raised her glass. "Here's to landing the big one."

Just after toasting and draining the wine from their plastic motel glasses, they heard a bed thumping and a woman moaning over the music next door. They dissolved into barely suppressed giggles.

"Love those Colorado gummies. Lucky I had my drug test today," Susan said.

More giggles.

"Stop. You're killing me," Jen said, rocking back and forth.

Susan looked up with tears in her eyes. "Oh, oh man, I needed this, girlfriend. This little trip to southern Utah has been plenty stressful." She pressed the left sleeve of her shirt into her eyes and then focused on Jen. "You still okay with being involved?"

"Oh yeah. My jump this morning was a great adrenaline rush but can't compare with spending even twenty-four hours Private Eyeing with you and Jake. I'm loving it."

"Okay, but you have to agree to say so if you get, as Jake would say, a private *eyeful* and it becomes too much."

More moaning from the next room, only louder, resulting in more giggles. Susan put her hand over Jen's mouth to control her.

Jen composed herself somewhat. "Oh, my. I haven't laughed so hard in years." She ran to the bathroom for a tissue and returned and sat and wiped her eyes. "Ah, me." She took a deep breath. "Soooo, how's Dwayne? Still gorgeous after all these years?"

"Oh . . . yes."

"If memory serves, you had quite the crush on him in Phoenix."

"Memory always serves you in that department, girl. You would forget your mother's name before you would forget a detail like that."

"But you told me nothing happened."

"And I'm still telling you nothing happened. The heat was intense, and I'm not talking about the Arizona heat, but the hard, fast 'partners don't get involved' rule kept us honest."

"Feel any residual heat today?"

Susan fanned herself. "I think I could be in a nursing home, and if they wheeled in Dwayne, I would still feel the heat."

"So how hot is he? On the Zullie scale: leaf-pile fire, dumpster fire, house fire, forest fire?"

"Dwayne is burning-down-trees hot. Think the other Dwayne, 'the Rock,' only smaller in stature. Dwayne Williams is a 'nine.' Lose the mustache—a 'ten.'"

"Whoa. That's hot. I'd have the Rock's bambinos."

"We had some close calls in Phoenix."

"Brush burns. I know all about those."

"You know, Jen, more importantly, today I was being looked at as a good cop again. I felt honored and important. I felt somehow larger with Dwayne's praise."

Jen refilled their glasses and held the empty bottle up to Susan's face. "Tell me, Investigator Brand, what are your first few days on the UHP going to look like?"

"Well, thank you for asking that, Jennifer. I suppose I will need to check in with my partner, Jake, and then we will begin to systematically remove every scumbag from the streets, arroyos, and buttes of southern Utah. Of course, I will be flashing my shiny new badge at every opportunity."

"What sort of danger do you face in this line of work?"

"Well, Jennifer, there is always the serious danger of mistaking my Taser for my vibrator."

Jen put her head on her forearm, shoulders shaking with suppressed laughter. She sat back up, cleared her throat, and, trying to stay in character, continued. "It is said you particularly have it out for a certain mining concern from central Pennsylvania."

"Oh, your media types are so savvy. Yes, top of the list. There *is* a mine owner named 'Blowhard' for whom we have plans to excavate a new asshole."

Bottle still in Susan's face, "Well now, Investigator Brand of the Utah Highway Patrol, that sounds rather ambitious, don't you think?"

"No, Anchor Jennifer of the evening 'snooze,' on the contrary. Especially if I can find enough of this white stuff around here." Susan grabbed Jen's glass and sucked down the contents, spilling half on her T-shirt. They both hooted.

Jen ran to the bathroom, returned with a small towel, and began daubing at Susan's chest. Susan flopped on her back, Jen tumbling with her.

Susan had initially covered Jen's hand with hers but then let her hands flop down by her side.

Jen noticed a hard bump under Susan's wet shirt and bra. She slid her hand slowly under the shirt and over her ribs and, while staring into her eyes, cupped her right breast, compressing the hard nipple gently through the material. Then Jen leaned down for a kiss. A kiss that began with mild mutual curiosity but soon developed into a thorough investigation.

Susan slid quietly out of Jen's bed and dug into her duffel bag on the bureau for a clean top. She found a dark T-shirt, slid it over her head, and tugged it down over her bare breasts. It was on backward and had to be adjusted.

She glanced at the clock: 2:05 a.m. In five hours, she was scheduled to run with Dwayne. A 5K would normally not be very challenging, but the evening's activities could make performing in the morning more difficult.

She slid into her bed. Jen breathed quietly in hers. So lovely and peaceful.

Ah yes, this evening's activities. It had finally happened. And it was nice. No big deal, really, as long as Jake didn't find out. It had just been a few kisses and hands, after all. Like a massage. An intimate massage.

Just hands, but expert hands. A woman's hands. Wise hands. Jen's fire-hardened hands—rough but gentle—leading to sweet, shuddering relief.

And it's not like things had been great in bed with Jake recently—sort of a dry spell since Pennsylvania. Not that the sex there had been anything to write home about.

But this was a one-off. Jen would surely understand this couldn't happen again. Susan thought hard about it. She had no regrets. Just as long as Jen understood the boundaries and Jake didn't find out.

She tucked the whole experience into its compartment and drifted off to sleep.

December 4
Sunday

Rustic Rig Haven, just outside the small town of Bluff, was more isolated than Temple Time in Saint George. The park was set back off the main highway, poorly lit, and wide open. In short, it was a location that invited an attack. Exactly what Jake and Susan wanted.

The park was divided into two sections of gravel RV sites with the requisite one-story, clapboard office and restroom/shower building in the center, the bathrooms being connected to the office by a covered pass-through breezeway.

Jake had stayed at the park before and knew the owner closed her office promptly at 5:00 p.m. every day, allowing late arrivals to fend for themselves.

Because he was certain any uninvited visitors would come well after dark, he was not concerned the owner or, for that matter, the occupants of the few rigs spread throughout the park, would get sucked into any nastiness.

The day before, Saturday, had been interesting. Whether intentional or accidental, Jen and Susan kept busy with their own stuff for most of the morning and had not seen much of each other. Around noon, Jake had picked them up in Cedar City to return Saint George. The talk in the car remained safely centered on Susan's exciting new role with the Utah Highway Patrol. Jake mentioned he had lunch with Trey Fleishman, their friend the pathologist, in Salt Lake and that Trey was getting married. It seemed a new female assistant technician had joined his lab, and they had fallen in love over specimen samples. Jake said Trey called his betrothed his "nerdy lover," and she referred to him as a "lovable nerd." A perfect match.

After Jen, Susan, and Jake arrived in Saint George, everyone had been busy packing the trailer for Bluff. That had offered a convenient excuse for the two women to avoid eye contact.

Their last night in Saint George was made even less memorable by a dinner at Denny's. They had all slept in the trailer with weaponry close—Jake and Susan in the double bed with pistols under their pillows, and Jen on the dinette bed, curled around her bear spray.

Early Sunday morning they had hooked up Majestic and left—the maroon Suburban hauling the trailer as usual. But in convoluted canyon country, there are no direct routes.

The trip took longer than expected, dipping down into Arizona twice. They had arrived in Bluff midafternoon.

Now Majestic, shiny and alluring, sat unhitched in a pull-through site on the part of the park closest to the entrance road and adjacent to, and parallel to, the office. The door to the trailer faced away from the building.

Jake was returning from the men's room when he noticed the garden hose was dripping where it attached to the trailer. He pulled a blue plastic bucket out of the back of his car parked in front of the trailer and placed it below the drip with the intention of emptying it periodically on the few spindly trees and shrubs that separated the RV sites.

After bending down to place the bucket, he stood, stretched his back, and took in the view. Once again, they were surrounded by wild, rocky country, but this time with far less city detracting from the beauty and serenity.

If only we were here to study the geology and absorb the natural beauty, Jake thought, gazing off toward the sheer varnish-covered red rock cliffs above the south side of the San Juan River. The bluffs were crowned with an afterglow of orange and pink as the sun tucked in behind them. He turned to look the other direction. Across the highway was a high bluff, still bathed in golden light, that marked the northern edge of the river valley. It had been obvious, especially as they had dropped down the steep highway into town through those bluffs, that they were the geographical element for which the little town had been named.

Studying the highway in the foreground and seeing his Airstream was clearly visible from it as planned, Jake realized Bluff, the town's name, was perfect for what they had in store for Team Dickhead, Melissa's captors, captained by—almost certainly—Raymond Beauford of Beauford Oil and Gas.

He gave Majestic a little pat on her shiny rump and silently thanked her for serving him so well for so long. He went around to the front of the trailer and removed the propane tank cover, lifted out the two propane tanks, placed them in the rear of the car, and then replaced the tank cover on the hitch. Now they had one more thing he needed to do.

Susan was happy she had caught Amy for FaceTime on her cell. She sat inside the trailer at the table while Jen was off jogging and Jake fiddled around outside. Susan filled Amy in on her new role with the Utah Highway Patrol and the move to Bluff, and then asked, "How are things in Park City?"

"Great, Mom. Too bad I'm not available. Lots of cute boys."

"And you know this how, sweetie?"

"The only way I can get Mandy away from her computer is to get her outside. And one of our favorite activities is window-shopping in town. As soon as the ski resorts open, I'll do some snowboarding, but for now it's just about all there is to do."

"Activity, as in physical activity? Like exercise?"

"Yeah."

"Shopping for exercise?"

"The stores are all on pretty steep hills."

"Uh-huh."

"It counts."

"And you meet boys that way?"

"All the time. It helps keep Mandy distracted. I'm even teaching her a few moves."

"Hmm. And how is Mandy holding up?"

"Oh, before I answer that, I almost forgot. She got a WhatsApp message about a pop-up protest. A One Degree rally right here in Park City this afternoon. We went. Lots of kids. It was about the film industry's carbon footprint and impact on climate. Kinda cool."

"Aren't you turning into a radical."

"Not a radical, just an activist. Tell Jake, okay?"

"Sure, honey; I'm proud of you. Now tell me about Mandy."

"She is one tough cookie, but like I said, glued to the computer—constantly digging on the internet for information that might help Melissa."

"And Ben?"

"Really sad. He just . . . looks worried all the time. This has aged him a lot."

"Maybe we can take those years off him by reuniting his family."

"If anyone can do it, Mom, I mean, Madam Investigator, you can. You and Jake are a good team."

Silence.

"Mom, you still there?"

"Yes, sorry, honey, I was thinking about what you just said. Yeah, we are a very good team."

"Well, whatever you two have cooked up, be super careful, okay. I love you guys."

"I love you too, Amers. Gotta go. Jake needs me to drive him to Monticello."

Majestic sat stolidly reflecting a bit of dull yellow light from the park office building. The moon was a sliver in the eastern sky. Stars glittered like sequins on black silk.

The gusting wind, although silent, carried a winter desert chill.

After the Rustic Rig Haven office closed, a small teardrop trailer had entered and occupied the site the farthest from the building on the same side as Majestic. Also, a large red bus had pulled in, unhooked the Jeep it was towing, and set up for the night one site over from the teardrop trailer. There were several empty sites and then the site next to Majestic, which had been occupied by a late-arriving, boxy rental RV parked facing the wrong direction in the pull-though site. It had scenic pictures painted on the sides and something on the door. Its windows were dark.

The Airstream sat alone—no tow vehicle in sight. But activity inside the trailer was surprisingly high for after 11:00 p.m. Two people, one man and one woman, were either playing cards or reading at the dinette. Their silhouettes were visible through the shade as they periodically moved their heads and arms. The other people in the party could not be seen and were presumed to be in bed.

At least that is what Fishing Hat and Ball Cap assumed as they snuck up on the trailer. They hid their car behind a steakhouse on the highway and walked in the dark the few hundred yards to Rustic Rig Haven. Fishing Hat carried a can of gasoline and a two-by-four. The shorter Ball Cap lugged a large canvas bag full of straw—all that was required to block the exits and burn the trailer to the ground, killing all inside.

They lurked in the shadows off the entrance road on the edge of the park. Nothing stirred. The night was deathly quiet except for the deep call of a great horned owl from the trees closer to the river and the hum of the RVs' furnaces kicking on and off. Except for the Airstream, the rigs scattered about the park were dark and still.

Fishing Hat gestured for Ball Cap to move the bag of straw closer to the trailer. Ball Cap pulled handfuls of straw out of the canvas bag and spread them evenly under the rig from front to back, ducking when he went in front of the illuminated window. Fishing Hat stayed back in the shadows and quietly walked around the trailer to confirm what they had suspected. The windows were either the type that didn't open at all, or if they did open, were too small for a grown person to crawl through. The trailer was a death trap. Fishing Hat grabbed the can, approached the trailer, and silently poured gas on the straw and on the trailer's tires, sides, and fender.

When finished, he stood up and studied the window with the people sitting inside. They did not appear to suspect anything as they continued to move as before.

Ball Cap grabbed the gas can and dripped a line of gas back away from the soaked straw at the rear of the trailer to the edge of the light from the building. He stood ready with a lit match cupped in his hand. Fishing Hat propped the short stout board between the bottom of the door and the base of a tree at the edge of the site. He hurried to Ball Cap's side, certain the occupants would have heard or at the very least felt that last action. But no one stirred.

Ball Cap looked at Fishing Hat. Fishing Hat nodded. Ball Cap dropped the match at his feet—the line of gasoline ignited, and fire traveled the ten feet to the straw under the trailer. There was a thump. The straw burst into flames. A draught of wind fanned the blaze.

In moments, the tires were in flames. The smell of the burning tires, rubber hoses, and burning insulation under the trailer was overpowering as a black cloud rose into the dark sky. Flames rose higher up the sides of Majestic and were now licking at the windows. The intense heat breached the bottom of the old trailer. Fire was now inside. First the floor burned and then the furnishings. Finally, the shade ignited and the two figures beside it slumped and caught fire. The arsonists looked on in amazement at their work.

There was a frantic pounding on the inside of the trailer's door, but the propped board kept it from opening. Then a blow from inside splintered the small opaque window on the door. A fire axe began tearing at the aluminum below the shattered window. After several strikes, the axe split the door wide open.

A human figure engulfed in flames spread the two halves of the cleaved door, jumped out, ran through the trees, and fell still burning to the ground beside the rental RV.

Ball Cap and Fishing Hat both felt a pistol jabbed into their backs and heard a demand to show their hands. They slowly raised them in confusion.

Jake burst out of the RV next-door to the Airstream with a CO_2 fire extinguisher. He sprayed the burning figure as she rolled on the ground. When the fire was out, it was evident she was wearing full protective firefighter's gear with a hardhat, face shield, and breathing tube.

Jen stood up unharmed and removed her helmet. She turned toward the arsonists with a huge "gotcha" grin. Out of her belt she pulled two crossed sticks, the kind puppeteers use, with pieces of burned fishing line hanging off the ends.

"Fire is my thing," Jen said. She opened the rental's door, entered, and returned with a fire extinguisher.

Susan, holding both her Glock and Jake's Browning 9 mm, demanded, "Down on the ground. Both of you. Hands over your heads. Do it."

The two men dropped slowly to their knees and placed their hands above their heads.

"I'm Susan Brand. I'm an investigator for the Utah Highway Patrol." She shoved Jake's Browning into her belt so she could badge the perpetrators with her free hand.

Jake and Jen worked with a garden hose and fire extinguishers to put out the fire. Then they stood back for a moment and stared at what was left of the trailer Jake had owned since living in it during his college days.

It was clear as she smoked and smoldered, Majestic was a total loss in the line of duty.

The distant sound of sirens shook Jake back to the present. He hid the gas can and the charred board that had been propped on the door, then, taking the guns from Susan, ordered the men to get up and climb into the rental RV. Susan remained outside, expecting company at any moment. The sirens were louder now.

Melissa had never felt so alone. Her faith was waning. Her courage was leaking out of her like sand from a torn burlap sack.

Beauford was sweet and conciliatory one minute and wild the next. When she heard him approaching her cell, with the frighteningly familiar tapping of that infernal golf club, she never knew what to expect, Jekyll or Hyde. If he liked the report and information Ben had just given him, he was all sugar and spice. If he didn't, he was a raging bull. Sometimes he was both.

Hopefully Ben had offered enough factual personal information on opponents of the monument reduction to appease Beauford but not enough to expose the people to danger.

She wondered if her messages about the move to Bears Ears and warning of Beauford's threat to burn the trailer had been discovered. She was worried to the point of nausea about Mandy. She tried to push down the fear inherent in her knowledge that the messages constituted her only hope and represented a slender thread at best. She felt utterly abandoned by Ben and Jake and Susan. She wanted to trust but found it harder and harder to do so.

She paced across her cell. Six steps one direction. Eight steps the other. No window, just a vent pipe for heat and air, a cot, a plastic bedpan, and a door. The lights were controlled from outside. At least in the first prison she could mark the walls. In this one the walls were solid rock.

She felt irrelevant, helpless, buried. Already dead.

There was at least one consolation: none of the three men had touched her sexually. And she prayed to a god she had never much believed in that wouldn't change. And more importantly, that it had been true for Mandy.

Jake and Jen sat in the dark inside the rental RV across the dinette table from the two men, each of whom had his hands zip-tied to the table leg and feet zip-tied together. Red and blue lights strafed the walls. Jake held his pistol on the guests just to insure their silence. The pungent odor of burning rubber permeated the RV. They could overhear a conversation from outside.

Susan was explaining to the chief of the Bluff Volunteer Fire Department—who had just turned into the park accompanied by several vehicles, lights flaring and sirens blaring—that she had been camping at the Rustic Rig Haven with her husband when the fire had occurred and they had put it out. She said the Airstream belonged to her husband and had fortunately been unoccupied. She also showed her badge and said she had been in contact with her captain, Dwayne Williams, in Cedar City, and he had put her in charge of investigating the fire. All of which was true. She added that they had seen no sign of anyone or any foul play, which was not true. She promised to keep the chief informed if he would tell the sheriff in Monticello, whom she assumed had been called, that everything was in her hands and that he could go back to bed.

The firefighting vehicles left the park quietly. A small group of onlookers from other RVs, all senior in age, had come over when they heard the fire trucks enter the park. Susan answered a few questions, again showed her shield, assured them they were in no danger, and urged them to go back to sleep.

Susan came inside, freed the perpetrators' hands, and read them their rights. She stood by the sink.

Jen had had enough excitement. She was yawning and stretching her back. She got up from the table, stripped, dropped the rest of her protective clothing on the floor, and kicked it into the bottom of a floor-level storage space; then, showing zero self-consciousness in her underwear, she said good-night and went back in the RV's bedroom to sleep.

Jake reached across the table and ripped off Ball Cap's ball cap. "You destroyed my vintage Airstream trailer, asshole." The asshole formerly in the ball cap just grunted. He had been hiding a bald spot as large as a yarmulke. The patch of scalp was ringed by stringy reddish hair not particularly well styled.

"What's your name?"

Silence.

"You two losers were clearly filmed on a video camera on night mode, committing arson and attempting murder," Susan said, grabbing the GoPro sitting on the galley counter. "Now help yourselves by helping us."

"What are your names?" Jake demanded. He yanked off Fishing Hat's fishing hat. It had been hiding a stubby gray ponytail held by a rubber band.

"Here's the deal, gentlemen," Susan said, approaching the table and leaning on it with both hands. "I repeat: you've been caught on film committing serious felonies. We can also prove you are kidnappers, times two. We've been dancing together long enough to know you're performing these nefarious deeds for an employer who we think is Raymond Beauford. You have a choice. Work with us. Mitigate the charges against you. Or stonewall us. Take the fall for your boss. I'm guessing that's a fall that could put you away for twenty to twenty-five years." She paused to let that fact sink in. "Now, let's begin with answering Jake's simple—and I might add, given the circumstances of what you just did to his baby, civil—question. Please introduce yourselves."

"Harold," muttered Ball Cap, glancing with resignation at his partner.

"And do you have a last name, Harold?" Jake asked.

"Fink. And call me Harry."

"Harry Fink. Nice to meet you, Mr. Fink," Jake said. "And now you, sir?"

"Jan Wozniak."

"Mr. Wozniak," Jake said, nodding.

"Okay, Harry and Jan. Our second question has to do with your boss," Jake said. "Just for the record, his name, please."

"Beauford," Fink said. "You had da right."

"Is it just the three of you?" Susan asked.

"There's another guy works security for Beauford, and at the school back east. Not sure what his name is," Wozniak said.

"As we suspected," Jake said. "Now we know for absolute certain who we're dealing with. But you can help us by solving one other mystery. The calls to Ben Fry regarding first his daughter's abduction, and then his wife's imprisonment, were made by someone else. Based on his voice, a man we have not met yet. Who is that?"

Wozniak and Fink exchanged a blank look.

"No idea," Fink said.

Wozniak added, "Could be anybody. He talks to people in na mine business all a time on his cell."

"You have no idea who else might be working with him?" Jake asked. The two men shook their heads in unison.

"And how is Melissa? For all your sakes, I hope she has recovered," Susan said.

"Beauford has taken pretty good care of her since he almost strangled her to impress you'uns," Fink said. "But . . ."

"But what?" Jake asked.

"Who knows what he had planned for her after we reported back?"

"That is, after you reported that we were all dead, right?" Jake said.

"Yeah. Can I have my hat back?" Jake handed Fink's hat to him, and he jerked it onto his head. Jake tossed Wozniak his fishing hat, but the captive left it lying on the table.

"That's good news about Melissa and will work in your favor in the long run," Susan said.

"Now, gentlemen, what will also work in your favor is what we are going to discuss next. That is, where Melissa is being held, and how you two are going to help us get her out unharmed," Jake said.

"How do we know we can trust you'uns to do what you say?" Fink asked. "I mean to help us."

"Truth be told, you will be throwing the dice in that regard. But half a chance is better than no chance at all. I mean, you did try to kill us, after all," Jake said.

"This will seem foreign to you, given the steaming pile of dog shit line of work you have chosen," Susan said. "But we are giving you our word, and Jake and I actually keep our word. Plus, I have a direct line to Captain Dwayne Williams of the Utah Highway Patrol. He holds your future in his hands. I have Dwayne's ear. Wanna play, or do we take you straight to Cedar City for booking?"

The two men exchanged a glance. "Boss has her in a gol' mine in a wash near here," Fink said.

Jake opened his computer on the table.

December 5
Monday

Jen was the only member of the crew to get any sleep, but the PIs felt she had earned it and then some. Susan had tried to dissuade her from performing the very dangerous duties of the puppet master, as they had begun to call it during the planning hours. But Jen had insisted fire was her element and that she was the right person to pull the strings on the mannequins Jake had purchased in Salt Lake City.

Besides, Jake had failed to be specific when he asked her to borrow the protective suit from her firefighter friends in Cedar City, and she had, by force of habit, requested a medium. There was no hope of it fitting Jake, and even Susan being slightly taller than Jen would have been a stretch. As Jen pointed out, large gaps in a protective fire suit, like between jobs, sexual encounters, and front teeth, are not good things.

Jake and Susan spent the night alternating between preparing for the rescue attempt—they had logged on to Rustic Rig Haven's Wi-Fi to study the target area on Google Earth and had Wozniak draw a crude map of the interior of the mine—and standing guard over the two men sitting side by side at the table, feet still tied, until they were finally snoring with their hats over their faces.

The last thing Jake did, over fresh cups of coffee and granola bars, was write a note to Jennifer. He told her what to tell the park owner when she arrived, which was pretty much what Susan had told the fire chief.

He thanked her again, reminded her where the keys to the Suburban were, and that it was parked on the other side of the office building. Susan tacked on a note, urging her to be careful but to enjoy a free day of exploration.

A dim dawn light illuminated the eastern cliffs. It was time. Jake woke Wozniak and Fink.

The four left the trailer, walked past the charred and blown-out rubble that was Majestic's sad remains, and headed out the entrance road toward the hidden car.

It was cold, as the high desert in winter tends to be before the sun thankfully returns.

Jake and Susan carried backpacks, wore loose-fitting parkas, and charcoal knitted caps. Jake had the GoPro on his shoulder harness.

The men behaved. Jake's having demonstrated that the hand in his right parka pocket was firmly wrapped around the grip of his pistol served as a constant reminder to do so.

They all climbed into the brown car. Wozniak drove. Jake sat behind him; Susan sat on Jake's right. Jake held his pistol on his thigh.

They went west away from town on the main highway and after a few miles took a right on a dirt road heading north. The sun was finally warming the valley floor.

The road passed through a small group of cattle in the sagebrush being tended by two black-hatted cowboys on horseback with coiled lariats on their saddles.

Soon the track became much rougher and wound down several switchbacks to the floor of a wash. Had it not been for the other tire tracks, it would have been impossible to tell the car was still on a road at all. They alternated between soft sand, causing minor spinning and fishtailing, and hard pack. Sticks and leaves from flash floods were trapped behind branches and boulders on the upstream side, which was the direction they were traveling—toward Bears Ears National Monument and away from the San Juan River.

They drove by a large red rock panel covered with carvings—animal, bird, and human figures—and passed by a sign indicating the petroglyphs' archeological significance. The sign urged people to respect antiquities.

After rounding a few bends, they saw a second sign commemorating early Mormon pioneers who had found an Ancient Puebloan trail in the area and had improved it to get themselves and their animals up out of the wash. The second *m* in Mormon had been scratched out twice on the sign.

"Oh my God, look at that," Susan said, pointing to a cliff dwelling to the left of the car, tucked under a massive cap rock. The rock above the ruin appeared to be boiling in flames.

"That's Flame House Ruin," Jake said. "Pretty spectacular in the morning light. Sad thing is, it's no longer protected if the monument reductions aren't reversed."

Unlike the ruin that had been built by ancient ancestors by following nature's contours and tucking walls of rock and mortar into the naturally occurring crevices, several barely accessible rectangular openings dotted the bluffs overlooking the wash. *Nature eschews straight lines,* Jake mused; the man-made passageways were portals into the dreams and aspirations—mostly failed—of hard rock miners of the past.

After several more twists and turns in the gulch, they approached a side canyon, which entered from the right.

"We change here. Car don't make it to the mine," Fink said.

Wozniak pulled into the mouth of the side wash, behind a fin of rock, and stopped beside a dust-covered white Ford F-250 with a crew cab. Beauford's Buick was parked fifty feet ahead in the shade of the walls where the canyon began to narrow.

"So only four-wheel-drive from here?" Susan asked.

"Yeah, rough track," Wozniak said over his shoulder while switching off the ignition.

"How many of these four-wheel vehicles service the gold mine?" Jake asked.

"Just this un," Fink said. Wozniak started to open his door.

"Wait. A few more questions before we switch," Jake said. "If this is the only truck going in and out, Beauford and Melissa are stuck there right now. What are they doing for food?"

"When we arrived, the boss showed us a storage vault next to the landing area off the shaft with the elevator. Has tons of dried food. Said it was good for a few years."

"Dried food requires water. Where does that come from?" Susan asked.

"A tanker truck; many served the mine when it was operating," Fink said. "It's used to fill a storage tank. With only a few people living there, one tank lasts for months."

"Bathroom? What does Melissa do for a bathroom?" Susan asked.

"Twice a day we bring her up to the surface to the miner's change house. Bathrooms in there," Wozniak said.

"Is Beauford armed?" Jake asked.

"I think that survival storage area had some guns in it too. Not exactly sure what," Fink said.

"Okay, gentlemen. Appreciate your cooperation. Let's go," Jake said.

He and Susan grabbed their backpacks and switched to the rear seat of the Ford truck. The truck was hot from sitting in the sun. They stripped off their hats and parkas and stuffed them in their backpacks. Everybody assumed the same position as in the car. Jake checked the camera to make sure it was ready to go.

Wozniak retrieved the keys from behind the visor, fired up the motor, and drove around the fin to the main wash. Within minutes, the going got much rougher.

"Are there surveillance cameras outside the mine?" Susan asked as they bounced over a flat boulder. "Your health and well-being going forward depend on continued cooperation and honest answers."

Fink turned in the passenger seat. "Nothing that high tech. Mine played out in the '80s before all that security shit. Boss had us on rotating watch from the mine plant up top."

"So if he and Melissa are below, he is essentially blind right now," Susan added.

"Yeah, pretty much," Wozniak said, glancing in the rearview.

"'Cause if you think about it, our assignment was to remove you'uns as a threat, but you'uns somehow got lucky and seen it coming," Fink added, chuckling.

"Oh yeah, that's true. We just got lucky," Jake said. "Now that I think about it." He tapped Fink on the shoulder with the pistol and grinned at him.

Susan leaned forward. "Here's another truth, Harold. I see a camera up there at the mine, I'll put a bullet in your belly at close range and claim you went for my gun. And I promise you won't see that coming." That shut Harold up.

The main wash led to a steep face of approximately one hundred feet of concave rock capped by a rounded rock lip. A slanting track around it to the left zigzagged up the bank.

As the truck ground up the slope, Susan looked down from her window at the large boulders in the wash below and then at Jake with mock wide eyes. But Wozniak maneuvered the Ford pickup to the top and back into the wash above the rock lip without incident.

"How does your boss, being from central Pennsylvania, happen to have access to a gold mine in Utah?" Jake asked.

"His dream has always been to strike it rich out west where he says the real money is," Wozniak said. "But his ties to family business have stopped him there."

Fink added, "Boss talks about it constantly. His old college roommate at Colorado School of Mines and him got into this here gold mine in the 1980s, based on the 'Bluff excitement' back in the 1890s. Very fine-grained gold was found on the surface, which was what all the excitement was about, but nothing come of it back then. He and his buddy figured that gold had to have a source underground, and technology had improved with the cyanide leaching process and shit like that. So they tried their luck. Beauford says he was a silent partner."

"Hard to imagine him silent about anything," Wozniak said.

"What became of that?" Susan asked.

"Boss says they created a few jobs, made expenses and enough to buy a new set of golf clubs. Plus, they were left with a mighty fine bomb shelter," Wozniak said.

"You want to know what else they did?" Jake said. "Heavy-metal mining is one of the most toxic extractive industries in the US because it leaches heavy metals and poisons like cyanide into groundwater."

"Yeah, well, 'toxic' is Raymond Beauford's middle name," Fink said.

"Speaking of that, does this buddy have a name?" Susan asked.

"Best I can remember he just calls him his buddy. His Mormon buddy," Wozniak said. "You catch a name, Harry?"

Fink shook his head. "Mormon buddy. At's all I remember."

"Tell us about the connection to Blake Wilson," Jake said.

"Wilson! Shit," Wozniak said. "Hicks for hire."

"Don't know their asses from their exhaust pipes," Fink added. "There it is, ahead on the right."

The hills pulled back a little and the wash began to spread out into a wider drainage area. Up on the bluff to the east, a wooden structure came into view. Power poles snaked over the ridge, and the lines terminated at the building. The next most obvious feature of Beauford's failed venture was a huge pile of rock waste mill tailings, which spilled down from the mine into the wash.

Around the man-made mound, the road wound up to a chain-link fence festooned with signs cautioning against trespassing. Wozniak stopped the truck, and Fink opened the glove box and extracted a set of keys. He slid out to unlock the gate.

Jake lowered his window. "Leave it unlocked."

Fink pulled back the gate, and Wozniak drove through and stopped. Fink closed the gate behind the truck and wound the chain through it without attaching the lock.

They pulled up and stopped on a flat gravel parking area carved out of the hillside, adjacent to the building.

The wooden-plank mine building had several wooden doors and many cracked and broken windows. The building sat next to four ore storage bunkers, now empty. According to Wozniak's crude map, the building housed a machine shop, a compressor house, a miner's change house, and an office.

Just above the parking lot, a military tanker truck painted camo sat on six huge rubber tires beside a metal storage tank on stilts. The grounds surrounding the building and enclosed by the chain-link fence were littered with discarded rebar, broken glass, chunks of concrete, disintegrating wooden beams, and various unidentifiable metal parts and pieces.

The four of them got out of the truck and walked onto the dilapidated deck of the mine plant. Jake kept his pistol aimed at the men's backs. Susan walked backward, Glock at the ready, eyeing the buildings and surrounding bluffs. Connected to the main building by the decking was a small open elevator, covered by a roof on support beams, that served the mine main access shaft. That was also, judging by the power lines, where electricity entered the mine. A concrete ramp parallel with the deck led up to the mineshaft and elevator.

Wozniak pushed open the door to the office and they all entered. They walked around a dirty, rectangular library table and past two gunmetal-gray filing cabinets. Sitting on an antique rolltop desk was a phone, vintage 1980s.

"What do you want me to say?" Wozniak asked.

"Tell him the truth. You ran into some complications. It took longer than anticipated, but you burned the trailer as ordered," Jake said.

Wozniak picked up the phone and punched a few numbers. After a pause he said, "Boss . . . yeah, uh, well, we're, uh . . . we're here. Yeah. Did it like . . . like you said. Coming down." He hung up.

Susan and Jake reviewed the sketch of the interior of the mine with Wozniak, then zip-tied them both hand and foot to two pipes running from the plank floor to the tin ceiling by the rear wall.

Jake turned on his camera and started filming.

They walked through a door to the shaft with the elevator.

It was a wooden platform surrounded by a metal cage. They entered through the waist-high gate and clicked it shut. The lift swayed under their weight. Susan pushed "1" on a small metal panel as instructed by Wozniak. The elevator bumped, screeched metal on metal, and began to descend. The shaft was well lit; an iron ladder bolted to the rock wall ran the length of it. Water flowing from fractures in the rock and down the face behind the ladder stained the gray stone orange. The lift traveled several hundred feet. It slowly passed a horizontal, crosscut tunnel that was dark and then descended several hundred more feet before jerking to a stop. A large cavern had been blasted out of the rock, what Wozniak had called the landing area, a staging area for men and equipment.

Susan opened the gate, and they crossed the cavern to a tunnel held up by a combination of metal and wooden inverted U-shaped support structures. The rock floor was worn smooth from the operation of small rubber-tired mining vehicles; a pipe ran along its edge. Conduits for power cables hugged the edge of the rough surface of the ceiling. Jake pulled out the sketch and turned it in his hands.

"Should be right down there."

Susan led, pistol braced.

Soon they came to a large wooden door with a crosshatch of metal strapping. Susan looked over her shoulder at Jake. He nodded.

Susan yanked open the door and they rushed in, guns first. Their eyes searched a fairly large living space including a couch, several single beds, and a dining table, behind which Beauford stood with Melissa clamped in his left arm. He had a Beretta M9 pointed at her head. His 7-iron lay on top of the table. There was a second door behind him.

"Well, well, well, face-to-face at last. Not even a pane of glass between us," Beauford said. "But . . ." He drilled the pistol into the back of Melissa's skull. "Looks like another standoff."

"How did you know we were coming?" Susan demanded.

"We're not as dumb as we look. Wozniak on the phone," he nodded toward a phone on the table by the golf club. "Says 'we're back.' Means we're alone. 'We're here.' Means we're not alone."

"Let her go and you walk out of here," Susan said.

"Ha! You come down here to suggest that. Very funny. No, that's not happening," Beauford said. "What is *abaut* to happen is you sliding your guns over here and getting on the floor with your hands on your heads."

"Beauford, we—" Jake started.

"Now, goddammit, or she dies!" He wrenched Melissa's waist. Her whole body jerked.

Jake and Susan looked at each other, knowing they had no choice. Jake slowly dropped to his knees and slid his pistol across the wooden floorboards toward the table. Susan followed suit. They both placed their hands behind their necks.

Melissa fainted in Beauford's arms, her body slumping toward the floor. He struggled to retain control but lost his grip on her. She hit the planks, wriggled free, leaped up, grabbed the grip of the golf club in both hands, and swung it like a baseball bat against the side of his head—the effort causing her to collapse to the floor again. Beauford staggered back and, grabbing at his bloody temple, fumbled his gun, then fell stunned to his knees. Jake dove for the table and their pistols. Beauford felt around for his Beretta, located it, and crawled out the back door to the room, kicking the door shut.

Susan went to Melissa and lifted her head into her arms.

"Oh my God. Oh my God." Melissa struggled to catch her breath. Her hands fluttered at her chest.

"You're safe now, Melissa." Susan put her hand on the side of her face. "You teed off on him, woman."

"Go after him," Melissa said. "He's getting away."

"You're our first concern," Susan said.

Jake, never taking his eyes off the door, crossed over behind the table and knelt by his wife. He laid her Glock by her side.

"No. Catch him. He has to be punished for what he has done to my family and to, and to . . . the . . ."

Susan looked up at Jake.

"I'll go after him. You get her up to the truck." He pulled his backpack off and dug around in a top pocket for an extra mag, jammed it in his jeans pocket, slung his pack on, and was through the door with his pistol in the low ready position.

The tunnel on the other side of the room was identical to the one they had entered through from the elevator. It was well lit but curved upward, obstructing Jake's view. There was no sign of Beauford.

"Beauford, give it up. You can't escape."

His voice was as muted as if he were shouting in a soundproof room. He felt a breeze coming down the tunnel toward him. Each overhead beam had an electric light attached. Plastic conduits ran between the lights. There was a faint mechanical sound, a sort of whirring in the distance. He pulled the sketch from his pocket and saw that beyond the chamber the tunnel connected to the ventilation system.

He started to pursue. The first hundred yards of tunnel were slightly uphill but easy going. Then the incline began to increase dramatically. Jake's legs felt heavy and his arms ached from holding his pistol in front of him.

The incline increased again; he found himself laboring up the slope, holding his gun in his right hand while grabbing support beams with his free hand to aid his climb.

So far, the rock had been uniform in color, a sort of crystalline gray. But now the tunnel came to a dead end at a sheer headwall of black rock. A ladder with several dozen iron rungs ascended the face and terminated at an opening chiseled out of the rock layer above.

Jake tucked his pistol into the black nylon holster on his hip and started up cautiously. When he was just below the opening, a foot shot out from above and glanced off the side of his head, causing him to fall back, body swinging away from the ladder. He dangled over the space below, held up only by his right hand. The metal bit into his palm. He heard footsteps receding above.

He swung his body around and tried to grab with his left hand and get purchase with his feet. But his pack had snagged on the rungs, causing him to miss, and he swung back around again over the drop. Desperate to find secure footing, he jerked his legs and twisted his body. This time his left hand caught the second rung and his feet connected with the ladder below.

Soon he was up and out in the higher tunnel. He sat back against the wall with his pack between his knees, catching his breath and rubbing his sore right palm. He wondered why Beauford had tried to kick him off the ladder. Why hadn't he just shot him? In fact, why hadn't he fired his pistol at all? Could he possibly be out of ammunition? It struck Jake as odd, but he immediately cautioned himself against taking extra risks based on that assumption. It might be false. And it could be fatal.

The mechanical hum stopped. Jake listened intently, trying to determine the cause of the change when the lights flickered and went out. Blackness. Stillness. Jake had never been in such profound and total darkness in his life. And the air was suddenly thickening.

Cradling her head in her lap, Susan ran her hands over Melissa's arms. She looked into her pupils, checked her neck and temples, and asked questions to determine her mental state. It was a crude and rudimentary examination, but sufficient to determine whether it was safe for Melissa to move under her own power.

Melissa appeared to be lucid. In a few minutes, she stopped shaking. After a few more minutes of catching her breath, she stood up with Susan's help and said she was ready to go.

There was no noise from behind the door Beauford had used to escape. All Susan could do was hope for the best for Jake and try to concentrate on Melissa's safety.

With her left arm around Melissa's waist to steady her and her Glock in her right hand, Susan pushed through the large entrance door. The tunnel was clear. They shuffled down the bore to the landing area and slowly opened the waist high gate and boarded the elevator.

Susan hit "3." The elevator jerked, groaned, and started to climb. She kept Melissa's body braced against hers as they ascended. They passed the unlit tunnel, indicating they were halfway, and entered a section of blank rock wall; the only sound was the creaking of the lift and water gurgling against the face. And then, without warning, the elevator shuddered to a halt and the shaft went dark.

Jake found the control button on the GoPro and switched it off. He felt around for the zipper on his pack and opened the top. He pulled out his parka and groped around inside for his headlamp, praying he hadn't forgotten it. Jake's hand landed on an elastic band and he jerked it out. He examined the elastic with his fingers, felt a circle of material, but there was no headlamp attached. He realized what he held in his hand was a GoPro accessory for wearing the camera on a helmet. Jake folded the band and searched blindly for a side pocket to tuck it in. His hand landed on a water bottle. He removed it and took a long drink, then returned the bottle to the pocket and resumed his sightless search for the headlamp. It was not in the main compartment. He stuffed his parka back in and closed the top. Thinking his eyes might have adjusted, he held a hand in front of his face. Nothing. Pitch-black dark.

He tried to keep panic at bay. The thought of blindly floundering around in the mine was terrifying. There was one more possibility. He felt around for the zipper and unzipped the small pocket in the lower front portion of the pack. The headlamp was there. If only the batteries were good. He found the toggle. Light. Jake slipped the elastic band over his head. Every direction he moved his eyes a beam illuminated the rock walls. Time to push on.

Except for a faint light at the top of the shaft, the two women on the stalled elevator were enveloped in total darkness. When the machine halted and the lights went out, Melissa crumpled to the floor of the lift. Now Susan sat beside Melissa with her arms around her, listening to her quiet sobbing.

"I'm . . . so . . . so sorry. It's . . . it's just the last straw. I'm done."

"I've got you, Melissa, and I promise I'm getting you out of this hellhole and back to your family. End of story."

"But how, in this dark with no . . . ?"

"Do you remember Jake and me telling you about the time I climbed down off the butte with Lyn Burke in Nevada?"

"Yes, yes, that's right. Amy said it was quite a feat for you."

"I would much rather climb up than down any day. When you're ready, we will climb the ladder to the top and freedom."

"I can't. I just can't do that," Melissa said.

Susan felt carefully in the dark, took Melissa's face in her hands, and pressed their foreheads together. "I believe you can, and I suggest with every rung you think about Mandy and her courage, the courage that she obviously got from her parents."

Susan hugged Melissa, willing strength into the exhausted woman's body.

The tunnel continued on, horizontally, for a few hundred yards, turning occasionally. At each blind bend, Jake followed protocol, his pistol held in both hands in the high ready position. And each time he turned a corner the way ahead was clear.

He noticed places where his headlamp illuminated irregularities in the rock wall that had been worked a bit, presumably to test for the presence of gold and other valuable metals.

Since the ladder incident there had been no sign of Beauford. In addition to the passageway getting smaller, the only change since the power went out was the air. The air was now heavy and oppressive. Jake's breathing had become labored way out of proportion to his physical effort, and he was sweating.

He turned another corner. The tunnel slanted up to daylight.

With the walls closing in, he covered the last one hundred yards on his hands and knees—pistol close at hand in the waistband of his jeans with his pack scraping the rock above.

Jake squeezed through a metal frame in an adit in the rock no larger than a car window. A fan lay on the ground, wires still attached, evidence Beauford had escaped this way. It was also a perfect place for an ambush. Goddard jumped to his feet, pulled his pistol, and scanned 360 degrees. He was alone.

He stood blinking in the intense sunlight and removed and stowed his headlamp. Sagebrush slopes rolled away below, converging in an arroyo. He was on the backside of the bluff and could see the top of the mine plant above.

Susan had helped Melissa over the gate and promised her she would be right below her. She had even kept a hand on Melissa's leg to reassure her. Getting Melissa onto the ladder had been fairly easy, but then she froze. She had not climbed a single rung, and her legs were shaking. Susan remembered Lyn Burke, an accomplished rock climber, had referred to that as sewing machine leg, or even funnier, Elvis leg. Susan had experienced it herself many times in tense situations—the body's uncanny and unfunny ability to make a bad situation worse.

But if Melissa didn't start climbing, they were in serious trouble. She presented a vague outline of a figure in the dim light from above. A rag doll made flesh, clinging to the wall. Susan wished she could see her better. She chastised herself for not packing her headlamp as Jake had urged. Stupid move.

"I can't . . . I just can't." Melissa said. "I can't make my legs move."

"Melissa, I'm right below you. I'll be with you all the way. You have got to dig deep," Susan said. "And only look up. Don't look down."

Silence. Melissa's legs continued to vibrate on the rung. The only things Susan could hear were the water gentling splashing down the face behind the ladder and Melissa's breathing. That gave her an idea.

"Do you do yoga?"

"Yes . . . for years."

"I want to you to take three cleansing yoga breaths before each move, and just as you're pulling up a rung, think of someone or something you can't wait to see at home."

"Okay, I'll try."

"Start breathing."

Melissa paused and then began. Susan counted three breaths. "Go!"

Melissa grunted and pushed up.

"Good girl! Again."

Another set of breaths, another grunt, another rung. Finally, there was room for Susan to put her hands on the ladder below Melissa.

Jake scrambled up the hill to just outside the mine plant building. He darted into an empty ore bunker and crouched behind the high, weed-covered wall at the far end. That provided cover as well as a view of the building. Nothing was stirring. He leaped over the wall and sprinted across the fifteen yards to the rear of the structure and sat against the wall, catching his breath. He could see through a cracked window; Fink and Wozniak were still tied up inside. For some reason Beauford hadn't released them.

That was some good news. The odds were still even. But where was Beauford?

Jake was easing around the end of the building in a crouch when he heard a diesel engine crank to life, followed by splashing water. He stood, back flattened against the wall, and cautiously peeked around the corner. The military tanker bucked and then started to back up the hill toward the concrete ramp that led to the elevator shaft. Water was gushing out of the pipes on the rear fender.

Susan's suggestion was working. Melissa had forced her way halfway up the face. And she was getting stronger and more confident with each rung on the ladder. Susan encouraged her from below. She patted the heel of Melissa's running shoes with each move up.

A blast of air and rush of sound caused Susan to look up just as a cascade of water from above almost knocked Melissa off her perch. Both women were suddenly caught in a waterfall that drenched them and pounded them, making it impossible to breathe. Melissa was flattened against the ladder, flailing to hang on.

Susan tried to move her head out of the torrent to catch a breath. She failed. And there was no way to communicate with Melissa. She could hear the water splashing on the deck of the elevator far below.

Susan fought against the force of the water one grueling rung at a time. First her head was at Melissa's knees, then at her waist. Finally, Susan's hands were beside Melissa's and her feet were outside Melissa's feet. Susan used her whole body to press Melissa into the ladder. That small fight upward against the pounding current had required great effort. Susan's body screamed for oxygen. She felt Melissa's body weight slump back against her. She could sense that Melissa's fingers were beginning to slip. Susan clamped her hands over Melissa's. She coughed out water and blinked fluid out of her eyes. She placed her cheek against Melissa's wet hair to reassure her, but Susan was getting light-headed and could feel her own grip weakening.

Jake leaped up on the porch and rushed the tanker with his pistol raised. When Beauford saw him coming, he thrust the huge five-ton into second gear and lumbered down the ramp. Jake squeezed off three rounds at the tires. The bullets sparked off the metal chassis. The tanker crashed down the hill, bouncing over debris piles, engine roaring and black smoke belching out of its stack. Water continued to flow out behind.

The massive vehicle veered over into the parking lot and slammed into the side of the Ford truck, pushing it sideways for ten yards. Then the truck backed up, turned, and bounced downhill, smashing through the fence and driving onto the mine road.

Jake ran to the elevator shaft, dropped to his knees in a puddle of water, and called, "Susan, are you down there?" Nothing. "Susan!"

A cough echoed up from below. "Yes. We're on the ladder."

"Are you and Melissa okay?"

"Okay, Jake. Need to rest. Catch our breath. But then we can make it. We can make it, right, Melissa?"

"I want to go home."

"Fink and Wozniak?" Susan called.

"Still tied up. Beauford is trying to escape in the tanker truck."

"Go. Be careful," Susan shouted. "I love you, Jake."

Jake ran down the hill toward the Ford. Just above the parking lot, the tanker's water had turned the soil to gumbo. Jake went down in the mud, slid for several feet, regained his footing, and ran on.

He could see the truck turning the corner in the wash below. Beauford had apparently shut off the valves because the truck was no longer spraying water.

196 • GREGORY ZEIGLER

As Jake got closer to the pickup, he saw the damage the tanker had done, a huge dent on the driver's side running from hood to bed. But the impact looked to be a body blow and with any luck had not damaged the engine.

He dug the keys out of his pocket and tried to open the driver's side door. It would not budge. He ran around to the other side, got in, and crawled over the console. The truck roared to life immediately. Jake was off, down the hill and through the flattened gate.

At first Jake was lagging far behind, only glimpsing the military truck as it bucketed around bends. But Jake slowly increased his speed and, being the lighter, faster vehicle, began gaining on Beauford. After a bounce over a boulder jammed his head into the roof of the cab, Jake buckled his seat belt.

Several turns in the wash later, Jake caught up to the lumbering, five-ton tanker. He tailgated it for a mile or so, mirroring its every move. Both vehicles fishtailed in areas of deep sand and bucked violently over sections of hard rock. Brush lining the wash flew by Jake's window. Intermittent sunlight glinted through the windshield.

The streambed widened enough for Jake to back his truck off a little, swerve right, lower the glass, and fire a left-handed shot out the driver's side window in the off chance his 9 mm round could actually penetrate one of the big tires on the five-ton. Just as he squeezed the trigger, the Ford hit a hard bump and his shot went high. The bullet smashed into the side-view mirror on the tanker, shattering it. That must have distracted Beauford long enough that he forgot the cliff face in the wash dead ahead.

When he did finally grasp the approaching danger, his brake lights lit up. The panic braking caused the heavy truck to fishtail left and then fishtail right on the slick, sand-covered rock.

The tanker appeared to have come to a full stop just in time. The truck was poised momentarily on the rock lip as if in a freeze-frame; then some force caused it to teeter. Gravity took over and tipped the heavy front end. Beauford plunged the one-hundred-plus feet to the rocks below.

Jake heard the crash. He braked to a stop and, at the top of the drop, jumped out and peered over the edge. The truck was on its side, engine running and rear wheels spinning. Water leaked out of the burst tank. There was no other movement.

Jake drove the side road to the bottom. He got out and cautiously approached the tanker. The impact had blown out the side windows. Beauford was still in the driver's seat, lying against the door. He was not wearing a seat belt. The windshield had a bloody spiderweb crack where Beauford's head had evidently smashed into it. Blood dripped down his face, covering his nose and mouth. The collar of his white shirt was turning crimson with his blood. Although his body was facing forward, his head and neck were twisted ninety degrees over his right shoulder. His blank eyes stared up at Jake in a grotesque mask of death.

Jake ran to the Ford and retrieved his pack. He covered the edge of the passenger window with his parka to provide a modicum of protection from broken glass. With his gun in his left hand, he lowered his upper body down into the cab through the passenger side window and switched off the engine. He stretched a finger to Beauford's carotid. It confirmed what he had suspected when he first looked into the truck. No pulse. He noticed the Beretta behind Beauford's head and retrieved and inspected it. No magazine. Nothing in the chamber. It was not loaded. It had all been a bluff.

Jake pushed the pickup hard back to the mine. When he raced through the fence, he was relieved to see Susan and Melissa sitting in the sun on the steps to the deck of the building. Susan had her arm around Melissa's waist. Melissa sat with her head on Susan's shoulder. Jake gave each a hug and then sagged down beside them and took a long drink of water from the bottle he had carried in his pack. Melissa accepted his offer to wear his parka over her wet clothes. Susan palpated the swelling on the side of his head where he had been kicked. She also gently inspected his raw hand. The wind was picking up a little and debris skittered across the ground.

Jake recounted what had happened. Neither woman was particularly heartbroken by the news of Beauford's death.

"It was the strangest thing. The truck was completely stopped on the edge for a split second. But then something jarred it over the lip. My theory is that after speeding up and causing the water weight to shift to the rear of the tank, Beauford locked down that panic stop at the brink and he was fine for a moment. But when the water corrected and slammed forward, it tipped the truck just enough for gravity to take over. Bizarre."

"I'll take it, and offer my thanks to the God of Physics, whoever that is," Susan said.

"As soon as we've caught our breath here, we need to get to cell service and report Beauford's whereabouts to Dwayne Williams and have him send the appropriate responders," Jake said. "And Melissa, I imagine you're looking forward to calling your husband and daughter."

"What about the phone in the mine office?" Melissa asked.

"It doesn't have a connection out," Jake said.

"And even though you seem fine, and like you said earlier, they didn't molest you, we need to get you checked out at a hospital in Blanding," Susan said.

"Beauford's pistol was not loaded. What do you make of that?" Jake asked.

"Don't know what to make of it. Melissa, do you have any ideas? Anything you overheard?"

"No clue, but had I known that I would have clobbered him much sooner."

"Maybe an oversight when they stocked the storage area," Susan said.

"Serious oversight—weaponry with no ammo," Jake said.

"That's a mystery that may never be solved. And believe me, speaking from experience"—Melissa touched her neck—"Beauford's golf club was plenty lethal."

"Speaking of mysteries, did he mention his partner in this mine?"
"No."

"Hey, got an idea. We could look for the power cutoff that Beauford tripped, turn it back on, call for the elevator, and go search for answers down below," Jake said, smiling.

"Thanks, but I think I'll pass." Melissa stared down at her boots for a few silent moments. "I have a confession." She looked up with wet eyes. "I was skeptical when Ben hired you to find Mandy." She cleared her throat. "I was so wrong."

"Thank you, but that's enough of that," Susan said, standing. "What do we do with the two hog-tied lackeys?"

"Good question," Jake said. "On the one hand they helped us—under duress, of course—but the information Fink and Wozniak provided did figure greatly in the rescue. On the other hand, the men were responsible for us walking into a trap. And then there's Majestic."

"Dealing with those two losers will eat up valuable time and take up valuable space in the truck. I don't want to sit beside them. I say fuck 'em," Susan said. "What do you say, Melissa?"

"Double fuck 'em."

After a quick check of their restraints, Wozniak and Fink, looking sullen and dejected, were left tied up in the office to be dealt with by the troopers when they arrived.

The Ford pickup headed down the wash for the last time.

As the truck neared Bluff, text messages began stacking up on Susan's screen. One was from Jen, thanking her for the rest day, saying that she hoped they were safe and had Melissa, and as soon as the dust settled, they needed to talk. One was from Dwayne, just checking in. The rest were from Amy, and they were troubling to say the least. Because they were in reference to Mandy, Susan decided to ignore them until they got Melissa checked into the Blue Mountain Hospital in Blanding, which was thirty minutes from Bluff.

Susan urged Jake to forego stopping at the RV park, and just keep going to Blanding in the truck, allowing Melisa to sleep in the back seat.

They drove through the town of Bluff past the Cottonwood Steakhouse where Wozniak had hidden his car, then past the rustic Recapture Lodge and finally the Twin Rocks Café, tucked into the base of a vermillion cliff topped by twin, humanlike rock pillars. Actually, Susan thought as they drove past, the twins look more like the blocky LEGO version of the human form.

The highway climbed through the bluffs above Bluff and up onto the sagebrush flats, providing a view of the snowcapped Abajo Mountains to the northwest.

The wind whipped with even more strength up on the exposed terrain above the river valley and occasionally jarred the truck. But the day was crystal clear with a sky blue enough to compete with the Abajo Mountains.

Susan called Dwayne en route and filled him in. He commended her. Thanked her for proving him right in choosing her for this duty. Asked her to thank Jake and said he would immediately dispatch the appropriate people to the wash and the mine.

Jake waited in the truck outside the Blue Mountain Hospital while Susan got Melissa checked in. He was unwinding and yawning incessantly.

The hospital was a modern, faux-adobe building with a blue metal roof and trim. Jake noticed the parking lot was almost empty. He had always considered a vacant hospital parking lot a good thing.

Susan came out the double glass doors, and as she approached the truck, the smile on her face morphed into a look of intense worry. She slid in on the passenger side.

"Melissa's in good hands in there. But my elation is short-lived, as is so often the case when you have a fourteen-year-old child." She stared at her phone in her right hand.

"What's up with Amy, sweetie?"

Susan looked out the window for a few seconds and shook her head as if trying to wrap her mind around this new information. "I have several text messages from our daughter indicating that she and Mandy are on their way to Moab in Melissa's car. One reason I didn't bring this up in front of Melissa."

"Whatever it is, Melissa will probably find out when she gets to a phone in there and calls Ben."

"Yeah, well, let's hope that takes a while."

"Why? Is he busy driving the girls to Moab?"

"Uh, nope. Uh, apparently Mandy is driving. And when Amy couldn't talk her out of driving to Moab without a driver's license, she decided the right thing to do was accompany her." Susan glared at Jake as if an explanation were written between his eyes.

Jake leaned forward in his seat and dropped his forehead into his hands. "Holy shit."

She studied her phone. "Oh, it gets better. Amy says, and I quote"— she scrolled—"'Mandy has insane computer skills. She cracked the password on Melissa's computer and studied her research on Beauford's business and on his board members. Then she dug around online and discovered a past board member from Utah who is super skanky.'"

"Yeah, so?"

"Let's see, da da da da, skipping down . . . oh, here we go. 'Dallin Hanson is his name, and Mandy is convinced he's been Beauford's business partner as well as a member of his board and was most likely the voice with no accent on the calls to the Fry house.'"

"Then a few more down. Lord, that girl can text! 'Hanson is a Mormon, but he's on Interpol's Red Notices list and the FBI's Ten Most Wanted list as a convicted Russian spy who escaped and disappeared after being indicted. Mandy's online investigation has convinced her Hanson is hiding in plain sight under an alias as a janitor at the Moab High School. We're on our way to confront him.'" She looked up. "Two fourteen-year-old girls on their way to confront a man on Interpol's most wanted list. Oh . . . my . . . God." She slumped back in her seat. "We've created a monster."

She hit autodial for Amy. It went to voicemail. "Amy if you get this message, call me immediately," Susan said.

She put her phone down. "Tell me this is not happening, Jake."

Mandy had her hands on the wheel at ten o'clock and two o'clock, just as the YouTube videos had instructed. Her neck was stiff, and her head hurt. So far there had been only one close call. She had to swerve to miss a pedestrian in a crosswalk in Price, but the near miss had gotten her full attention. She had not taken her eyes off the road for a moment since.

They had just passed the entrance to Arches National Park in Melissa's green Volvo and descended a long hill to a bridge where the highway crossed the Colorado just beyond where the river emerged from between sheer sandstone walls.

Amy had been navigating with the GPS on Mandy's phone because her phone had died shortly after the stop in Price. According to the app, Moab High School was up on a plateau overlooking the northwest end of the town.

"Turn left in a few blocks on Uranium at the Stubbs Coffee Shop and it should take us up to the high school."

"Thanks. Help me watch for Uranium, okay."

"How do you know when Hanson, aka Templeton, gets off work?"

They passed a business on the right advertising red rock safaris. Red Jeeps with canvas tops surrounded the building.

Mandy did not answer. "Mandy?" Amy prompted.

Mandy stared straight ahead, "Oh, sorry. I'm concentrating on staying two seconds behind that silver SUV ahead of us as indicated by the instructional videos. I got it from the school website. Under the 'Staff' banner. George Templeton's hours were listed as 6:00 a.m. to 2:00 p.m. What time is it now?"

"There's a digital clock right there on the dashboard."

"I know, but I'm scared to take my eyes off the road." The SUV slowed and Mandy hit her brakes a little too hard, causing Amy to lurch forward against her seatbelt. "Whoops. My bad."

"It's one thirty, and I could sure use something to eat."

"We can't risk missing him." Mandy tensed as they approached an intersection with a light that had just turned yellow. She white-knuckled through. A car to her right honked angrily.

"Oh, crap. Bad timing." She exhaled audibly. "And I think I just blew by Uranium."

"It's okay, don't worry about it. The GPS will reroute us. We'll get there in plenty of time." Traffic was heavy for early afternoon. "But are you sure you want to do this? Still not certain what we're supposed to say to the jerk if we do find him."

"I don't know, really. Just going to follow my new mantra, WWGD. What Would Greta Do?" Mandy accidentally turned on the wipers.

"It never rains in Moab," Amy joked.

"Dammit," Mandy said, turning the wipers off and finding the correct lever to signal a move into the turning lane to take the next left. "Beauford and Hanson are criminals and major polluters. Think about people who do not have access to clean air and water. Think about all the children impacted by severe weather, drought, forest fires, and flooding. Think about the Indian tribes and the loss of protection for their sacred monuments. Think about my mom."

The GPS led them to the high school parking lots. Mandy drove through the student parking area next to the football field. Some of the cars had students hanging around them talking. Then she drove past the baseball field and around the side of the main building to a lot labeled STAFF PARKING. Although the lot was almost full, she found an empty space, flawlessly pulled into it, and put the Volvo in park. The parking space was perfectly flat, but she applied the emergency brake just in case, switched off the engine, and exhaled.

"Bravo, you did it. We survived," Amy said.

Mandy smiled. "Phew." She adjusted her red headband and scratched above her left ear. She stretched both arms above the wheel all the way to the windshield, bent her back, and inhaled again and relaxed back into her seat.

"I really appreciate you coming along, Amy."

"Watching you drive after a cram course on YouTube. Wouldn't miss it for the world."

"I know we weren't the best of buds at school."

"I've figured out you're kinda cool . . . in your own batshit kinda way. And nobody would ever question your guts."

Mandy smiled at her, placed her head back against the headrest, and closed her eyes. The dashboard clock displayed 1:47.

Amy searched the school building with her eyes. It was a flat-roof construction, made of brown brick. One part of the roof was much higher; she assumed that was the auditorium and stage area. There was also a high, blank wall with nothing but an emergency exit, probably the gym. There was little ornamentation except for an occasional brick archway and a few clusters of trees. Dumpsters lined the staff parking lot. The windows on the building in the lower sections that she assumed held classrooms were small and lined up like gun turrets. A shame, she thought, considering the stunning view from the school of the beautiful surrounding red rock. She saw a sign by the gym: WELCOME TO THE HOME OF THE RED DEVILS.

Amy realized she was feeling more nervous as 2:00 p.m. approached. Mandy, however, seemed fine. In fact, she appeared to have dozed off.

Mandy had printed the FBI's Ten Most Wanted poster of Hanson/ Templeton and brought it along on the trip. To pass the time, Amy studied it. He was clean-shaven, white, and had blond hair and green eyes. He was smiling in the picture, and his smug grin creeped Amy out. He was either fifty or forty-eight years old, depending on which date of birth he had used in the past. Several aliases were listed, but Templeton was not one of them. The poster showed the same shot of Hanson in various hair lengths and disguises. It said Hanson had completed his Mormon mission in Saint Petersburg, Russia, where it was thought he was recruited by FIS. Later he attended School of Mines and then got a master's degree in International Business at the University of South Dakota. His business connections, especially in the mining industry, had required many trips to Russia. He had been indicted for trying to film military installations in Utah. He had escaped while being transported to a federal prison in Colorado.

At the bottom of the poster, a gray band with words written in all red caps sent a shiver down Amy's spine: SHOULD BE CONSIDERED ARMED AND DANGEROUS.

Amy asked herself for the hundredth time: just what the hell did she and Mandy think they were doing?

Still sitting outside the hospital, Jake stared at the GPS on his phone. "We're an hour and a half from Moab right now. When did Amy send her last message?"

"Let's see. The last one mentions they stopped in Price, and that was sent two hours ago. Oh, great. And she says her battery is dying, and knowing my daughter, no way she has a charger with her." She dialed Amy again. Voicemail. "Goddammit, Amy!" She slammed the dash with her palm.

Jake tapped on his phone. "Price is two hours from Moab. They could be getting close." He rubbed his jaw with his right hand. "What have we got? We've got Melissa recovering here in the hospital. We have Jen babysitting a burned-out trailer. We have us sleep-deprived and close to crashing. We have a damaged truck and no idea how reliable it is. We have two girls an hour and a half away from us, walking into a very dangerous situation. And Ben. Where the hell is Ben in all this? He can't possibly know. I'll call him right now."

"We need help, Jake. I'm calling Dwayne back."

They both got on their cell phones.

There was no more time to fret about the reasons for coming to Moab. A man dressed in a short-sleeved gray shirt and darker gray pants exited the school building through the door on the large blank wall and walked toward the parking lot. He carried a bulging black garbage bag in one hand and a blue canvas tool bag in the other.

Amy shook Mandy awake. By now the man was close enough to the car that the girls could see he matched the height and weight stipulated on the most-wanted fugitive poster. However, he had longer hair than depicted, a goatee and mustache, and large glasses.

"Do you think it's him?" Amy asked handing Mandy the poster.

She studied it. "It definitely could be."

The man paused at the dumpsters to dispose of his garbage.

Taking no notice of the car with two girls hunched down in it, he walked past them and toward the middle of the parking lot.

"He has a name patch on his shirt," Amy said. Before Mandy could respond, Amy was opening her door. "I'm going to ask him an innocent question and read that name tag."

206 • GREGORY ZEIGLER

Mandy watched Amy approach and speak to the man. He pointed at the building; she smiled and nodded, then walked back to the car and slid in.

"It's him. Name tag says 'Templeton.'"

"I've got an idea. It's a long shot, but . . ." Mandy typed furiously on her phone.

Hanson leaned into the back of his pickup, adjusting something in the bed.

Mandy tossed her phone into a cupholder. "Let's go," she said.

The two girls jumped out of the car and approached. When they got within twenty feet, Mandy called out, "Hanson!"

Hanson jolted in recognition, turning quickly toward them, and then tried to cover. "Sorry, you must have the wrong guy. My name is George Templeton."

He started to open his truck door.

"Templeton is one of your names. But you were born Dallin Hanson," Mandy said. She held up the poster.

"Says right here on your portrait that adorns every post office. Where are you holding Melissa Fry?"

Hanson slammed his door shut, swung around to the pickup's bed, and reached into his tool bag. He extracted a heavy wrench as long as his forearm and turned toward the two girls.

Behind Hanson, four students appeared from the direction of the student parking lot. Another ten were running over from the gym door. Then students started pouring out of the arches that led to the classrooms. Before Hanson could make a move, a throng of students had surrounded him in the parking lot. Several dozen students had gathered. And the number kept rising. A few even pulled up in cars and got out to join the crowd.

A large boy in a red-and-black Red Devils football jersey called out from the crowd, "Hey, Templeton. I just got a message saying you are a major contributor to climate change and a wanted criminal. What's up with that, dude?"

A girl added, "You fracking with our future, Templeton?"

Another girl shouted, "We will not stand for actions harmful to our planet."

Someone started the One Degree chant, "One, two, three degrees, a crime against humanity." And the crowd joined in. The pop-up demonstration Mandy had called for with her WhatsApp broadcast list was in full swing.

Hanson circled like a cornered animal, but although he threatened with his wrench, he did not attack.

The numbers were just too great. Resistance was futile. Escape was not an option.

Another boy: "Drop the wrench. You're surrounded." Laughter rippled through the group.

"You can stop a few of us, but you can't stop all of us, Hanson," Mandy shouted.

A male school official ran up to the students to try and restore order just as two Utah Highway Patrol cars pulled into the lot. Dwayne Williams got out of the lead car.

Jake and Susan waited in the battered truck outside the Blue Mountain Hospital. Behind the building and angling low in the western sky, the sun poured down on the snow slopes and tree-green ridges of the mountains like molten gold. They had called Jen and asked her to bring the Suburban to Blanding. That was all they had managed to do. What else could they do but worry? They were exhausted. All they could muster was the hope Dwayne had successfully sent troopers to intercept the girls in Moab. Susan's phone rang. She put it on speaker.

"Dwayne, Dwayne, what did you find out?" Susan asked.

"Fortunately, I was near Moab when you called. I immediately went to the high school with another unit for backup."

"Are the girls okay?" Susan asked.

Dwayne chuckled. "Okay? The apple doesn't fall far . . . when we arrived, we found over a hundred students surrounding Dallin Hanson, aka George Templeton. Mandy and Amy had mobilized an army with the tap of a button."

"So, Mandy had it right? Hanson is Beauford's business partner and an escaped prisoner?" Jake said.

"And probably involved in the kidnapping. Hanson has been arrested without incident. No one got hurt. The girls are fine."

Jake and Susan simultaneously sat back against their seats.

"Bless you, Wayne. We will see you in Moab as soon as we can get a reliable vehicle," Susan said.

Just after Susan had hung up, Jake's phone trilled. It was Ben. He put him on speaker.

"Ben, where the hell are you?" Jake said.

"Hello, Jake. Sorry, I'm driving to Bluff to try and catch up with our daughters. I was at a board meeting in Salt Lake City, and when I returned home, I discovered they had taken off with Melissa's car."

"Melissa is fine. Mandy is fine."

"Oh my God. Oh, thank God."

"As soon as we are certain Melissa is resting comfortably at the hospital here in Blanding, we're going to head up to the Utah Highway Patrol headquarters in Moab to pick up the girls," Jake said.

"That's assuming Dwayne Williams hasn't locked them up and thrown away the key," Susan said.

"Hi, Susan," Ben said. "I've been worried sick. I tried calling you earlier, Jake, but it went to voicemail."

"And I tried calling you, but you must have been out of range. Where are you now?" Jake asked.

"Green River, about an hour north of Moab. I can't imagine what got into my daughter, driving down there like that."

"No, Ben, trust me, you really can't imagine. We'll let the girls fill you in," Susan said.

"We'll meet you in Moab at the UHP," Jake said.

He ended the call.

Now all they had to do was wait for Jen. She had agreed to take over with Melissa so Jake and Susan could head north in the Suburban.

Dwayne sat in his formal brown uniform in a meeting room at the Section 13 Utah Highway Patrol offices on East Center Street in Moab. His trooper's hat rested on the end of a rectangular, wooden table that the group had gathered around.

Susan studied the cramped room. She concluded a severely depressed person must have decorated it with a few spare items and with bilious green as the paint of choice. The one exception adorned the wall above Dwayne's head. It was a beautiful, framed photograph of the iconic Delicate Arch of Arches National Park. Beside the print, a large, generic, white-faced clock showed twenty minutes past five.

Susan was flanked by Jake on her right and Amy on her left. Across from them sat Ben with Mandy on his right.

"I just got a call from Blue Mountain Hospital," Dwayne said. "The chief administrator reports that Melissa is doing very well. Better than expected. I know you are all anxious to head down there, so I'll make this brief.

"Amanda, I gather that you found out about Hanson posing as Templeton from your online investigation, but how did you know for certain that he was the kidnapper on the phone?"

"I found a recording of his voice on a video made at his trial. I asked Dad to listen, and we both agreed that it sounded like the guy on the calls."

"And I tried to tell Jake that but couldn't reach him," Ben said. "Next thing I knew, my wife's car, my daughter, and Amy were gone."

"Yes, we will address that matter momentarily. First, I need to update you all about the scene at the mine where Melissa was being held captive. I assume you girls—excuse me, you young women—can handle the gruesome details after what you've been through," Dwayne said.

"I'm sure my daughter can, Captain Williams," Susan said.

Ben Fry nodded and patted Mandy's back.

"Raymond Beauford was extracted from his wrecked vehicle and pronounced dead at the scene—cause of death a broken neck and severed spine as a result of massive trauma from the impact of the head on the windshield. We are awaiting the family's instructions re: claiming and disposing of the body.

"My troopers found Jan Wozniak and Harold Fink in restraints in the mine plant office. They were fine if a bit hot and thirsty. They are being held here in Moab, awaiting arraignment. Once they heard Beauford was dead, they offered up anything and anyone they thought might save a portion of their skin. Fink identified a workman at Saint Michael's School who was involved. The local police chief and the school head in Pennsylvania have been notified."

"That is, no doubt, Mandy's original attacker," Jake said.

"Hanson is sitting in a cell here, awaiting transport to a federal prison in Colorado. This time he will be under double guard, as he is a known escapee."

Dwayne's face took on a more serious demeanor. "Now, to the matter of the stolen car and driving without a license."

"Yes, we three parents have been very curious about how you might proceed regarding that *very serious* issue, Captain Williams," Susan said.

Mandy and Amy glanced at each other, their faces communicating volumes. He had their attention.

"I'm duty bound by the oath I took when I was awarded this badge." He tapped the multipoint metal badge above his left breast pocket. "That oath requires me to uphold the laws of the state of Utah, and the state makes no provision for driving under the age of fifteen except in the case of extreme hardship such as incapacitated parents. Have either of you young women been issued a hardship license?"

The young women were uncharacteristically silent.

"I take that as a no.

"The standard punishment in this case if I turned it over to a judge is loss of driving privilege until the age of twenty-one, a fine of a maximum of two thousand dollars, and one hundred hours of community service."

Now the young women's silence could only be described as stunned.

"However, the law gratefully offers me some leeway with minors in these matters. There is one condition that could allow me to resolve this issue right here today." He paused for emphasis. "If you give me your word, Miss Fry, that you will never drive again before doing so legally. And if you, Miss Brand, will promise me you will never again knowingly ride with an unlicensed driver, I have the authority to adjust your penalty to one hundred hours of community service. That punishment will be split evenly between the two of you and supervised by your parents. And it should be done in support of the youth organization known as One Degree. Agreed?"

Amy and Mandy smiled in relief and nodded their heads vigorously.

"Then it is settled. I want to thank you all for your service to the state of Utah and to the country. I must add, you have all been outstanding, but you two young women, the matter of the car notwithstanding, have been nothing short of amazing." He rose and picked up his hat. They all stood to walk out.

"Ms. Brand, a word, please." When they were alone, Susan closed the door.

"Oscar-worthy performance, Dwayne."

He grinned. "Seemed like I got their attention."

"I know my daughter; that was Amy *at* attention." She reached into her rear pocket, slipped out her badge, and placed it on the table. "Thanks again for this."

"Any time you're ready to jump back in, darlin', it'll be waiting for you."

"That means more than you will ever know, old friend."

"I'm as serious as a dead man. Cops don't come any better than you. Partner Jake is pretty impressive too."

"Do you suppose I could hug the captain without violating his oath of office, causing a Me Too incident, or getting stabbed by his badge?"

"Let's risk it."

December 16
Friday

Amy and Mandy put their heads together a few days after Melissa returned home and cooked up a plan to fly back for the last week of school before winter break.

They were now at the end of that week, and the school holiday was slated to begin the next day.

The Saint Michael's Theater was decked out with a menorah at the entrance, wreaths connected by boughs above the proscenium, and a large, fully decorated Christmas tree on stage. Students and parents were gathered for a special award presentation, which was to be followed by a choral program and several holiday skits performed by the lower grades.

Mandy was sitting in the front row between Melissa and Ben Fry, and right next to them sat Susan, Amy, and Amy's friend Will, who was secretly holding Amy's hand between their seats. The students were all dressed in their formal school uniforms. Khaki pants and green blazers with white dress shirts and ties for the boys; kilts, green blazers, and white blouses for the girls.

Joan Bailey stood on the stage behind a microphone stand, holding two plaques in her hand, her white pantsuit glowing in the spotlight. She called for everyone's attention.

"I wish Jake had made it," Amy said to Susan.

"So do I, sweetheart. I'm sure he's sorry to miss it."

"Ladies and gentlemen, students, it is a great pleasure to have you here this evening to help Saint Michael's celebrate the end of a productive first semester and the beginning of a well-earned winter break. And both the boys' and girls' varsity basketball teams won their games today. Woo-hoo!"

Applause filled the theater.

"We start this evening with some sad news. But it is sad news resulting in good news. Last month, for the first time in this safe rural school's one-hundred-plus-year history, we had a student assaulted by an employee, a member of our maintenance staff. That man has been terminated and in fact has been arrested by local police. That student, freshman Amanda Fry, in the long tradition of tenacious Mikes, was investigating an oil well that is close to our campus boundary and was polluting our beautiful river and threatening the health and safety of our students. Unbeknownst to us, the employee in question also worked security for the well and was operating under the well owner's orders.

"Mandy, who was later joined by her friend and classmate, Amy Brand, proved the company and its leadership were corrupt and in violation of innumerable regulations and codes. The well has since been shut down; so, for that matter, has the entire company." Clapping from the audience. "And it gets better. As a part of Amy and Mandy's, and their parents'— Ben Fry, Melissa Fry, Jake Goddard, and Susan Brand—investigation into the corrupt mining company, they helped several Native American tribes and environmental organizations to block the federal government's attempt to reduce two important national monuments in Utah, Grand Staircase-Escalante and Bears Ears. Recent reports indicate that success could be imminent in restoring the monuments to their original size and thereby protecting their scenic beauty and archeological treasures."

The head held up the two plaques. "I want to honor Mandy and Amy tonight with this token of the school's appreciation for"—she pulled her glasses down off her head and read from the top plaque—"'selfless and courageous service to the school, the community, the state of Utah, and the planet.'" She peered out into the audience. "Amy and Mandy, please join me."

The students in the audience jumped to their feet, and the room exploded in applause as Amy and Mandy approached the steps to the stage.

December 20
Tuesday

Susan found Jake living in a second-floor walk-up, thirty-dollar-per-day room at the Virgin River Casino. She stood in his room by the door. He sat on the bed. An empty Jack Daniel's bottle lay under the flat-screen TV on the dresser. Chip bags and take-out containers littered the floor.

"How did you find me?"

"When pinging your phone didn't work"—she slid a phone out of her back pocket—"since you left it behind"—she placed the phone on a chair by the door—"Dwayne put out a BOLO. If seen, you were not to be stopped but reported to him. One of his troopers was in Mesquite on his day off and spotted your car."

"Great."

"Amy is home and she misses you. You would have been so proud of her, getting the award at school. Standing ovation for the two of them. She is all excited about climate justice now. I told her you were on a job in Nevada, but I don't think she believes me. She said you always call her when you are away working, and you haven't called."

"Why don't you tell her the truth? Tell her I walked in on you and Jen in the movie theater in Bicknell, making out like horny teenagers."

"We were not making out. It was her last night and the first time since . . . since that night that we had a chance to talk. We asked you to come to the movie, but you said, if I remember correctly, 'There's too much chick in that flick.' We didn't expect you to change your mind and show up. Neither one of us would ever want to hurt you, Jake. I've told you over and over again, it was a final kiss, a kiss goodbye. A kiss that said, 'I love you, but this can't happen again.'"

"You love her? You love Jen?"

"Yes. I love Jen. I love her like a sister. And Jen loves you like a brother."

"And how can I trust that it means never again when you admit you slept together in Cedar City?"

"You can trust it because I didn't try to hide it. I told you the truth. And I'm telling you it will not happen again."

"You told me the truth after I caught you sucking each other's faces."

"That's a nasty way to characterize a beautiful friendship. That must be the alcohol talking. Jen loves both of us, and she is really distraught right now. Come home. Amy and I miss you and we need you."

"I'm not finished here."

"Not finished doing what? Gambling away most of the money we earned on the Fry case? How much have you lost, Jake?"

"That's none of your damn business. Leave me alone."

"I'm not leaving Mesquite without you. You are not staying here through Christmas. Look at this room. It's a pigsty. And you look like shit. I have apologized. Now I'm begging for your forgiveness. I made a huge mistake. It will never ever happen again. Now please come home. Amy and I can't live without you."

"Get out."

"Please, Jake. Forgive me. Please."

"I said, get out!"

Susan turned at the door in tears. "Just ask yourself: are you punishing me or are you punishing yourself? And you are certainly punishing Amy. I'll be back tomorrow. I screwed up, but I'm never giving up on us. I'm not going back to Boulder without you."

She departed.

December 21
Wednesday

Susan spent a sleepless night at the Mesquite Hampton Inn. She got up, took a walk to get a coffee and to clear her head, and went in search of her husband.

She found Jake in the bar at the Virgin River Casino. It was just after 10:00 a.m. He was nursing a beer. There were only three other people at the bar—two men and one woman. They all looked a little desperate, including Jake. That broke Susan's heart.

She sat on his left. "I was hoping you might still be sober this early in the morning."

"You're about an hour too late. Already lost a hundred bucks too. Guess they're determined to get my last dime."

"Alcohol and gambling, Jake. Why not just put one in the cylinder, spin it, and take your chances?"

"It occurred to me."

"Before we talk about us, I want to update you on a few things."

"Us? Work your way down the bar and see if you can find someone who cares about us."

Susan chose to ignore that. "What Melissa learned from that blowhard Beauford was enough for Southwest Wild's lawyers to threaten the government with even more complicated and drawn-out legal action. The administration and the Bureau of Land Management got caught with their hands in the cookie jar. Or in the rare earth metals jar, so to speak. With national elections looming, they are scrambling to control the fallout. Melissa thinks the tide has shifted and the monuments will be preserved as originally created."

"Well, that's something. anyhow," Jake said.

"Remember Beauford's nephew whom we busted for swinging freshmen?"

"The one who accosted Amy for tardiness?"

"Yeah, that jerk. He lost his prefect status and was moved back to the senior dorm, but the malicious prick couldn't stop harassing younger students. They caught him in the freshman dorm in the middle of the night, grabbing boys' mattresses and flipping them over."

"Poor kids. That should have been Beauford's last strike," Jake said, lifting his beer bottle.

"Like Joan said, zero tolerance for bullying. He's out. Kicked out. Middle of his senior year. I must say, that's a relief. I was afraid of payback against Amy and Mandy after all that had happened to his uncle."

"Didn't you say something about hoping for justice in that little corner of the world?"

"And remember Blake Wilson and the monster truckers?"

"How could I forget?"

"They pled out. Blake got two to five as the organizer and driver of the truck that injured that boy. Sentence was lessened for ratting out his buddies. His buddies each got one to three. They'll all be locked up together at Point of the Mountain in Draper."

"Speaking of payback, Wilson better watch his shiny rat's ass."

Susan inhaled and looked around the casino. Blinking, plinking neon everywhere, vying for the attention of the handful of morning gamblers. "Now, in the matter of Susan Brand's major screw-up." She leaned forward on her elbows on the bar and stared up into his face. "I will do anything to win back your trust. We need you at home. What can I do to convince you of how sorry I am?"

Silent sipping.

"Look, let's get out of this place, okay? There's nothing but negative energy."

Jake stared down at the bar. Susan got up from her stool.

"Come with me. Just give me an hour."

"No way."

"Please, sweetheart."

He pulled down the brim of his ball cap and reached for his beer. "Nope."

"If I have to go to my truck and get my Glock and take you out of here at gunpoint, I will. I swear . . . to God, I will, Jake."

Silence.

"Like they say in the cop shows, wanna go the easy way or the hard way? One hour. That's all I'm asking. You have my word."

Jake put down his beer, pushed two fives toward the bartender, and slowly rose from his stool and followed Susan out.

The truck climbed up the street above town to the north. They passed a subdivision of modern homes painted in earth tones. They topped a hill and approached a sign that read *Mesquite Sports Complex*. Susan parked in a large lot. No one else was around. The complex included several buildings flanked by picnic ramadas with tables and charcoal barbecues. Two strips of grass stretched away side by side like runways. The lush green athletic fields were surrounded by barren dirt and rock. A sheer bare butte rose to the west of the complex.

Susan walked out onto the closest field and sat in the grass. Jake stood towering over her. She patted the turf beside her. He sat.

Neither spoke. Susan ran her fingers through the grass. Jake wrapped his arms around his bent knees.

They looked south across sere benches cracked with arroyos leading down to a serpentine golf course of incongruous green. Beyond that were more houses, the interstate running next to an industrial park, and, paralleling the highway, a strip of emerald along the winding Virgin River. In the distance lay more barren foothills leading up to hazy mountains shaded pale olive as they rose in elevation and topped out with a dusting of snow.

"How did you find this place?" Jake asked.

"You're not the only one who can use Google Earth."

"Nice view."

"I thought you might find it a little more attuned to who you are—in your heart—than motel walls, backbars, and casinos."

"You hurt me," Jake said.

Susan stood and went behind him. She wriggled in with her legs outside his hips and her arms wrapped around his arms. "Yes, I did." She said, with her cheek pressed against his back. "And I've never regretted anything so much in my life." She brushed at her right eye and then hugged his arms with her arms again. "I can't stand to see you like this. I will do everything in my power to assure it will never happen again. I promise."

Jake's front left jeans pocket vibrated audibly. Susan reached down with her left hand and squeezed through the fabric. "Is that a phone in your pocket or are you just happy to see me?"

Jake smiled. Then he chuckled. Then he dropped his head on his arms.

Susan jumped up, yanked off his ball cap, pulled him backwards on the grass, spun around, and straddled him.

Staring into his eyes, Susan said, "Can we please just start over?"

She stretched out on top of him, pressed her chest against his, and gave him a kiss on the mouth intended to erase any doubt about the sincerity of her promise.

Jake kissed back.

Acknowledgements

Rare as Earth is a work of fiction. Mistakes are mine and mine alone. Perceived political opinions are figments of my imagination and my imagination alone.

I continue to marvel at the support old friends and new acquaintances offer in the process of creating a novel.

My journey for *Rare as Earth* began with a writer's residency at Kiski School in Saltsburg, Pennsylvania, supported by school head Chris Brueningsen and assistant head and senior English teacher Mark Novom. My thanks to the Kiski students who made me feel welcome during my stay on campus, and for their insights into how fourteen-year-olds think.

The journey ended with old friends, Chuck Shepard and Leslie Poston, acting as beta readers and offering invaluable suggestions—and with a new friend, author Anne Hillerman, reading my novel and writing the cover endorsement. I'm grateful.

Once again, I'm indebted to my wife Dimmie for her unselfish support in all aspects of my writing projects. And I'm grateful to my writer daughter Jameson Laurens for daily inspiration.

I want to thank Sienna Taylor and her fellow Jackson student protesters for the planet (International Youth Climate Strike, 3/15/19). Those passionate students are inspired by Greta Thunberg, as am I.

I wish to acknowledge my two partners in crime (writing) Pam Beason and Dave Butler (FreeRangeWriters.com) for their support and professional guidance. Thanks are also due to my editor, Karen Brown. Little escapes Karen's editorial attention.

Finally, I want to again recognize cover artist, Jane Lavino—whose skill ensures my novels are instant works of art—and Bronwyn Minton for assisting Jane.

About the Author

Gregory Zeigler is a life-long educator, writer, speaker, and environmentalist. He is a former National Outdoor Leadership School instructor and Executive Director of the Teton Science School in Jackson, Wyoming, where he currently resides with his wife, Dimmie. Gregory served as a teacher, coach, administrator, and ultimately as the head of several independent schools.

Zeigler has acted professionally on stage and in film, including appearing alongside NFL great Lynn Swann in an Instructional Television production, "Arts Alive." Zeigler wrote and appears in the short award-winning documentary about John Steinbeck, "Steinbeck Country." The film is available for viewing on vimeo.com.

CPSIA information can be obtained
at www.ICGtesting.com
Printed in the USA
FSHW022209180720
71816FS